SWEET TIME

GRAHAM REILLY

HODDER

With thanks to the following for permission to reproduce excerpts:

Easy Rider copyright © 1969, renewed 1997, Columbia Pictures Industries Inc. Courtesy of Columbia Pictures.

Gunfight At The O.K.Corral copyright © Paramount Pictures. All Rights Reserved. Excerpts used with permission.

The Treasure of Sierra Madre, courtesy of Warner Bros.

'Macarthur Park' (Jimmy Webb) copyright © Universal Music Publishing. Reproduced by kind permission of Universal Music Publishing.

'Ruby, Don't Take Your Love To Town' (Mel Tillis) copyright © Universal Music Publishing. Reproduced by kind permission of Universal Music Publishing.

'Fly Me To The Moon' (Bart Howard) copyright © Essex Music. Reproduced by kind permission of Essex Music.

'Rootie Tootie' words and music by Fred Rose. Copyright © Acuff Rose Music Limited. Campbell Connelly & Company Limited. All Rights Reserved. International copyright Secured.

'When You're Tired of Breaking Hearts' words and music by Hank Williams. Copyright © Acuff Rose Music Limited. All Rights Reserved. International copyright Secured.

A Hodder Book

Published in Australia and New Zealand in 2004
by Hodder Headline Australia Pty Limited
(A member of the Hodder Headline Group)
Level 17, 207 Kent Street, Sydney NSW 2000
Website: www.hha.com.au

National Library of Australia
Cataloguing-in-Publication data

Reilly, Graham, 1956- .
  Sweet time.

  ISBN 0 7336 1713 1 (pbk.).

  1. Immigrants - Victoria - Melbourne - Fiction. I. Title.

A823.4

Text design and typesetting by Bookhouse, Sydney
Printed in Australia by Griffin Press, Adelaide

For my friend Helen Rechter

As the train pulled slowly out of Glasgow Central, Kirstin Fairbanks waved. She waved so hard she thought her arm would drop off. Because of the state she was in, she was surprised she could wave and cry at the same time. It was a bit like that old trick where you rubbed your stomach and patted the top of your head simultaneously. She didn't bother to dab at her tears; she just let them flow, as her mother was doing on the platform. There seemed to be a lot of tears accompanying emigration. You only had to say the word and your friends and various members of your family started to weep. Mention the promise of a new life and the hankies came out like sails at the first suggestion of a breeze.

A new life! Can you imagine that? Few people ever got the chance to start again. But she had and she was going to make the most of it, and by the look of Douglas, with his head out the window, smiling at his sisters and their weans, he was too. At least she hoped so. She hoped that when he departed these shores he'd leave his demons stranded behind him.

Sometimes she couldn't believe it. Here she was, a woman married to an ex-priest, and there he was, a man who'd traded in his collar for an agnostic with a wise-cracking disrespect for anything Catholic or biblical, and indeed, black tailoring in general. It wasn't how she thought her life would turn out, at all.

Kirstin caught her mother's eye. She had thought that by virtue of her age her mother could have been forgiven if she'd looked vulnerable and abandoned as her eldest daughter chugged out of her life. But she didn't. She looked sad, but not heartbroken. She had been left before, she said, and she had survived. Besides, she still had two other daughters to nag and to offer the benefit of her many years' experience of life, love and expensive footwear. And she knew a bargain when she saw one. Two tickets to the colonies for twenty quid! You couldn't ask for more than that.

As the train shuddered into life, Kirstin felt her whole body shudder along with it. The station felt like a giant echo chamber, amplifying every sound, every emotion. Everything thundered and hissed and clanged in unison with her hopes and fears about their future. Why were they leaving behind everything they knew, everything to which they belonged? But perhaps, as she and Douglas had discussed many times already, they didn't belong in Glasgow any more. Perhaps they needed a new place to belong to, a place to reinvent themselves, and preferably a place that didn't serve chips with every meal and rain with every summer.

She watched the light from the midmorning sun filter through the glass roof of the station and seemingly parachute to the ground, particle by meandering particle. It was as if it was still making up its mind about whether it really wanted to come into the station or not. Everything seemed hesitant. All the colours were muted, like in the old photographs on her mother's mantelpiece. She blew her mother a kiss, then stuck her thumbs in her mouth and pulled the sides wide apart, pushing her eyelids up with her fingers. It was the 'scary' face she had always made when she was wee. She watched her mother laugh and admonish her with a wag of her finger. Kirstin knew what she was saying, even though her words were drowned out by the train's hiss and thunder.

'The wind might change and your face will be stuck like that forever!'

Kirstin held her mother's eye and they both laughed. She waved again, this time with more regret than enthusiasm.

She looked at Douglas, still hanging out the window, which he'd lowered to just below the level of his armpits. He was swaddled in a thick black overcoat, the only part of the uniform he'd retained from his former life. She had wanted him to burn all his black clothes, but he wouldn't. He didn't agree that it would be a symbolic gesture, just a thoughtless one when so many folk in his parish had so few clothes to wear. So he gave them away, all except for the coat. He said you probably wouldn't be able to get a coat like that in Australia. Kirstin had replied that it was unlikely to get so cold there that you would ever need one. He took her point but kept the coat anyway.

He was waving at his sisters and the few friends from the church who were still talking to him. He was playing cowboys and Indians with a couple of his nephews who were firing their Colt 45s and their Winchester repeating rifles at him while he shot off arrow after arrow with what appeared to be no success whatsoever. His nephews kept scampering about, avoiding his assault and hiding behind benches, poles and the occasional relative. Douglas obviously decided that it was about time he took a bullet and did so quite dramatically by being shot in the left eye. Blinded, he was unable to return fire. He waved his white handkerchief in surrender.

Watching all this, it suddenly occurred to Kirstin that she had said her goodbyes. There was no going back. There would be no more conversations about when you might catch up for a cup of tea or coffee, a movie, a walk in the park. This realisation left her catching her breath. She felt time stand still, just for a moment, before it lurched ahead.

She was startled by young Iain dashing along the platform waving something of his own.

'Uncle Douglas! Uncle Douglas!'

Douglas leaned further out the window. The boy had a good pair of legs on him and was catching up to the departing London-bound train. But he'd have to be quick or he'd run out of platform. 'What son? What is it?'

Iain held a five pound note aloft as he continued to run. 'Ma mammy says here's the five pound she owes ye. She says she's awfy sorry, she nearly forgot.'

'Ach, away,' Douglas chuckled as the train gathered speed. 'Tell your mammy I'll get it when you all come to Australia for a holiday,' he shouted.

'Naw, she says I have tae gie it tae ye, honest.'

'I'm sorry, Iain, I can't hear you.'

The boy stopped running and stood on the platform, hands on hips and breathless. All of a sudden, like an afterthought, he waved the five pound note in the air. 'See ye, Uncle Douglas,' he shouted. 'Have a good Australia!'

'A man cannot live on waitresses alone, Andrew,' Douglas said, casting a curious eye around the busy Melbourne pub, so different from the gloomy little caves back home. It had clear glass windows for a start, and light coursed happily through them, designating this as a place in which all were free to enjoy themselves, rather than being a dank and smoke-filled den of drink, dominoes and dirty socks.

'Oh, I don't know, I haven't been doing so bad. I like waitresses. They're very sociable. Good conversationalists. I prefer them. They're women who're no what they seem.'

'Is that right?' Douglas raised his eyebrows in mock exclamation at his cousin.

'Aye, it is. They're very mysterious, your waitresses. There's always so much more to them than meets the eye. They're generally women who always want to be something else, or be somewhere else. They're works in progress, aye. Flowers yet to bloom. They're standing at the bus stop of life waiting for the next Greyhound coach to adventure. They're always on a journey and that's what makes them attractive, a wee bit exotic even. They know stuff, have experienced things that your average punter hasn't.'

'What's so exotic about a strange woman in a black dress bringing you your dinner? Our granny fits that category just as well.'

'Aye, but you don't want to have it away wi' your granny, Douglas. At least I hope no.'

Andrew sat back in his chair, and squinted at Douglas, his head tilted slightly to one side. He appraised his cousin like a man about to put a deposit down on a new car. He was a dark horse was our Douglas, and not just because of his preference for dark clothing—trousers, socks, jackets, ties. But then, that could be a product of his previous life as a fully paid-up shepherd of the Lord's wee Catholic flock here on earth.

It was difficult to know what went on inside Douglas's head. Perhaps he didn't know himself. You know what they say about priests. They go into the seminary as emotionally immature seventeen year olds and come out ten years later as emotionally immature twenty-seven year olds. He was always a bit finicky, was Douglas. When he was a wee boy back in Glasgow he had a bath twice a week, Saturday and Wednesday. Once a week, ten days at the outside, was enough for the everyone else. And he was always collecting things. Comics, toy soldiers, football cards, stamps, birds' eggs, all categorised according to age, shape, size, colour and place of origin. Not a shell out of place or a dog-eared *Beano* to be found anywhere in the house.

'Here, you don't have one of yon Oedipus complexes, where you want to kill your father and have sex wi' your mother or your mother's mother or something?' Andrew joked.

Douglas laughed, shaking his head. 'Would you have had sex with our granny?'

'Och, I don't know,' Andrew said, pausing for thought. 'If she took her curlers out and put her teeth in, I might.'

'You're a sick man, Andrew Fairbanks,' Douglas said, forever amazed at the workings of his cousin's brain. Andrew had created his own logic, his very own set of rules by which he governed his life. It was a unique canon that owed nothing to any religion or moral code, eastern, western or from outer space. His brain was a pigeon cote of self-contained compartments which allowed no intercourse between thoughts or acts and the moral justifications for them. In this way, anything he did or thought could be sanctioned without any sense of folly or, above all, guilt. He could enjoy the pleasures of an Italian waitress from Calabria one night and profess an admittedly sudden but nonetheless deep-felt love for an Athenian goddess serving him a plate of souvlakia the next, without feeling compromised or manipulative. Indeed, what he felt at a particular moment was what he felt. On the rare occasions when he doubted his own sincerity, saw truth legging it up the high street, he could quickly convince himself otherwise and rope it back onto a nice comfy chair in front of the fire. The word justification was not to be found in Andrew's dictionary.

Andrew smiled. He was always amused, and occasionally concerned, that Douglas's former life with the white dog collar strung around his neck still dictated his approach to the world. Somewhere out there, the big guy in the sky still whispered in his ear hole, 'No, that's not right.' It was like that old hymn they were forced to sing at school every Friday afternoon when they were weans. Breathe on me breath of God. Well, him up there was still breathing all over poor Douglas. Bad breath as far as

Andrew was concerned. The Father, Son and Holy Ghost needed to give their teeth a good scrub, a decent floss, scrape all that muck off their furry tongues and give Douglas a break. Stop breathing on him for a few minutes, months, bloody well years so he could finally get a clear view of life and what was important. Catechism, dogma, hymns, holy fuckin' pictures, hands soft as a kitten's—they'd done the poor bloke's head in. Although, to give him his due, Douglas was fighting back. Most days he came out of the blue corner, chin down, guard up, keeping his distance and looking for a wee gap in the Big Yin's defences. Other times he was flat on his back on the canvas.

'I am not, as you put it, a sick man, Douglas. I just happen to believe in the mystery and allure that all women possess, curlers, chilblains and hairy legs included. And this is particularly true of waitresses. You see, dear cousin of mine,' Andrew said, tipping himself further into the small table, 'as you'll no doubt become aware, Australia is not like Scotland. There's more to this place than boiled potatoes and pints of warm beer. This is a multicultural society with multicultural cuisine and multicultural women to bring it to your table wi' a smile. Women that smell faintly of olive oil and eastern spices that tantalise the senses. Underneath their black or white or stripy aprons these are women that promise hitherto unknown pleasures. A kiwifruit of dripping sensuality, a ripe mango of luscious love, a soft juicy pear of tongue-licking tenderness. No boiled cabbage snogging here, pal. No bloody brussels sprouts of limpid passion.'

'Sounds more like Frankie Disabato's dad's fruit stall at the Victoria Market to me,' Douglas laughed.

Douglas again surveyed his cousin, took in that wide confident grin of his, like a sudden and unexpected burst of sunshine on a grey day, and knew at once why he was doing so well in this country, why he had taken to it and it to him. Like Australia, he was fresh, like a child ready to embrace the new day. He hadn't been broken by ancient and redundant class barriers and weather that soaked your spirit in gloom and resignation. And he did have a way with the opposite sex, no doubt about it. Even from when he was a little boy running around the swing park, the girls always gave him a lick of their lollipops, if not the whole spit-sodden lot. From there, it wasn't long until he could lick whatever he liked.

'And these girls, these waitresses, they like you?' Douglas inquired.

'They seem to.'

'I don't know why. You're still full of shite. Australia hasn't cured you of that particular predilection,' Douglas said, grinning.

'Aye, well, changing countries doesn't necessarily change your personality. You see, Douglas son, women like men who talk to them. But you know what most men are like.'

'No, what are most men like, Andrew?'

'Most men can't talk about anything they feel, so when a bletherhead like me comes along, women just lap it up. Women like to talk about feelings, no doings.'

'Really? Listen, if you know so much about women, can you tell me why they take so long to spend a penny?' Douglas asked, eyeing the door in the corner of the lounge bar, its frosted glass emblazoned with a female figure gaily twirling a parasol. 'I mean, what do they do in there? There's something they're no telling us, Andrew. They must have some extra bits they have to wash or attend to or something. Mysterious extra bits that men don't know about.'

'Don't talk daft. There's no extra bits. Trust me, I know, I've been there. Many times, and wi' mysterious women from mysterious places. A few had hairy nipples, but nothing more esoteric than that.'

'I'm not so sure. There must be something going on.'

'I worry about your view of women sometimes, Douglas,' Andrew sighed. 'I mean, your Church, its always been a bit afraid of women, has it no? Terrified of their sexuality. You know, I read somewhere that the Church used to execute priests' concubines and their children. That's taking things a bit far, don't you think?'

'That was a long time ago. Things have changed.'

'Oh aye. It just does them in other ways, if you ask me.'

'No one's asking you, Andrew,' Douglas snapped, not wishing to get into another prolonged and fruitless discussion about the Church he had left. He knew why he had wrenched himself away from it and he didn't need to be reminded of it by Andrew, who tended to see everything in black and white and failed to appreciate that sometimes there were shades of grey.

'They're probably just in the cubicle, having a wee chat,' Andrew said, smiling.

'God, I don't know how they do that,' Douglas said, uncomfortable with the idea that such bodily functions were not a private event but rather a social occasion. 'They're a bit weird, women, don't you think?'

'No, not at all. I think they're God's most perfect creation.'

'Ah. So you're admitting there is a God then?'

'What I meant to say was if there was a God, women would be his most perfect creation.'

'Is that right? Perfect?'

'Aye. You know, Douglas, there are just so many women who are just so bloody perfect. You know, they've got their perfect breasts that perk up just the right amount and their perfect little bottoms that fill out their tight skirts but no too much, and their perfect lips that are full but no too full. And then there's ones wi' a little mole by the side of their mouth that can drive you crazy, and some, especially those Mediterranean lassies, Douglas, that have those big black eyes and a little bit of hair on their upper lips—God I love that—and then there's the way they walk wi' their hips swinging all about the place . . .'

'I can't believe they don't have any faults, Andrew.'

'Ach, sometimes when they're doing the washing. They mix up the coloureds wi' the whites. I hate when you get blue bits on your white shirt.'

'You know, Andrew, I don't think there is any such thing as perfection. Not me, not you, not Sophia bloody Loren. Not God even. For me, it's the flaws in someone that makes them interesting.'

'Aye, sure, but as long as they can give good head,' Andrew said, his gaze shifting from a deflated Douglas to the corner of the busy pub. 'Look, here they come now.'

Andrew beamed at his latest flame, his smile resembling the clown over the entrance to Luna Park. Douglas raised the corner of his mouth in a lopsided half-moon of a smile as the two women chuckled their way across the obscenely floralled carpet, leaning on each other like a couple of old friends at the end of a long memory-filled night on the town.

Douglas watched his wife, her long shapely legs somehow longer and finer, her blue eyes bluer and brighter by the day, her skin no longer pale and tired but brown and blushing with health as if it had been set free after years of internment in a cold and dark place where the sun made only intermittent appearances in the cheerless sky. Glasgow in summer. After only a few months in Melbourne, she was a different person. She had gathered this new country into her arms and clung to it, not out of fear that it might slip from her embrace, but out of the joy and wonder of having found it at all. And she was doing her best to encourage Douglas to cling to it as well.

It was not so long ago that Andrew had written to Douglas saying there was a position going at his school and that with his experience in the Catholic education system in Glasgow, he fitted the bill perfectly. As for Kirstin, with her time in the property department at the Glasgow council, it wouldn't take her long to find a job because the real estate market in the western suburbs of Melbourne was about to take off, that's what those in the know said anyway. And Andrew was right. The headmaster of the Catholic boys' school was more than impressed with Douglas's qualifications and offered him the job right way as head of English. And having been in the God game for a while didn't do him any harm either, unlike in some countries where the Church did all it could to keep ex-priests out of the Catholic system.

Andrew's predictions about Kirstin's employment prospects also proved correct when a local real estate company offered her a job within a couple of weeks of their arrival. Clive Peterson, the director, said he found her as enchanting as her Scottish accent and no doubt the customers would too. The ability to charm without subsiding into puke-green insincerity and stomach-churning sleaziness was all-important in that business, and if you knew your stuff, you couldn't fail. He gave her responsibility for two suburbs he said were about to soar in value and wished her luck.

'Nineteen sixty-nine will be a big year for property in the west,' he'd said. Believe me, I know what I'm talking about.'

Several weeks on, the luck had certainly gone her way and people were heading out to Baytown for the cheap land and housing. Life was one fat, belly-caressing commission and she loved it.

Andrew's fingers reached out to take the hand of his new girlfriend. She was a waitress at a French restaurant in the city, and was a dab hand with a frog's leg. 'Francine, hen, what took you so long in there? Douglas was getting worried.'

'Oh, nothing, just talking. You know, women's talk,' she said, giving Andrew an enigmatic smile.

'And what have you two boys being talking about?' Kirstin said, making herself comfortable in her chair and pulling her skirt away from her thighs. She had bought it in Glasgow and it was a bit heavy for Melbourne's weather.

'Oh, you know, nothing, just men's talk,' Andrew smirked, pursing his lips and batting his eyelashes.

'And what exactly is this men's talk?' she asked.

'God and sex.'

'They're two very big subjects, Andrew,' Kirstin said. 'I'm impressed. Not like you two at all.'

'Well, your husband and I are only interested in the big issues, the stuff of life an a' that, isn't that right, Douglas?' he said turning to his cousin. 'I mean, for two men of the world like ourselves, what else is there?'

'Football,' Douglas replied.

'Jesus, Mary and Joseph! What time is it?' Andrew said, displaying an uncharacteristic flash of panic.

'A quarter to eight,' Kirstin said, holding out her watch for all to see.

'Right, we'd better get a move on, Douglas son. He'll be waiting for us.'

'Who'll be waiting for you, Douglas?' Kirstin asked, eyebrows raised.

'Ach, sorry. I forgot to tell you. We have to meet Angus tonight and decide on the best spot for the new soccer pitch.'

'Oh aye. Football, I should have known,' Kirstin said, shaking her head. 'Some things you never leave behind. You two could be living on top of Mount Everest and you'd still want to kick a ball around. Off you go then, don't mind us, we'll look after ourselves. Another drink, Francine?'

The two women watched the men hurry out the door busily rifling through their various pockets for car keys, cigarettes, matches, change and important bits of paper without which life would be impossible to navigate.

'Don't get too involved with Scottish men, Francine. They're football crazy. They're obsessed, sick in the head,' Kirstin said as she gestured to the barman for two more.

'Maybe,' Francine said softly. 'But I like them. At least they wait until you come.'

Kirstin smiled like the knowledgeable elder sister, the village 'rl who'd gone to the big city and returned older and wiser to ile her friends with stories of forbidden love and steamy ' of passion and intrigue. 'Not all of them, sweetheart,' she 'Not all of them.'

'Fucksake!' Andrew exclaimed as he took in the devastating scene before him. Sections of the temporary wire fence the Baytown City Council had erected to keep out inquisitive passers-by, wandering domestic pets, and the occasional farm animal and miscreant youth, had been wrenched from the ground like weeds from the vicar's prize rose bed. Several of the tall metal stanchions that had supported the fence, which ran the entire length of the site designated for the soccer pitches he, Douglas and 'Aberdeen' Angus McDonald had planned to discuss that very evening, lay across the footpath and part of the road. The few pedestrians out in the street gingerly stepped around them, and passing cars slowed to take a longer look. The once perfectly straight barrier was now as undulating as a drunk's late-night stagger.

'Fucksake, right enough,' Douglas responded, not quite able to believe his eyes. 'Why would anyone do this? I don't understand, it's just a fence. Why would you vandalise a fence?'

'Ye do whit yer thinking,' Angus said, dropping on one knee to inspect the damage more closely. 'Aye, they do that.'

'I'm not with you,' Andrew said.

'The actions of men betray their inner thoughts,' Douglas explained.

'It's a waste, whatever they're thinking,' Andrew replied, shaking his head. 'At least in Glasgow they would have stolen the entire thing and sold it on to some bloke in the building game, not just wrecked it. It's worth a fair few bob, this fence, so it is.'

'I never thought this sort of stuff went on in Australia,' Douglas said. 'But I suppose that was a bit naive of me. Maybe it's not the paradise it was made out to be on the television back home.'

'I think you're overreacting, Douglas. It's probably just some boys who did it for a laugh. Besides, what do you expect for ten quid? The Bahamas?' Andrew laughed. Sometimes his cousin took things too seriously.

'Och, I don't know, Douglas might well be right,' Angus puffed as he extended his hand to be helped upright. 'Whoever did this was serious about it, I can tell ye that.' He presented some long dun-coloured fibres he had removed from around one stanchion. 'Somebody's tied a rope around these here poles and just torn them out ae the ground. And they must have used something very powerful to do it.'

'A large vehicle of some sort, I would think,' Andrew suggested.

The three men stood in silence, unsure of what do next. They hadn't even got the soccer club properly underway and already they'd had a setback, Douglas thought. Perhaps it was just a bit of bad luck. The moon aligned with the stars aligned with a couple of young idiots with a big car with a decent sized towbar to sling a rope around. They'd most likely had a few drinks as well. The drink will do that to you. Make you do things you wouldn't normally do.

'Well, we'd better get on wi' it then. We'll call the council in the morning. There's nothing we can do about it now,' Andrew said, trying to sound encouraging. 'It's getting late. We should have a look at this ground before it gets dark.'

They turned away from the battered fence and back towards the vacant land. They carefully walked its length and breadth, taking note of any incline or decline that could affect the quality of a pitch or the effectiveness of its drainage.

'What do you think, Angus?' Douglas asked.

'It's fine piece ae ground, there's nae doubt about that,' Aberdeen Angus pronounced as he chipped away dods of grass with the toe of his wellington boot. He picked up the bits of earth and grass he'd dislodged before giving them a right good two-nostril sniff, a wine buff savouring the delicious and complex aromas of a glass of old shiraz.

'Slightly acidic,' Angus said, handing a brown lump to Andrew. 'Here have a smell ae that.'

Andrew took a quick whiff, like a man smelling his armpit before a big date. 'Aye, so it is.'

If there was a man to assess the soil of their planned soccer pitch it was Angus, a former farmer from Aberdeen who knew the dirt under his foot like the back of his hand.

In his mind Douglas could picture the spot where the clubhouse would be—on the west side, a bit back from the road. Nothing flash at first, just weatherboard perhaps, with a couple of changing rooms for the home and away teams, and maybe even a small meeting room doubling as a bar. A public toilet, of course, although with a time limit for female fans. There was probably even enough room for two pitches. The east side sloped right away though, down to the marshy ground by the old dried-up lake bed. But that could be fixed. They'd have to get a new fence up and put in some trees around the perimeter for a bit of a windbreak. Goalposts, corner posts and flags, a bloody big lawnmower, grass seed, lime and fertilisers. They'd have to get all that stuff too. What they needed was a fundraiser. A dinner dance maybe. With a raffle.

He could see it all before him; a glorious Saturday afternoon as the teams run out onto the pitch, the sun warm on their faces, nervously anticipating the game ahead, the first thud of leather against leather as the players kick the ball between themselves. And there at the centre of the field for the toss of the coin is Douglas Fairbanks, team captain, former Glasgow Schoolboys player, the old hand, the elder statesman of the game. The crowd bloody well roars.

'So Angus, what do you think?' Douglas asked, returning to the task at hand. 'Will this make a good football pitch, will the grass grow, will it be subject to flooding and can we correct the slight decline on the east side?'

Angus raised himself to his full six feet three inches, removed his pipe from the inside of his jacket and began tapping it against the side of his boot. He slowly and carefully filled it, and after a few pensive moments punctuated by the sounds of sucking, popping and relieved and contented exhalations of rum-flavoured tobacco with a hint of peachy fruit, he bent down and gathered another handful of soil. He rubbed it between his thick farmer's fingers, like a pastry chef preparing the casing for an apple tart.

'Easy texture, fine consistency, rich, fertile. We can fix slight acidity, nae bother. And the downhill slope will be nae problem if we manage tae borrow Vincent Vella's grader. This, my wee pals, will be a fine soccer field, a fine soccer field indeed.'

'Well thank God for that,' Douglas said, smiling at him. 'What shall we call it then, the club?'

The three men stood in the dark, nodding to themselves, scratching and probing at the damp earth with their shoes.

'How about the Baytown Soccer Club?' Douglas finally suggested, as no one else appeared to be about to come up with anything at all.

'That's a bit obvious, is it no?' Andrew said.

'You think so? Well, where do we live?' Douglas asked, slightly wounded that his suggestion had been so quickly dismissed.

'Baytown,' Andrew replied cautiously.

'Right. And what are we trying to establish here, for us and the weans about the place?'

'A soccer club.'

'Right again. So don't you think the Baytown Soccer Club captures all the relevant information?'

'Aye, I suppose you're right, Douglas. It does get to the point,' Andrew conceded. 'What do you think, Angus?'

'Aye, aye,' the big man said, nodding to the now dark and star-filled sky. 'It's a good name at that. But ye know, a wee thought just occurred tae me. How about the Baytown Soccer and Sheep Trial Club? Remember that programme on the television, *A Dog's Life*. It was awfy popular in Scotland and England, mind. We could have sheep trials every other Sunday. All those border cheviots and border Leicesters running about the place. What a sight that would be, eh? It would be a sight tae behold, so it would. And it would be another wee string to our bow, so tae speak.'

Douglas pursed his lips together and shook his head in a parody of profound thought and soul-searching. He folded his arms across his chest and nodded some more, a wee plastic dog in the back window of a 1963 Ford Anglia on the way to Blackpool for the Fair Fortnight.

'It's not a bad idea, don't get me wrong. But I don't think we should bite off more than we can chew, Angus. Let's start with soccer balls, and maybe sheepdogs can come into the picture down the road a wee bit. Why don't we wait until we get properly established and have got into the higher divisions of the state league and have a junior programme going and a permanent clubhouse built, that sort of thing. Then we can give some thought to border collies and the like.'

Angus emptied the tobacco from his pipe into the palm of his hand. 'Aye, maybe you're right. A blind man's wife needs nae painting, that's what they say.'

'What?' Andrew said, raising his eyebrows at Douglas.

'Don't carry out unnecessary tasks. It's an old Scottish saying.'

'Och, aye. Well said, Angus.'

The three men shook hands, happy that some decisions had been made, and walked quietly across the lumpy and weed-strewn patch of ground that would one day be the proud home of soccer in Baytown by the sea.

'Mind, there's nothing quite like a man and his dog and a wee tin whistle trying to coax a flock of sheep into a pen on a warm Saturday afternoon,' Angus sighed. 'It's takes a lot of skill, ye know. Aye, a lot of skill right enough.'

'One day, Angus, one day,' Douglas said, reassuring the big man. 'Let's get this fence sorted out first, then we can think about sheep.'

As he headed towards his car Douglas glanced back at the broken wire and fallen poles. 'I can't believe someone would do that,' he said.

'Your problem, Douglas,' Andrew said, stopping and taking another look himself, 'is that you've lost touch with the real world. The sad fact is, some people are just right bastards.'

Kirstin was already in bed when Douglas arrived home. As he pulled up in the driveway he could see the soft light from the small bedside lamp through the bedroom window, but by the time he'd entered the house she'd switched it off. He breathed in the day's-end quiet of the house; nothing stirred and even the smallest sounds were magnified in their resonance and clarity, like listening to music with headphones on. It was as if the ticking of the clock was keeping time with the beat of his heart. He hung his jacket on the back of a chair and slipped off his shoes. They smelled of what he hoped would become hallowed ground.

He scanned the shelves for something to eat, but couldn't see anything he fancied. After some more poking around and shifting tins and jars this way and that, he settled on a couple of long swigs from an open bottle of milk. He watched his reflection in the black screen of the kitchen window, his Adam's apple rising and falling, falling and rising, as he gulped down the soothing nectar. It was a familiar image. Him, sitting up late and alone, hoping somehow the silence would wash over him and cleanse his soul, make him new, different; that it would expurgate his demons, soothe his regrets and fears in a healing balm of absolution. Her, asleep in their bed, her knees tucked into her stomach, her thin brown arms clasping her pillow for dear life, as if it could somehow steal away while she slept. What was she dreaming about? Their old life in Scotland? What was she trying to capture with her tight embrace? The Douglas she thought she knew? A new life in Melbourne? A fresh start perhaps? She was a clean slate awaiting those first tentative chalk marks. Sometimes, as he undressed, Douglas saw her momentarily illuminated by the headlights of a passing car sweeping though the blinds like a train though a deserted station at midnight. She looked so small, so childlike, curled up there in bed, wrapped around herself like a shell from the sea.

'Hello.'

Douglas jumped, a shiver running through his body like a current of electricity through a taut wire. He spilt some milk on his shirt and rubbed at it.

Kirstin stood framed in the kitchen doorway, her satin dressing-gown tied loosely around her waist and held in place by her arms hugging her breasts. Her thick red hair fell across her forehead in a lush strawberry cascade.

'Sorry, love, I didn't mean to scare you,' she said. 'How'd it go?'

'Ach, fine. Well, not fine, really. Good and bad. The land should be okay. It's a wee bit swampy but we'll get the council to put some drainage in. Once we level it out it should be good enough.'

'And?'

'Somebody tore down sections of the fence.'

Kirstin looked puzzled. 'What?'

'Aye, I know. I couldn't quite believe it either.'

'Any idea who did it?'

Douglas shrugged and took another swig of milk. 'No, not really. Somebody with a big car, a tow bar and a rope. That's what Angus thinks, at any rate.'

'That's strange, eh. It was probably some bad boys who did it and ran away,' Kirstin laughed. 'That's what my sister and I always told our mother when something untoward happened, like when we broke the vase she got as a wedding present. It was from Venice, I think. She still hasn't forgiven me.' Kirstin shuddered at the memory of it.

'Well, whoever did this didn't run away, that's for sure. They drove off, and in a bit of a hurry at that.'

'What are you going to do?'

'Ach, Andrew said he'd ring the council in the morning.'

Kirstin took the bottle of milk from her husband had a sip. 'What did Angus think?'

'Of the fence?'

'No, of the ground.'

Douglas smiled. 'Angus thinks with a wee bit of work the ground will be just fine. But he wanted to have sheep trials every other week as an added attraction. He thinks football by itself won't be enough to pull in the crowds. He thinks border collies and sheep shite are the way to go.'

'Well, he's still a farmer at heart,' she laughed, pulling her dressing-gown tighter around herself and lifting her heels up and down from the cold floor tiles.

'Aye, I think he misses his place something terrible.'

'What happened with that anyway?' Kirstin asked.

'Och, typical farmer thing. Too much debt and the bank stepped in as banks do and relieved him of his property and his livelihood. I think there was a bit of bad weather and foot and mouth disease.'

'Do sheep get foot and mouth disease?'

'Well it was some crazy affliction his sheep got, I can't remember what it was called.'

Kirstin slipped her arms around her husband's waist and burrowed into his flesh, looking for the warmest, most comfortable place. 'The club will be good for Angus, I think. It'll be a new interest.'

Douglas pulled away from Kirstin's embrace. 'Did you stay on much longer at the pub?'

'No, just for one more drink. Francine is a nice girl, but a bit on the young side for us two to really have much to talk about. She thinks Andrew is the bee's knees though.'

'Yes she says they have many—what did she call it?—sweet times, together.'

Douglas nodded towards the book on the coffee table. 'Have you been reading?'

'For a wee while. I watched the last bit of a program about life on Mars. Apparently some scientists have found traces of ancient microscopic life in magnetic crystals from a Martian meteorite that fell to earth.'

Douglas snorted. 'Aye, well, these scientists are always coming up with fragments of organic material that point to something or other that has wee legs and pointy antennae. They're just kidding themselves.'

'You should have more faith, Douglas.'

'Aye, well I lost faith in a few things quite a while ago. When they find a rusty old shopping trolley or a used betting slip then I'll start to give life on Mars some serious consideration.'

'Yes, well, you do that. I'm away to my bed. Are you coming?'

'No, I've got a few papers to correct for the morning.'

'Don't stay up too late then. Goodnight,' she said, kissing him lightly on the cheek and gently squeezing his groin, unable to contain her laughter as he pulled away in surprise.

Douglas prised open the venetian blinds, two fingers revealing his new world. He should've gone to bed, he knew that, but he still couldn't free himself from the solitary cell of his former existence. Just him down here, Him upstairs, and too much altar wine. Sometimes he could still feel the pristine collar around his neck, could sense its absence, like an amputee who still felt his missing limb. He knew he had spent too many of his formative years on his knees, the wooden rail rendering them comfortably numb, consolidating a monastic, female-free sense of himself and his place in God's world. He should join Kirstin in bed; he should leave his books and his solitude and go and be with her. After all, that was part of the reason why he left the priesthood. He needed intimacy; he needed to feel loved.

He watched his friend and next-door neighbour taking his greyhound for its late-night stroll, regular as clockwork. 'Ayrshire' Archie Thompson had always meant to race the animal but somehow had never got around to it. Now, in the dark stillness, Douglas observed Archie with his lopsided gait and his dog with its steady rhythmic patter quietly and determinedly making their way down the street, symbiosis in motion, both vaguely aware there had been some original purpose to their nightly march, but not particularly concerned that any higher thoughts of glory they once harboured had quietly left them. They were content in the comfort of their own company and the liberating feeling of being without ambition.

A man and his dog, a man and his God. D-O-G. G-O-D. Was there that much of a difference? Douglas laughed to himself, the window fogging up from the closeness of his breath. Not one of the great metaphysical questions of all time, but one that may in the end reveal that the former relationship made more sense, although with the latter you did save on tins of Pal and vet's fees. Maybe he should get Archie involved with the soccer club. He wasn't such a bad bloke for a Protestant. And he could play that guitar, as Chuck Berry put it, like ringing a bell. Maybe he and his dog could walk the players around the pitch, that little extra bit of training to keep the lads in prime condition.

Douglas watched Archie merge with the enveloping darkness. The empty gloom they left behind reminded him of when he was a boy, wandering the streets in the cold night, escaping from the screaming turmoil of his home. A tentative creep down the stairs of the black close, for yet again some bastard had stolen the light bulb, all the while trying to shut out the hysterical battle his mother and father were waging in their top-floor flat. At first, they always tried to keep it down, lest the neighbours should hear. The vicious acid-tongued whispers were like a bad dream in the addled minutes before waking. They ripped at your stomach and scratched at your skin. They pushed and squeezed their way though the gap between your bedroom door and the linoleum and slid under your bedclothes, and no matter where you tried to hide, no matter how many damp pillows you clamped panic-stricken to your head, they found a way through to clatter and thump inside your brain. By the time he reached the bottom of the stone stairs, his heart beating fast, his gut a tight knot of pain, their voices were explosions that echoed out through the walls and the curtained windows into the street below. They no longer cared about what the neighbours heard or thought, or whether the boys from his school would imitate his mother's screams at playtime. They didn't care who heard and they let the world know they didn't care. It was an expression of their defiance in the face of their helplessness. The enemy was in sight and rushing over the ramparts but they had no weapons to repel it. They could only scream and shout and yell and tear their insides out in the pitiful hope that it would help. But it never did, and week after week, year after year it would go on. Not enough money, too much drink, not enough love, too many bad memories. The past was too miserable and blood-stained to look back upon, the future too grim to contemplate. And Douglas would stand at the bottom of the close and stare up at the window of their home, his home, at the paradoxically warm glow that blushed through it, and feel the rain of abuse falling through the sky and soaking his head with tears and confusion.

'All right son?' people would always say as they walked past, the collar of their coat drawn high and tight around them. 'A wee boy like you shouldn't be out at this time of night. You'd better be off home to yer bed. Your mammy will be worried about ye.'

'Aye, I'll be going up in minute,' Douglas would say, before turning down the path for a slow head-hung walk to nowhere in particular.

More often than not he'd end up at St Catherine's. If he arrived there early enough or late enough—his parents tended to go at each other either when they first woke up or when they'd finished the day's chores and had a few drinks in them—he would be the only person in the chapel. It would be just him and the cavernous silence. It was new, built from money raised from the parish, a parish of breadline working people barely able to feed themselves and keep their weans in cornflakes and school shoes, never mind fork out for a new chapel. Whenever Douglas clinked his penny or his threepenny bit into the collection plate on a Sunday morning, he could sense his mother at home listening to it drop and thinking what else she could have done with it. As far as she was concerned, it was not money well spent. She said there was not a Catholic priest in the Glasgow schemes who was as poor as the people they were supposed to serve. You didn't see them out borrowing money on a Tuesday night to tide them over until payday. She had no time for priests, or the chapel, or the Pope for that matter.

But Douglas didn't feel the same way. He treasured the silence when it was just him alone on the pews. It caressed his face, warmed his insides, even on a freezing winter's morning when he could barely keep himself from crying from the coldness of it. He'd push open the big door and genuflect before the giant wooden crucifix with Christ dying on it, and he'd be protected from life outside for a few minutes at least.

Once his mother had come and dragged him out of the chapel after he'd run away. She'd tried to take him and his sisters off to their grandmother's house for a while. She and his father had had a terrible fight the night before when she'd told him she hated his fuckin' guts and having sex with him made her sick to the stomach. But she had only been able to hold the hands of the other two weans and when he'd got the chance Douglas had slipped away down an alley and headed for the chapel.

It was always the same. Every time his parents had a huge screaming match his mother would pack up the weans in the morning after his father had gone to work and they'd all trudge off to his grandmother's on the other side of the town. It took ages to get there. You had to take two buses, then there was a long walk up a hill. When they got to their granny's house Douglas and his sisters couldn't go to school so they'd end up just sitting around the living room or playing out the back, which stank from the brewery up the road. Then, after a few days, his father would come and the weans would be sent into the other room while their parents talked and made up, and after a while they were told it was all right to come out and have a cup of tea and a ham and tomato sandwich their granny had made. Then they'd all have to walk back down the hill to the bus stop with their bags and get the two buses home. But after a few months it just happened all over again. So what was the point? Douglas felt he might as well stay with his father in his own house and keep to his routine. Up early for school in the morning, stop off at the chapel, his dinner in the school hall, football training at a quarter past three, then some tea and toast in front of the television before he started on his homework.

That's why he'd made a run for it that day and gone to sit in the chapel. But he'd turned as he heard the croak of the big door opening and watched her march down the aisle. She'd slapped him on the face right then and there and pushed him out the door. She hadn't even genuflected or anything. Then they all went home and she made some tea and bread and butter. Later, she took the other two and left him behind with his father. So he was able to keep up his routine and could enjoy the quiet of the chapel in the morning.

Douglas closed the blinds, drawing the strings tight. He sat down by the coffee table and drew a long breath of silence into his lungs and exhaled it slowly. He picked up an exercise book from the pile in front of him and removed the top of his pen.

Shane 'Shazza' McGowan woke up, sat on the side of the bed and scratched his arse. Bleary-eyed, he squinted at the sun belting in through his bedroom window and ran his fingers through his long, lank blond hair. He let out a slow gaseous burp and rubbed at the stubble on his cheeks. He raised both arms above his head and stretched till he could feel the vertebrae in his upper back and neck strain and creak and click like a wooden fishing boat on the water. He yawned long and wide and smacked the roof of his mouth with his tongue to knock some life into oral cells that had been rendered comatose by too much beer and too many cigarettes. He breathed hard on his palm and smelled it. 'Fuck,' he moaned.

He pulled on a pair of black footy shorts and stumbled out into the hallway and into the kitchen where the cat was curled up asleep in a spotlight of sun by the kitchen table.

'Slack bitch,' he muttered to himself as he pulled open the fridge door. 'Fuck, no fuckin' milk,' he swore, shaking a bottle of orange juice, sniffing it, and swallowing most of it in one long Brownlow Medal-winning gulp.

He rustled around the bottom right-hand kitchen cupboard until, in the mysterious gloom of the furthest corner, he found a crumpled box of cornflakes which he inched out with his fingertips. He examined the packet, noting a few specks of mould, but nonetheless poured what was lurking in the bottom of the box into a plastic bowl. Cornflakes in hand, he returned to the fridge and ran his bloodshot eyes over the sparsely populated shelves.

'Fuck,' he said. 'No fuckin' milk.'

He poured what was left of the bottle of orange juice into his cereal and made his way to the table, giving the sleeping cat a kick in the guts before sitting down to his breakfast. The cat shrieked and padded into the living room, her hackles raised and her tail in the air.

Shane cleared a space for his bowl amid the rubble of previous epicurean experiences and slurped at his food. He picked up the new edition of the local rag and slowly began to turn the pages. He skipped past stories about the latest council meeting, reports of drainage problems in the west ward, and rumours of a new housing estate at the old swamp, before lingering on a human interest story about an old couple who'd been married for seventy-five years and who declared the secret of their longevity to be their faith in the Lord and a rollicking good sex life.

'Filthy old bastards,' he laughed to himself.

He spent a few minutes with the comics and flipped the paper over to the sport on the back page. He skimmed through the Little Athletics report, noticing happily that his niece Tiffany had come second in the under-10 triple jump, till he found the article he was looking for. It was a report on how he, Shazza McGowan, had led the Baytown Football Club to a thumping forty-eight point victory over Spotswood at the Baytown Oval on Saturday. The article described his five screaming goals, the last of which, the journalist noted, was preceded by a mark reminiscent of the very best of Alex Jesualenko.

'Good on ya, Jezza,' Shane exclaimed to no one in particular, spitting sodden lumps of what were once crispy golden flakes of corn on to page 12.

Amid his quiet pleasure in himself and his strong footballer's thighs so admired by the sheilas in the unofficial cheer squad, his eye was caught by a three-deck double column headline in the bottom right-hand corner of the page. BAYTOWN TO GET ITS OWN SOCCER CLUB? it said. Shane immediately stopped chewing, his mouth hanging open like an overflowing rubbish bin without a lid, and read on with startled and groin-crushing disbelief. The council had all but approved an application from certain parties to lease a parcel of land near the old lake for the purpose of establishing a soccer club for the benefit of the community in general. Councillor Brian Myers had spoken against the proposal but other council members seemed to be in favour of it. Any public objections were to be lodged with the town clerk within one month. Shane rattled and rumbled like lava inside a volcano. Wogball in Baytown! He couldn't believe it.

'Objections!' he roared. 'I'll give them fuckin' objections, the cunts!'

Bloody hell, Douglas swore to himself. One of these days he was going to take that Malcolm Myers down to the boiler room and give him a good kicking. Some folk just didn't respond to prayer. He'd never met a student so incapable of sitting still for one minute, or of holding his tongue for more than the time it took to formulate another smirk-laced inquiry about matters juicily physiological.

This was always the problem with Health Education; it got the boys all worked up into a state, especially the ones that had been short-changed on the brain cell front but had been generously shot up with an overdose of hormones that left them purple pimpled and priapic. They could barely keep their hands off it during class hours, while recesses and lunchtimes were a frenzy of venial sin in the toilets, which only the giant factory pistons of the early Industrial Revolution could have matched in terms of frenetic hydraulic activity.

Douglas swore that on a windy day these boys could smell the girls at St Joseph's three blocks away and a female teacher two floors down through reinforced concrete and vinyl floor tiles as thick as sliced sandwich bread. Should Mrs Konieczny, Mrs Tamara Konieczny, short, raven-haired, full-lipped, swivel-hipped sex bomb of a music teacher possessed of a body that was riddled with heavenly breasts, suddenly emerge from the safe haven of the staffroom, the boys would welcome her into their sperm-charged world with a symphonic banging of a few hundred locker doors which mimicked the mini explosions taking place in their bodies as every corpuscle, brain cell and hormonal emission sprinted to the fertile territory between their legs. As the students, gripped by a ferocious, teeth-baring horniness they could hardly contain, dribbled their way to their next class, every teacher knew that was it for their powers of concentration for the rest of the day.

The Konieczny Effect was only a half-head in front of the Health Education Effect, for what the class lacked in real live caressable flesh, it made up for in joltingly explicit charts and diagrams, a virtual Royal Automobile Club guide to getting to the places you want to go with the minimum of fuss. The good priests and brothers of the religious order that ran the school had only recently introduced the HE program as a response to the growing influence of television on the sexual awareness of the students. Programmes such as *The Beverly Hillbillies* had undoubtedly added fuel to the fire of the boys' lust-filled loins, inciting them to believe that they were the ones to stick it to a writhingly grateful Elly May Clampett, Granny if they were desperate.

Thus the order's elders has decided to set up the HE program to educate their vulnerable boys and enlighten them to the fact that life was not just one big drive-in romp in the back seat of an EJ Holden or a midnight snog on the Baytown back beach. They wanted their charges to be aware that there was a moral framework for all aspects of life and sexual relations or, as the good brothers liked to put it, the private and special relations between two people who loved each other very much.

Of course, the problem for the brothers was that very few of them had actually experienced any of these private and special relations themselves, except, rumour had it, with each other. Consequently, it was left to the lay teachers to deal with the more hairy bits of the HE curriculum, which included anything to do with human reproduction, masturbation (known as onanism to the brothers, who seemed to Douglas to be very knowledgeable about it) and personal hygiene, which Andrew had once described to Kirstin as getting the little pricks to wash their swollen knobs occasionally.

And so it was that Douglas found himself on the fourth period of a Monday morning faced by thirty drooling fifteen year olds and Malcolm Myers, sixteen, who was repeating fourth form, although Douglas couldn't quite understand why. The boy didn't seem stupid, just distracted. It was not a class that Douglas particularly looked forward to, given that his own experience in the cattle market of love and sex was scanty, to say the least. Entering a seminary at seventeen did tend to cramp your style in that department. At that time all he had to stroke his imagination was the *Catholic Weekly*, a movie poster of Doris Day in *Calamity Jane* and a picture of Correggio's famous and decidedly voluptuous painting, *Leda With The Swan*, which featured a very self-satisfied Leda looking as if she needed a postcoital cigarette, and a large white and sated bird of the species in question having a bit of a kip between her milky white thighs. As far as Douglas was concerned, it beat the hell out of a twelfth century Flemish triptych any day.

Douglas had occasionally thought of getting Andrew in to share with the class his experiences with the opposite sex, a guest speaker if you like; but he had decided no matter how wildly imaginative and palm-blistered his students were, they were not quite ready for that sort of exposition.

Douglas coughed and stared coldly at Malcolm Myers, who was surreptitiously drawing pictures of the female genitalia with his friend and fellow onanist, Brendan Spruce. If this was Scotland he would have given him a good belting and be done with it, but Australia had different, more humanitarian rules that proscribed that sort of behaviour, although he had noticed Brother Chuck, the physics teacher, appeared to be unaware of this. His frequent use of a long and thick bespoke leather strap to tan the hides of his more recalcitrant students was well known and occasionally applauded. As Andrew liked to say, Charlie didn't fuck around.

Douglas tapped his desk with a pointer. 'Okay,' he said, like Jesus on the Cross knowing that any minute that prick of a Roman soldier was going to stab him in the ribs with that bloody long spear of his, 'RE-PRO-DUC-TION.'

The class erupted in a grand final roar of approval. This was the one they had been waiting for, Chapter 11, 'The Physicality of Reproduction Among Homo Sapiens—A Moral Overview', or as the boys called it, The Rooting Chapter. For them, this was the much dreamed about night at the drive-in with their older brother's naked and big breasted girlfriend, a session on the sand with the horny eighteen-year-old daughter of the bloke who ran the fish and chip shop. Free love and free flake—what fifteen year old, perennially aroused adolescent boy could ask for anything more?

While the boys usually ignored the preparatory requirements of most of their lessons—at least the ones Douglas set them in English—they had studied The Rooting Chapter in the sort of depth Montgomery had dedicated to the map of the Sahara for his victorious desert campaign. Many intense hours had been spent reading, underlining and highlighting what they believed to be *the good bits*.

Douglas took a deep breath and began a detailed, if somewhat hesitant, elucidation of the process of arousal, coitus and conception, all the while illustrating his lesson with regular pointed-stick references to the diagram on the blackboard which he'd carefully drawn with five different colours of chalk. The rapt students had uncharacteristically given him their undivided attention, save for the occasional guffaw and guttural moan at the mention of certain key words that appeared to set alarm bells ringing in their chuckle zones.

After twenty-five seething and sweat-soaked minutes hacking his way through the steaming jungles of their ignorance and wonder, Douglas rested his pointer on the desk in front of him and, with considerable relief, gazed across the room of crimson-faced and occasionally salivating students. In one of his rare remaining priestly gestures, he pursed his lips and placed his fingertips together in the form of a miniature cathedral, the spire of which touched the base of his chin. He slowly filled his lungs with air, a dying man's final breath.

'Any questions?' he asked, readying himself for the inevitable.

The classroom hummed with anticipatory silence, the calm before the storm, the blissfully ignorant and innocent moments before a few thousand seriously disgruntled Sioux stormed over the hills at Little Big Horn and General Custer realised he wouldn't be home in time for dinner. A couple of chairs scraped across the floor, some muffled coughs broke the unearthly quiet, two boys giggled and whispered in the corner by the window overlooking the football field.

'Eh, sur, I've goat a question, like.'

Douglas immediately recognised the distinctive Glaswegian tones of Wullie Henderson, late of the East End, and only two weeks off the boat. When he'd first arrived at the school several mischievous, if unwise, fellow students had taken great joy in mocking young William's indecipherable accent and curious phlegm-ridden intonation, assuming his scrawny egg-and-chips-reared frame denoted an inability to defend himself from verbal or physical aggression. However, they soon discovered, much to their surprise and detriment, that wee Wullie was what was known as a Glasgow 'hard man'. He was a five foot four bandy-legged inner-city cowboy with a mod haircut, a force 10 scowl and a diminutive frame that served more as an encouragement to his potent fighting prowess than to a kowtowing inhibition. As a former member of one of the toughest gangs in one of the toughest schemes in one of the toughest cities in the world, he took no prisoners. He punched, bit, kicked, chewed, spat, gnarled and generally slaughtered any of the hapless innocents who dared to torment him. While some boys continued to mimic Wullie's mannerisms and speech, it was out of respect, and indeed, some of Wullie's more common sayings such as 'nae bother', 'that's the game' or 'yer bum's oot the windae' had become part of the school's playground lexicon. As far as many students were now concerned, Wullie Henderson was 'far oot'. He also possessed a brain as sharp as a cut-throat razor, a fact which he attempted to disguise by enthusiastic lashings of profanity in even the briefest of sentences. In the short time he had known Wullie, Douglas had become convinced he would end up either as a university professor or a serial killer.

'On you go, Wullie,' Douglas said with a doom-filled flick of his hand.

'Well, sur, ye know when a wummin hus a wean, gies birth tae it an' that, does it come oot her erse or oot her belly button?'

Douglas struggled to contain his amusement. Wullie Henderson always broke him up. He was tough but earnest. Wise beyond his years but innocent as a baby when it came to some matters. He gave him a tight smile.

'Neither, Wullie. We'll get to that next week when we finish the chapter, okay?'

Wullie snorted and shifted around in his seat. 'Well, no really sur, ye know, we might as well get on wi' it the noo, if ye know whit I mean. Time's marchin' on. I'll be fifteen next week.'

Douglas sighed. 'When a child is born it passes from the womb through the birth canal and exits through the vagina, Wullie. Usually headfirst. It's fairly straightforward.'

Wullie nodded away to himself for a few seconds, seemingly absorbing these revelations and mulling them over before further inquiry. He raised his hand in the air.

'Are ye sure, sur?'

'Aye, I'm sure, Wullie.'

Wullie shook his head in disgust, which quickly turned to anger.

'See that big brother ae mine, he told me it came oot her erse. Wait till ah see the cu—'

'Wullie!' Douglas quickly interjected. 'If you don't watch yourself, the only thing that will be sticking out your erse will be my foot.'

'Aye, sur, sorry sur, but ye know ma brother he's a right bast—'

'Any more questions?' Douglas said, moving on quickly.

The thick, bough-like and sweaty right arm of Malcolm Myers rose slowly upwards like a refuse-strewn stairway to a second-floor whorehouse. As this particular appendage rose, other more centrally located appendages within the room rose with it in anticipation of the predictably and sordidly carnal nature of his inquiry. Twenty-nine heads turned in his direction.

'Yes, sir,' Myers said, grinning like a Murray Grey bull that's just been let into the cow paddock. 'I have a question.'

'Is that right, Myers?' Douglas said, nodding his head slowly.

'Yes, sir. You know when you have, eh, what do you call it, intercourse. How far do you put it in, sir?'

As fast as a blade out of a flick knife, all eyes fixed on Douglas, then quickly reverted to a grinning Myers before sprinting back to Douglas again.

Douglas sighed. He scratched a little itchy spot behind his left ear. He drummed his fingers on his desk, Keith Moon in "My Generation". He closed his eyes and he sighed again. He licked his lips. He bowed his head and folded his arms across his chest. He returned young Malcolm's gaze with his own unrelenting stare. He exhaled heavily, like the sigh of a football pierced by a nail.

'All the way, Malcolm, all the way,' Douglas said, betraying only a minor hint of resignation. 'As far as it will go.'

As the lunchtime bell rang the boys let out an excited roar, and with the speed of bullets from a gun they rushed down the corridor and into the crowded toilets to exercise their fertile imaginations.

'Class dismissed,' Douglas moaned in their yelping wake. 'And don't forget your essays for English. A story from your childhood. You've got until the end of term.'

He dolefully packed up his papers and books and sighed away to himself. Not long till the end of term, his first term in Australia. Term. It sounded like a prison sentence and some days it felt like it.

'S'cuse me, sir.'

Douglas looked up to see Jeremy Spencer, the youngest, smoothest of cheek and most quietly spoken boy in the class, a freckle-faced innocent in a sea of throbbing pricks, standing meek and puzzled before him.

'Yes, Jeremy?'

'Well, sir,' he said hesitantly, his eyes bolted to the floor, 'All that stuff you said before, about reproduction and all that, was it all true?'

Douglas looked down at Jeremy and affectionately flicked the boy's blond fringe out of his pale blue eyes.

'Aye, Jeremy, I'm afraid it is.'

Jeremy nodded away to himself, still suspicious that it all might be a joke, and hiked his schoolbag over his shoulder.

'Who would have thought?' he said, his brow furrowed with incredulity.

'Not me, Jeremy, not me,' Douglas sighed, patting the young man on the shoulder.

Douglas trudged out into the corridor towards the staffroom for a much-needed cup of tea. As he was pouring the third teaspoonful of sugar into his cup of Lipton's, Andrew waltzed into the small but functional staff kitchen like a man without a care in the world.

'What are you so happy about?' Douglas asked, his voice thick with resentment.

'I'll tell you what I'm so happy about, my wee Glasgow friend. I went out last night wi' this gorgeous waitress who works at a Lebanese restaurant on Sydney Road. You would not believe what she could do wi' a couple of pieces of pitta bread and a tub of hummus.'

'I don't want to even think about it,' Douglas said.

'What's up wi' you?'

'Health Education, that's what's up with me.'

'My God, what class?'

'Four B.'

'Oh no. Malcolm Myers?'

'Aye. Malcolm bloody Myers.'

Douglas rested his cup of tea on the table and held his head in his hands. 'I'm not ready for this, Andrew, seriously I'm not. It wasn't so long ago that I was warning people about the sins of the flesh and encouraging them to use the rhythm method. Now I'm instructing them on what goes where and how to get lassies pregnant. Sometimes life goes too fast, Andrew, so it does.'

'Well, you've been through a lot in the last few years, Douglas, there's no doubt about that, what wi' leaving the priesthood and getting your end away on a regular basis, at least wi' someone other than that nice wee Sister Mary Frances . . . '

'I don't know how many times I've told you, Andrew, me and Sister Mary Frances never—'

'I know, Douglas, I know. I'm just kidding you on. You are a bit tetchy the day. Thank heavens it's the weekend, eh. So I'll see you and Kirstin at the fundraiser then?'

'Aye, eight o'clock at the council hall,' Douglas said, solemnly stirring an extra spoonful of sugar into his tea.

Sergeant Richard McDonald stood by the old stone wall that protected Pittenweem from the fury of the ocean. The grey and wintry water, bitterly cold even in summer, thrust and tumbled its way along the Firth of Forth and out into the freezing and frightening waters of the North Sea. Thinking back, it had been a hard year, what with Duncan Connolly proclaiming at the council meeting that the village should forget about fishing and concentrate on tourism. That was the way of the future, not haddock or cod. Fish were fucked, he'd said in a moment of passionate discourse that shocked some of the elderly female members of the ladies auxilliary who had chosen to attend the monthly meeting at the back of the Pittenweem Arms. There wasn't much on television given that *Dr Finlay's Casebook* was finished until the next series began in the new year.

Connolly's proclamation had divided the village into those who wanted to keep things as they were and those who preferred to look to the future. It was true that the local fishing industry had seen better days, but nobody was willing to admit that the life they had lead for so many generations could be coming to an end, that it might disappear into a circus of madly clicking cameras, short-sleeved shirts and violently checked trousers. Their history was precious to them and they didn't want to let it go. Better the devil you know, than the devil you don't, eh?

Some of the council members had all but laughed in Duncan's face. Why would rich Americans want to travel thousands of miles to an ancient and wee stone village by the sea to wander about its narrow meandering streets and drink at the only pub, which had had little done to it since it was built in 1743? They'd put an exhaust fan in the kitchen, and that had expired trying to cope with the fat-infused vapours from the chip pan. And the current publican's dad, Benny Buchanan, had replaced the toilet seat in 1939, just in case there was a shortage during the war. So they'd need to renovate the place and knock through some walls, put in a gas fire at least. Those Americans would expect all the latest amenities and a range of international lagers, not just the locally brewed ale. They'd want hot dogs, for fucksake, not home-made shepherd's pie and scotch trifle. 'Are ye daft, Duncan?' was the general response from the gallery as well.

Upon reflection, there was no doubt that Sergeant McDonald had had a difficult year, and was, he whispered to himself as he confronted the bathroom mirror each morning and at night before he trudged off to bed, as tired as a pit pony after a double shift. It was even more demanding than 1963 when the Rolling Stones, the Kinks and a whole caravan of up and coming pop stars came to the village as part of one of those huge roadshows that had more bands than the Edinburgh Tattoo and more hair than a barber shop floor. Richard had lost count of how many acts were on the bill. Young people had flocked to the local Palais from all over Fife and he'd had to get reinforcements sent in from Kircaldy. His brother Angus had lent a welcome hand with keeping the crowd in order. But they'd agreed afterwards that they were generally well behaved, although that Michael Jagger had been unnecessarily provocative, wiggling his skinny hips all night and pouting away as if he was waiting for some young lass to leap up and kiss him right there on the stage. Mrs Sinclair from the Co-op said he looked like a right toerag, and anyhow, it wouldn't last, this 'poppy music'. It was certainly a big change from the Alexander Brothers who'd come the year before, no doubt about that. 'Marie's Wedding' had gone down a treat that night but this time there wasn't a hint of an accordion all evening. Still, that's the way of life, Angus had said; nothing stays the same, even if you grab hold as tight as you can and refuse to let go. Life just takes a detour around you and leaves you behind, wondering where the hell you are and where the time went.

No, it wasn't always easy being the only representative of the regional constabulary in Pittenweem. And it was a lonely life some nights. There was only the pub and the telly. *Sunday Night at the London Palladium, Coronation Street, Z-Cars, Dixon of Dock Green*, you couldn't go past them, right enough. One night he'd even seen Des O'Connor on *Top of the Pops*. But still, you sat there in front of the box by yourself, with only a drink and your memories to keep you company, thinking that every strange noise, every click and whisper of wind under the door, every sound of laughter in the night, every distant whine of a car struggling up the hill, was her coming back as if she'd never left. It was as if she'd just march right in the door, take her coat off and put the kettle on.

Richard McDonald took one last look at the snug harbour filled with fishing boats and swooping gulls in full lament, finished his cigarette and placed the butt in his empty cigarette packet. Some people in this village treated the place like a midden, but not him. He'd put it in the bin outside Hughie Cameron's butcher shop. What will it be the night? Lamb chop? Pork chop? Mince and tatties maybe? Some beef links? The evening was just overflowing with culinary promise.

'Morning, Hughie,' Richard called as he entered the shop, the bell above the door tinkling behind him like a musical alarm. 'The polis is here. Don't anybody move. Drop that meat cleaver nice and easy, son. Nae funny business. I'm afraid I have to ask ye a few questions.'

The two men stared at each other, gunfighters at either end of a dusty deserted street in Dodge City. You could cut the air with a boning knife. Richard sniffed and made the first move.

'How are the sausages the day?' he asked, slowly peeling off his leather gloves.

'Freshly made this mornin',' the butcher said, fingering his meat cleaver, his gaze unwavering. 'Any fresher and they'd still be bellowing in the field.'

'Is that right? Well, I'll take half a dozen for my dinner,' Richard said, adjusting his truncheon for quick and easy access, should the need arise.

'Right ye are,' Hughie said, cutting six from the long string of home-made links that hung on a metal hook from the ceiling and wrapping them up in two sheets of paper. 'And when are ye away then?' he inquired, placing the parcel on the counter.

'First thing in the mornin'. I'll be taking the Edinburgh train down tae London and then the aeroplane tae Australia.'

'How long will it take tae get tae Melbourne?'

'Thirty-two hours!' Richard exclaimed, hardly able to believe it himself. It had once taken him five hours to get to Ullapool in his brother's old Morris Minor and that had seemed like an eternity.

'Jesus, Mary and Joseph! That's a gey long time. Will I wrap ye up some black pudding and a few potato scones for along the way. Ye'll be famished by the time ye get there,' Hughie said, already grabbing a handful of scones from the pile behind him.

The sergeant held up his hands. 'No, dinnae bother, they give ye yer dinner on the aeroplane.'

'Aye, but what kind of dinner might that be, Richard?'

'I'm sure it will be very tasty, whatever it is. It'd want to be given a' the money ye pay for the ticket.'

'Aye, yer right there, Richard. Yer international jet-settin's no cheap, is it? Is this yer first journey across the water?'

'No, not at all. I took my mother to Skye last summer,' Richard laughed.

'Away wi' ye. Ye know what I mean. Anyway, it'll be a right adventure, eh? Imagine that. All the way to Australia tae see Angus. A miracle, so it is. I hear they have kangaroos hopping down the middle of the streets in Australia. Is that right?'

'I dinnae ken about that, Hughie. Angus hasn't mentioned any kangaroos in his letters. He's mentioned something called possums, but. He says they've got intae the roof of his house and make an awfy racket at night.'

'Possums? Can you eat them?' Hughie inquired, casting a proud eye over the feast of fresh flesh laid out before him, like a cannibal's dinner party.

'That's something else I'll have tae ask Angus when I see him. Maybe we can catch one and send it back tae ye,' Richard laughed. 'You could put it one of yer pies, alang wi' all the other mysterious things ye put intae them.'

Hughie picked his meat cleaver and wielded it in a mock threat of imminent decapitation. 'Ye cheeky bugger ye. The sooner you're off to Australia the better, Richie.'

'Sergeant Richie, tae you,' he said, picking up his sausages and sauntering out the door into the frosty morning. 'I'll be seein' ye, Hughie. Mind ye behave yerself now.'

When Kirstin first met Douglas she couldn't get over how handsome he was, in a clean finger nails, ruddy-cheeked, black and white, highly polished shoes kind of way. His thick black hair was perfectly combed with a side parting as sharp and straight as the crease on a bishop's trousers. He seemed calm, serene, but quick to laugh. He even liked to tell jokes that chipped away at the sanctity of the priesthood. Priests were just like everybody else he said, only they mostly kept their thing in their trousers and did a lot of unpaid overtime. She was surprised by how open he was, how ready to talk, as if he needed to share his thoughts. He even whispered tales about the priests who had taught him at school, or the seminary, or had long since passed away and caught the Number 11 bus to the big chapel in the sky.

His elderly parish priest, Father Docherty, made him laugh, he said. Never was there a more devout man, a man whose vocation was as strong as the Firth of Forth Bridge, a visionary teacher of theology, a man who would close his eyes and feel the love of God warm his bones: but neither was there ever a man who could drink so much whisky and be able to wake up in the morning still breathing. He'd sit in that favourite chair of his, with a doily on it which his Irish mother had given him thirty years before, and turn up his Mozart as loud as it would go without shaking the old building from its foundations, and he would just laugh at the wonder of it. God, Mozart and Johnny Walker. The Holy Trinity.

Kirstin had gone to see Douglas in the first place because his parish was looking to find a building where they could open a child-minding centre. Some of the local working mothers didn't have unemployed husbands or obliging grannies on hand to look after their kids while they were at work, and there were also women who just had too much on their plate and needed a rest from the weans and the washing. They needed a couple of hours to themselves to shave their legs and get their heads together, as Douglas put it at that first meeting. Of course, as a woman, Kirstin greatly appreciated the idea and admired Douglas for pursuing it with the obvious enthusiasm he displayed. She thought he was quite ahead of his time. Douglas had telephoned Kirstin's boss at the council, who also happened to be a member of the parish welfare committee, to inquire whether he knew of any possible premises the church could rent which would not be too down-at-heel nor too expensive. The job had been given to Kirstin and she had spent a few hours over the next couple of weeks or so visiting the possibilities. She'd finally come up with something she thought would be, if not ideal then perfectly suitable, given the location and the price restrictions. It was an old house in the original village around which the scheme where Douglas now served had been built, like a net thrown around an unsuspecting fish quietly grazing on the riverbed.

Kirstin arranged to pick Douglas up in her car and together they drove to the building, him in the front seat next to her. She could smell his aftershave. After a bit of small talk about parish goings-on and possible mutual acquaintances, they got on to talking about what films they'd seen lately. He asked her if she liked westerns and whether she'd seen *Gunfight at the OK Corral*, the version with Burt Lancaster as Wyatt Earp. Although she hadn't, he quoted a few lines from it anyway, ones that Lancaster had addressed to a young Dennis Hopper. *'All gunfighters are lonely. They live in fear. They die without a woman, a dime or a friend.'* Then he laughed to himself, a half-hearted kind of laugh. 'Burt should be a priest,' he said. She wasn't quite sure what to make of that. She wondered whether he was just trying to be enigmatic, but then who had ever heard of an enigmatic priest? She was not at all religious herself, and the rituals of Catholicism were a complete mystery to her, but she would have thought priests would have to be quite the opposite if they were to do their jobs properly. If anything, they would need to be forthright and outgoing because they had a battlefield of barriers to break down before they could even get started with what most people would call normal conversation. As it was, most dialogue was usually dusted with deference, palpitation and a gnawing sense of guilt on the part of the nonclerical participant. Guilt for not going to the chapel three Sundays in a row, guilt for never going to confession, guilt for rarely putting anything in the plate when it was passed around like an unwanted orphan.

Kirstin wanted to come back with an equally impressive line from a famous movie but the only thing that came to mind was a song from *Calamity Jane* with Doris Day going on about the how the Windy City was mighty pretty but they ain't got what we got, I'm tellin' you boys, in the whole of Illinoize. But, changing from third to second as they headed up the hill past the old abandoned sewing-machine factory, she decided this would be best kept for another time.

As they drove on, Douglas seemed to grow more melancholy. He stared straight out the windscreen and said sometimes he felt just like Burt Lancaster in the movie, like an anachronism, a man out of time, out of place. He was part of the community he lived in, but separated from it by his celibacy and his relatively privileged existence. Unlike those around him, the people he laughingly described as his flock, there was always food on the table and wine and whisky to drink. There were no worries about paying the rent or having enough money to buy school shoes for the weans. It was a comfortable life. But when he went out visiting after his dinner he'd climb the cold stone stairs of the tenements to arrive unannounced at the home of one of the children at the school or a family he'd met at mass, and he could feel their unease. They sat nervous and upright, and politely made conversation with the man in his black suit in their small rooms smelling of cheap food and too many children. By the very nature of his vocation there would always be a barrier between them, like frosted glass on an office door. Sometimes when he was talking to them, endlessly rubbing his clean white hands together, he felt it was he who needed their help, not they his. He needed their help to become a part of the world he lived in, the streets he walked on, to become connected.

Then suddenly Douglas had laughed and, mimicking some drug-addled rock star he'd heard on the radio, had slurred that he was 'right out of it, man'. Kirstin hadn't known what to make of him at all.

When they reached the building, Kirstin and Douglas walked slowly around the four rooms, inspecting this and that, poking in corners and lifting the linoleum to see what was underneath. Douglas found an old copy of the *Daily Record*. He couldn't help but laugh when he picked it up and saw that the front-page article was about the Vatican II congress and how the Latin mass was to be dropped in favour of an English version. The article featured criticism of the move from some of the city's leading Catholics complaining about the end of tradition. But thank God that was one barrier that had broken down, he said. At least now he didn't have to preach to his flock in a foreign language. East End Glaswegian was foreign sounding enough.

They walked on and discussed where things could go, where the best places would be for the playroom, for cots and mattresses, a small office. They poked at walls and ran the water through the taps and speculated about colour schemes. Something soothing for the nursery, bright for the playroom and serious for the office. Yellow ceilings were best, Kirstin said. Like sunlight.

Douglas said he had been born in an old house like this one, although a fair bit smaller. He said the weather was terrible when he was born, and the snow was so thick that his mother couldn't get to the hospital so he came into the world in their Single End flat with the help of Mrs Murdoch from down the stair. The doctor had come afterwards to examine his mother and him and make sure everything was as it should be. Kirstin laughed and said her father was a doctor and he had had a practice in Dennistoun around that time and wouldn't it be funny if he was the one who'd called on them that night. She joked that this would probably make them related, like third cousins or something.

After a short discussion about leasing details and moving arrangements, they shook hands in an exaggeratedly formal manner, like children playing at grown-ups. They both laughed and then—to this day Kirstin didn't know why—she put her hand behind his neck and kissed him full on the mouth. For a moment, nothing existed outside that room.

'Oh my God,' she said, panic-stricken. 'Oh my God, is that, what do you call it, a mortal sin?'

The empty house suddenly seemed emptier, as if the walls and the floors had been stripped bare. They said nothing for a while. Douglas stepped back, shocked, but to his surprise, not displeased.

'I don't know whether it is or not, Kirstin. But if the way it felt is anything to go by, it probably should be.' He touched her hair and said they should get going.

And here they were again, three years later, looking at another house, but this time in another life in another country 11 000 miles away from the damp grey slate roofs of Glasgow. The sprawling, run-down Victorian house was a rarity in Baytown, which had developed in a rush in the 1950s and 1960s. The suburb was mostly a flat sprawl of modest two or three bedroom homes built by the migrants who'd found work in the local factories, slaughterhouses and petrochemical plants. The English and the Scots came first, then the Maltese and the Italians, followed by the Greeks and the Dutch. Chuck in the odd German and Pole and there you had it, a suburb for Everyman. Except, thanks to the White Australia policy, for blacks and Asians. There was one Indian doctor at the Baytown Clinic, but with his pukka accent and the stethoscope dangling around his neck, people seemed to assume he was some sort of honorary Englishman.

This house was one of the area's original farmhouses, built at a time when hundreds of thousands of sheep grazed almost all the way to Geelong. It had large airy rooms with leadlight windows, open fireplaces and a return veranda. It still had the original wood stove next to an ancient gas cooker whose untidily exposed pipes suggested it had been rigged up by some backyard plumber. It had a wooden dunny out the back, a good twenty yards from the house. Kirstin pointed out that you wouldn't want to be desperate because you might not make it in time. Douglas said they could move the dunny closer to the house or move the house closer to the dunny. Nonetheless, despite possible lavatorial difficulties, they agreed it would be a perfect house for them, giving them so much more space than the small house they presently rented next door to Archie and Joyce. 'There's room here for one or two more people,' Kirstin said pointedly.

The back door moaned as they made their way into the garden. One of the wooden steps was broken and Kirstin took hold of Douglas's arm to steady herself as she descended. She took a noisy breath of sea air and held it in her lungs until she almost choked. She loved the salty tang, the sense of the water being a powerful presence just a few minutes up the road.

Kirstin jumped up and grabbed hold of the Hills hoist, spinning it like a merry-go-round at the carnival. She closed her eyes and the bright sunlight painted colourful flashes on the insides of her eyelids. Douglas laughed as he watched her, he couldn't help himself. She looked like a young girl, her hair and skin illuminated, her body stretched and lithe as she hung there like a single puff of whipped cream cloud in the sky. Seeing her like this, he could almost admit to himself that it had all been worth it, the pain, the guilt, the terror of leaving the Church that had been the firmament of his entire adult life.

'I love this place, Douglas, I love it,' Kirstin said, laughing as the washing line gathered speed. She felt dizzy. 'You know, you can hang out the washing on this hoisty thing and it will be dry by the time your basket is empty. Did you know that?'

Douglas smiled to himself. 'I didn't know that, no.'

'It's true. Dry and crisp, and all the white things bleached by the sun. Back in Glasgow it would take two weeks to dry out there on the line, that's if someone didn't steal it. But no one can steal your washing here, Douglas, no, not if you have your very own backyard with its very own hilly hoist. In this country, your smalls are sacrosanct. In Glasgow they were public property. This place is civilised, that's why I love it. And you can wake up in the morning with a wee bit of hope in your heart. And the sound of sprinklers spreading all that lovely cool water on the grass makes you feel like you're waking up in a Garden of Eden or something.'

'Well, I wouldn't go so far as to call this grass,' Douglas said, kicking at the thick sponge-like layer of couch that had clamped itself to the ground like a rampant parasitic creeper to a tree. 'It's more like an invasion from outer space.'

'You know what I mean, Douglas. At least it's green and more than you ever had when you were a wee boy.'

Although her arms were tiring, Kirstin continued to drift on her merry-go-round, her head hanging back, the sunlight dancing on her hair. 'I'd like to buy this house, Douglas, wouldn't you?'

'Aye, maybe. Is it for sale? How would we pay for it?'

'I'll talk to my mother. She would lend us some money, I know she would.'

'Won't it be a bit draughty?'

'Listen Douglas, people will be soon be falling over themselves to buy beautiful old houses like this, I'm telling you.'

'Aye, and the Pope will have a wife and five weans. I'll believe it when I see it.'

'Shall I ask the agent to look into it then?'

'You are the agent.'

'Ah yes, so I am. I will ask myself then,' she said, spinning faster before leaping off onto the long uncut grass. She lay still, spread-eagled like a fallen star, and stared at the deep blue never-ending sky. 'Yes Douglas, my love, I think we can be happy here. Do you?'

Douglas smiled and gave the Hills hoist a push and watched it spin. 'I hope so.'

Andrew and Douglas stood on each side of the main door to the council hall like a pair of Scots Guards outside Buckingham Palace. They nodded and smiled and joked with the people making their way into the hall for the fundraiser, an evening of food, drink and musical entertainment, featuring Valletta Vince, King of the Spin, and Ayrshire Archie and the Vandellas.

Douglas was forever amazed by people, the way they bobbed up with their hidden talents. As Father Docherty had always told him, never underestimate anybody for they will always surprise you. He had proved to be right. God bless him and rest his drink-sodden soul. If someone had told Douglas that a five foot four inch version of Elvis Presley hailing from the capital city of Malta could not only drive a one-ton grader around a field as if it were a toy car at the fair, but also possess the best record collection this side of Gozo and a silver-tongued patter any loquacious Glaswegian would be proud of, he would not have believed them. And if someone else had told him that a quietly spoken and bespectacled sexagenarian with a gammy leg, a pencil–thin moustache and a ten-gallon hat could play the meanest, finger-lickin' country and western guitar since Scotty Moore did the business for the boy from Tupelo, Mississippi, he wouldn't have believed them either.

But there they were on the poster stuck to the tinted window at the front of the club, and at other strategic points around the suburb as well, although why Andrew had insisted on gluing one to the clubhouse wall of the Baytown Football and Athletics Club, he'd never know. The posters seemed to have done the trick because the evening was a sell-out, and they'd even had to squeeze in a few extra tables so as not to disappoint the bricklayer brothers of Andrew's latest girlfriend, Gina, who worked in an Italian trattoria in Lygon Street, Carlton. The boys could each lay hundreds of bricks an hour and it was felt they might come in handy when the time came to build a pavillion for the soccer club. For her part, Gina could carry a bottle of chianti and four plates of spaghetti bolognaise without spilling a drop of sauce on her, or anybody else's, clean white blouse. And, according to Andrew, she also had huge Neapolitan nipples and thighs the colour of creamy drinking chocolate. The youngest boy, Paulo, was apparently a dashing centre-forward with a bullet-like right foot and an unerring eye for goal. 'What a family!' Andrew had laughed as he and Douglas arranged the chairs around the family's table in the corner.

'No a bad turnout, eh Douglas,' Andrew said, collecting another ticket and nodding to Perry McIntosh, a painter and decorator from Govan. He'd offered to paint the new clubroom when it was built. He explained his unusual name (at least for a Glaswegian) to Douglas as being due to his conception on the living room settee as his ma and da revelled in the tender tones of Perry Como singing 'Magic Moments'.

'Aye, very impressive. With the money we get from this we should be able to think about seeding the two pitches and maybe even buying some strips for the senior team.'

'What senior team?'

'Well, the senior team when we get it started,' Douglas said, waving at Kirstin who was holding on to the leash of Archie Thompson's greyhound, Hank, while he unloaded an old amplifier from the back of his Bedford van.

'Is the dog in the band as well?' Andrew asked, gesturing towards Douglas's neighbour.

'Aye, the dog's on tambourine and backing vocals. It can yodel as well, apparently. Good for some of those old Hank Williams songs Archie does.'

Douglas noticed a barrel of a man in a dark suit, loitering on the footpath and staring at them. His hair shone like an oil slick in the rain. He didn't look as if he was about to join the party. 'Who's that?'

Andrew squinted at the man, who was about fifteen yards away across the car park. He could just make out his features by the light from the street lamp behind him. He took a long look. He'd make a useful right-half, whoever he was. Broad shouldered and a chest like a landing pad. Perhaps a slight swelling around the waist, but a few laps around Cherry Lake would soon get that off him. 'No idea.'

'Well, he doesn't look too happy,' Douglas said.

All of a sudden they were hit by a rush of excited dinner dancers waving their tickets and laughing loudly as they went through the entrance. When Andrew and Douglas turned around again the man in the dark suit was gone.

The men had brandished their tickets as if they were chits to the promised land. Their shoes were polished, their hair combed and their ill-fitting jackets brushed free of dandruff and dust. A few had obviously done a couple of rounds with a bottle or two of the finest blended. With their flushed faces and self-satisfied smiles, they looked as happy as a fridge full of beer. As they walked through the door, into the hall and across the wooden dance floor to their tables arranged around the perimeter, one or two began humming along with the music and doing the odd solo snatch of improvised ballroom dancing. Some tilted slightly to the right because of the half-bottle of Grouse ensconced snugly in the side pockets of their jackets, which, Douglas couldn't help but notice, were machine crafted from a material completely foreign to that of their trousers.

Some of the older women from Glasgow, who still believed the biggest thing to have happened in popular music was when Sinatra played the Glasgow Empire in 1949, had teased their hair into a follicular fairy floss of home perm and hair spray. Now and again they patted it into some position of imaginary perfection, but it yielded not to touch of any kind, soft, medium or bone-crushing. Theirs were dos that defied disorder. Pink or white nylon blouses were the preferred upper garments for this particular group of females.

The former schemies from the East End of Glasgow wore adventurously ruffled and wickedly déshabillé tops that exposed a tripe-like ripple of plump and freckled bosom, while the gals from the more rural environs of Dumfries and Galloway wore their blouses buttoned right up to the neck to keep out any chilly draft that might be lurking somewhere in the hall just waiting for the right moment to make a flu-inducing dash for their cleavage. They kept their arms folded firmly across their ample chests like oak planks across the nunnery door. Some still had their cardigans on and were obviously no strangers to the comforting clack of crochet needles in front of the telly of an evening.

The Scots had covered their various tables with hand-embroidered tablecloths, except for the Glaswegians who had bought plastic ones from Coles. They laid out the salmon sandwiches, mutton pies, Forfar bridies, Dundee cake, Edinburgh scones and Abernethy biscuits. The schemies had brought a few pieces an' jam just in case.

The Italians arrived in various shades of black and white. They entered in a chattering and excited mass, like a flock of birds that had just flown in from colder climes and were relieved to be somewhere that didn't freeze your feathers off. Gina Coppola led them in like Caesar through Rome after a big win in Mesopotamia. She was closely followed by her mother, an older, broader and shorter version of herself, and what appeared to be two younger, equally buxom sisters. Between them and their beaming smiles they bore large plates piled with a *macelleria* of tasty Italian fare. Great cylinders of salami fuming with garlic and chili, ripe home-grown tomatoes and verdant cucumbers, creamy mozzarella cheese, whole red onions, jars of pickled vegetables, exquisitely thin slices of parma ham, cold cutlets of veal Milanese, some calamari fried in olive oil and a dish of golden-topped lasagna.

Behind them danced a festive trail of masculine family members headed by Signor Coppola with a veritable vat of home-made red wine under his arm, the three bricklaying boys, all with cigarettes dangling from their lips, and a lean, dark and unshaven man wearing a manky kerchief around his open neck and leading a young black and white goat tied to a piece of old rope.

'Who's that?' Douglas asked.

'That's Gina's cousin Carlo. He's just off the boat from Sicily. Got in yesterday morning. He's a farmer from some wee village near Caltanmissetta.'

'Aye, I know it well. What's with the goat?'

'I'm not sure. I think Carlo was hoping to put it on a spit and roast it,' Andrew shrugged.

'Well, we can't have a goat in the hall, the council will go crazy. We'd better tie it up round the back with Archie's greyhound. I'm sure they'll be all right together.'

'Well they'll either eat or fuck each other,' Andrew said. 'That's the way of all primitive life forms.'

'Aye, well, I'm sure there's a council by-law against that sort of thing as well,' Douglas replied as he poked his head into the hall to locate the whereabouts of the goatherd. He found him deep in a semaphore-heavy conversation with Aberdeen Angus who was peering into the baby goat's left ear hole and inspecting its teeth. He lifted its leg and peered at its little hoof, then nodded happily to himself before giving Carlo from Caltanmissetta a cheery thumbs up. Meanwhile the goat was shoving its head under Angus's kilt, no doubt in search of some tasty morsel to munch on.

The three-table strong Maltese contingent headed up by Valletta Vince, his wife and their nine children, were also taking a keen interest in the goings-on with the goat.

'Bloody beautiful goat, no worries,' Vince said to his wife Teresa, who nodded in affirmation. 'Bloody beautiful, Vincey,' she said.

'That's terrible that, those young people smoking,' Margaret Walker moaned to her husband Alec, a master carpenter from the northeast of England and a diehard Leeds United fan. 'If I were their mother I'd be giving them a right good seeing to, that I would. Eh, I tell you, me dad would never have put up wi' that if he were alive. He'd 'ave them muckin' out the cow shed quick smart, isn't that right, Alec?'

'Eh, that would be right, Margaret,' Alec said, loosening his collar and tie, looking for another bottle of stout, and grimly recollecting the many miserable drizzly days spent on Margaret's father's farm in the Yorkshire dales before they migrated to a dung-free life in Australia. Alec sighed and, surveying the grim picnic of curried egg sandwiches and fishcakes in front of him, made a mental note to introduce himself to the Italians across the way.

'All right Alec?' Douglas said as he and Andrew strolled past towards the stage, the duties at the door now over. 'How are those goalposts coming along?'

'Be ready next weekend, lad, no problem.'

'Good man.'

Andrew waved at the Svensens and the Ericssons, the only Swedish couples in Baytown, and mad soccer fans to boot. 'You know, Douglas, all Swedes look like Max Von Sydow. Have you noticed that?'

'Aye, even the men.'

Douglas and Andrew clambered up the small steps at the side of the stage. As members of the executive committee they had a few announcements to make concerning the progress of the club and the evening in general. Douglas tapped the microphone and was met with a reassuring thud from Ayrshire Archie's PA system. The old guitar plucker had built it himself out of bits of scrap wood and broken valve radios. As Andrew coughed loudly, waved his arms about and shouted at people to quieten down,

Douglas gazed across the room like Columbus over the New World. He still couldn't get over it, the way all these people from every corner of the planet, from the grey, rat-ridden slums in the East End of Glasgow to tumbledown stone cottages in the barren hills of Sicily, had left their families and their friends and everything they knew, everything that made them who and what they were, and set out for a new and uncertain life. They'd survived and mostly prospered with their fruit and vegetable shops, their joiner's sheds, their jobs at the petroleum refineries and the slaughterhouses and the local council. They'd carved out new homes with their boning knives, long-handled shovels, Sidchrome spanners and part-time jobs on the side. They were up early and home late till they saved up a deposit for a three-bedroom brick veneer or weatherboard house in quiet tree-lined street with a dunny out the back and a promise from the council that it wouldn't be long before the sewerage came in. Some blokes could even afford a brand new Kingswood or Fairlane, although Jimmy Staccato, who ran Baytown's premier fish and chip shop, had steadfastly refused to drive anything without fins, much to his wife Connie's distress. Sweating over a bubbling basket of dim sims and potato cakes she was often heard laughing that you could take the wog out of Naples but you couldn't take Naples out of the wog.

'Soy sauce with the dimmies, luv?' she would inquire, shaking her head with resignation.

Baytown was full of vegetable gardens, grapevines draped over carports, chook pens, and standard suburban houses that had been transformed into Mediterranean sun-drenched villas of a Greco-Roman persuasion. They had immaculate concrete driveways, which the owners had laid themselves, with a narrow strip down the middle for some mixed pebbles or grass. They stretched in a shark-grey shadow as far as the eye could see to the shed out the back which usually harboured an old car to be tinkered with on a Saturday afternoon.

In their modest castles, the Scots and the English and the Irish had covered every available, innocent inch of wall space with recklessly patterned wallpaper. Even the ceilings were papered. There were fitted carpets on the floor and apricot and apple trees in the backyard. And bungalows with grannies in them.

On Sundays the kids washed the windows, the dads washed their cars and the mums swept anything that was sweepable, including significant stretches of the street. It seemed as if people always had a hose in their hand and they hosed and hosed with joyful water-rich abandon, each sunlight-infused squirt a symbol of their new-found freedom and prosperity.

Everybody's kids looked healthy and had tanned legs and big appetites in this western suburb by the sea. The fumes from the refineries hung in the air like the scum on a freshly made pot of chicken stock, but it didn't bother them too much. They did bombs off the pier and lay in the park under the old pine trees and stuffed themselves with flake and chips and Chiko rolls and chocolate milkshakes. They lay in the scorching sun and their salt-encrusted skin sizzled and peeled away like bark from a eucalypt. At night they slept with a convention of mozzies buzzing around their heads, tossing and turning in the close heat, and when they awoke their sheets lay crumpled on the floor and their skin was thick with sweat. They walked the streets barefoot and rode their bicycles to the shops. They played cricket for hours until they were felled by sunstroke or unprotected shins bruised black and blue by tricky offspin bowling. It was a tangy world of cold cordial, baked beans on toast and refrigerators that hummed their own particular lullaby through the night. Some of the kids were off at university but still bringing their washing home. The eternal attraction of the nest, Douglas laughed to himself.

And here they were, all those races, skin colours and eating habits in the one room, united in their desire for a better life and the love of the greatest game ever known to mankind. And all would agree that football was not a matter of life and death—it was much more important than that. A club of their own would be the icing on the cake, the big grumbling donk in the Monaro, the checks on the Miller shirt, the bloody cat's pyjamas.

'All right, all right, could I have your attention please,' Douglas shouted into the microphone. 'I know you're all anxious to get the evening started and to enjoy some food and dancing, but I've got a few announcements I have to make before we can get on with it. So if I can have your indulgence for a few minutes, I'd be grateful. As you all know, the council has given us the go-ahead to use the land by the old lake and Vince Vella's already been up there wi' his grader and levelled it out a bit. Thanks Vince.'

'On ya, Vince!'

'You beauty, mate!'

Vince half raised himself from his chair and happily acknowledged the approbation and gratitude of the crowd, not unlike Elvis at his comeback concert on the telly the year before.

'Beautiful jacket, mate! Bloody beautiful!' someone yelled.

Douglas gestured for quiet with a downward push of his hands.

'All right, thank you. You may have noticed it you have driven past that the council has been back and repaired the fence. So a big hand for the council. If anyone hears anything about how it was torn down in the first place, get in touch with me or Andrew. Now, next Sunday fortnight we'll be having a big working bee and I hope I will be seeing you all there. We'll be getting underway at nine o'clock on the Sunday morning so go easy on the drink on Saturday night because we don't want anybody throwing upon on Vince's nicely levelled ground. Isn't that right, Vince? Bring some food and something to drink and we'll make a day of it. All right, that's enough from me. I'll just hand you over to Andrew here who's going to say a few words.'

'Did you hear the one about the woman who collapsed dead drunk at the bar?' Andrew said, relishing having the microphone in his hand and imagining he had a guest spot on *Rowan and Martin's Laugh-In*. 'The barman said to the bloke next to her, you'd better resuscitate her while I call a doctor. So the doctor arrives about five minutes later and this guy's down on his knees and blowing up her arse. So the doctor says, what the hell are you doing, you're supposed to blow into her mouth. So the guy says, "Aye I know, but have you smelt her breath?"'

Given that the audience had been into the beer and the wine and the whisky for a good hour or so, it was generally felt that this was one of the funniest jokes they'd heard in years and that Andrew was a right comedian, so he was. Margaret Walker and her sister-in-law Dorothy, who was married to Alec's brother Dennis, were not appreciative, however, and tut-tutted into their fishcakes, disappointed with the declining moral standards of young people and the nineteen sixties in general.

'Oh for a nice bit of Connie Francis, eh, Dot love?' Margaret moaned.

Andrew spread his arms in front of him in mock apology. He put the microphone back on the stand and read from a crumpled piece of paper.

'Right, the raffle will be drawn at ten o'clock. I hope you've all got your tickets. See Douglas or myself if you haven't, okay? Let me see here, aye, the second prize is a free do or haircut at Bettina's House of Beauty in Bay Street, courtesy of Bettina herself who's here tonight. Will you give her a big hand, ladies and gentlemen.'

Andrew put his hands together and the rest of the audience followed suit as Bettina stood up and acknowledged the applause with a slight quiver of her beehive.

Joyce Thompson let fly with a rollicking drum roll as Andrew prepared to announce the big prize for the night.

'Thanks Joyce, you were sounding a bit like Ginger Baker there for a minute. I'm no kidding. Right, the first prize for the Baytown Soccer Club's inaugural raffle, the big numero uno, is, wait for it, a garden shed, handcrafted out of the finest timber by the Walker brothers, Alec and Dennis.'

More applause and a few whistles.

'Right, I know you're all anxious to have your dinner, so let's get stuck in.'

Douglas had a quiet word in Andrew's ear, pointing to Carlo from Caltanmisetta who was waving from the Coppola table.

'Eh, wait a minute, wait a minute,' Andrew continued. 'Stop press. Gina's cousin Carlo wants to donate his wee billy goat, Alfredo di Stefano, for a third raffle prize. How about that? Only in the country a day and already he's giving away his livestock. That's what you call generosity. Thanks Carlo. Molto grazie. Right, that's it, away we go. Ladies and gentlemen, all the way from that nice wee house next door to Douglas's, live for one night only at the Baytown Council Hall, will you please put your hands together for Ayrshire Archie and the Vandellas. Take it away, Archie, ye old bugger ye!'

Happy that all the official business was finally over, everybody cheered and whistled and stomped their feet as Archie moved to the microphone with his distinctive swaggering limp, tipped his ten-gallon hat over his left eye, adjusted his tartan waistcoat, and with his silver Gibson guitar strapped high to his chest like a young Roy Orbison, belted into an old Hank Williams song he'd first heard way back when he was just a poor boy from Ochiltree. A one, a two, a one two three four.

'Met my future wife today, And her name is Cassie May,
Rootie tootie, rootie tootie,
Rootie tootie, she's my Sunday gal.

Feelin' dandy, doin' swell, my gal is the village belle,
Hotsy totsie, super dooper,
Rootie tootie, she's my Monday gal.'

The song had such an infectious beat, and Archie sang it with such ebullience that people were up on their feet before you could say lickity split, except for some of the teenagers who were hankering after a bit of something by the Master's Apprentices or the Easybeats.

73

'Archie sounds like he's straight out of Nashville,' Andrew said, tapping his foot. 'It's a bit odd, don't you think, for a bloke from Ayrshire?'

'Most people are a bit odd in their own way, Andrew. Archie just doesn't hide it. He is what he is and that's that as far as he's concerned. The closer you get to folk, when you watch them go about their business, when you commune across the kitchen table of their lives, the more their eccentricities come out—the things they eat, the stuff they think, the way they stick their fingers in their ears or up their nose or keep mysterious substances at the back of the fridge. A quiet weirdness is the norm, Andrew. Everybody is a little insane. I mean, how could you not be, with life the way it is? You wake up, eat your cornflakes, work like a bastard all day, clock off, drink beer, sleep, die.'

'Aye, I suppose you're right, Douglas,' said Andrew doubtfully. 'But country and western in this day and age?'

'Highland and western, Andrew. He calls it highland and western. He does a medley of Andy Stewart songs in the middle of his set.'

'Oh aye, but what's wi' this Vandellas bit. That's no very highland or western, is it?'

'No,' Douglas laughed, 'I suppose it isn't. Joyce used to love that Martha and the Vandellas, thought they were the business, and said she wouldn't be in the band unless Archie paid tribute to them and black women generally.'

'She's a bit of a women's libber, is she?'

'Aye, and she likes girl groups as well.'

Andrew scratched his nose. 'Do you think they'll ever be men's liberation then?'

'No, I don't think so.'

'Why not?'

'Because men are not seen to have anything to be liberated from. But I can tell you one thing for nothing, my father wouldn't have minded being liberated from his work down the pit, five and a half days a week for eleven pounds and fifteen pence. That job did his head in. By the time he retired he looked like a wee sparrow.'

'Aw aye, all my auld man needed liberating from was the bookie and the bevy.'

Andrew gazed at Joyce as she joyfully flicked her sticks, swinging her head from side to side like a pendulum clock, and sang along with Hank's great lyrics.

'She must be fifty-five if she's a day, Douglas.'

'Aye, but inside I bet she still feels like a young girl growing up in Airdrie and going up to Fort William with her pals and singing old Highland ballads on the bus. She says some mornings she wakes up she can still smell the hills and feel her favourite dress swish against her bare legs when she was a girl. If she closes her eyes she can see the pattern of the flowers on the hem and herself with not a care in the world as she runs and skips to the shops to get her mother's messages. She doesn't know where the time's gone.'

'How do you know all this, Douglas? Have you been having wee heart-to-hearts?'

'Well, she is my next-door neighbour. We hang over the back fence and gabble away like two old sweetie wives.'

'She's got a lovely pair of cowboy boots, anyhow,' Andrew said, watching her right foot rhythmically pumping the bass drum pedal. He rubbed his hands together in gleeful anticipation. 'Right, I'm away to see Gina and get some of that gorgeous Italian food. I'll see you later.'

'Wait,' Douglas said, holding his cousin's arm and pointing to the thickset man with the broad shoulders and shiny shoes. 'There's that man again, over by the door.'

'Aye, so it is. I wonder who it is. Wait a minute, I'm sure I've seen his picture in the paper. His name's on the tip of my tongue.'

'Perhaps he's interested in joining the club. We should invite him in.'

'Aye, we should,' Andrew said, catching the man's eye. But before he could take a step towards him, the man disappeared again into the darkness outside.

'Maybe he's shy,' Douglas said.

'Aye, maybe. A couple of drinks would have sorted him out, eh. No danger.'

Douglas gazed around the room. It seemed to crackle and bounce. 'Okay, I'd better go and see where Kirstin is, she'll think I've done a runner with one of yon Coppola lassies.'

'There she is, dancing with some bloke. Looks like she's enjoying herself as well. Who is he, anyhow?'

Douglas watched Kirstin twirl like a top under the confident hand of her partner. Suddenly he felt hollow, as if he hadn't eaten for days.

'That's Clive, her boss at the real estate agency. English. He loves football. Arsenal fan.'

'Arsenal! I can't say much for his choice of fitba team. He's a good dancer, but, eh.'

'Aye, I suppose he is.'

It was, many said later, a cracker of a night. Douglas spent most of it wandering from table to table, chatting and sampling the delicacies on offer. People reminisced about some of the great football games they had seen and talked of the memorable ones they would hopefully see in the future at their very own home ground. Folk drank and drank and drank some more until their modest little ground had become a giant stadium capable of seating 40 000 people in comfort, complete with floodlights for night games and a social club that was a million-dollar concern, with a bar as long as a twenty-five yard strike into the top right-hand corner of the net and a restaurant that did the finest pasta and the best egg and chips in town. In between sets from Ayrshire Archie and the King of the Spin, the kids, weary of country music and Elvis Presley, played their own records and jiggled and wafted around the dance floor to the likes of The Beatles and Billy Thorpe. Even a few tipsy parents got up and did the twist, much to the mortification of their offspring.

During a break from the dancing Kirstin even had a fishcake with the Walkers and had a brief chat with Alec's eighty year old father, Norman, who, although he dribbled slightly, appeared to be having a great old time sitting in his wheelchair and rattling his dentures to the beat.

'All right, granddad?' Kirstin smiled.

'Oh aye,' he said, peering down her blouse as she bent over in front of him. 'But I could do with some pussy. It's been seventeen years, you know.'

Kirstin patted him on the head and offered to get him a nice cup of tea and a biscuit.

The eagerly awaited raffle was drawn. Valletta Vince won the goat; Aberdeen Angus won the free hairdo at Bettina's House of Beauty; and 'Lively' Ernie Lovett, who conducted some mysterious business from the boot of a 1967 Ford Zephyr, had the lucky ticket for the handcrafted Walker Brothers shed. He was well pleased, he said to anyone who wandered within earshot. 'Very well pleased indeed,' he smiled, winking and tapping the side of his nose with his forefinger. 'Just what I need, a lovely big shed like that.'

Andrew and Douglas counted the takings in a room behind the stage. Douglas put eight hundred and forty-nine dollars and seventy-five cents into Kirstin's handbag.

'No a bad result, eh Andrew?' Douglas said.

'Aye, no bad at all, son. Better than we expected in fact. People seem really keen to get their own club up and running.'

'Aye, well, it's no surprising. There's some bits of your old life you want to take to the new one. It helps take away that big knot in your stomach when you think about what you've done, the people and the places you've left behind.'

'Aye, true enough. D'ye remember that Betty McFadyen from Glenpark Street? I'm no kidding, sometimes I wish I'd brought her along to my new life. The chest on her,' Andrew chuckled.

Douglas shook his head dolefully. 'If I was still a priest I'd be suggesting you get some counselling, Andrew. You're a sick man.'

'Away. You're the one who was celibate for all those years. If anyone needs help it's you.'

'Let's not start all that again. Here, I think I should go and have a wee turn around the floor,' Douglas said, catching the first few mournful bars of a country and western classic. 'Are you coming?'

'No thanks. I'm more of a Led Zeppelin man myself.'

'Led who?'

'Led Zeppelin. They're a new group from England.'

'Well, they'll never get anywhere with a name like that.'

Ayrshire Archie leaned into the microphone and poured his aching heart and tormented soul into this last number, his eyes wet with tears, his voice a forlorn quiver of love scorned.

'When you're tired of breakin' other hearts
Won't you come back again and break mine
When you're tired and alone in the garden
And your love light no longer shines

When your dreamworld falls around you
And you sit by yourself and pine
When you're tired of breakin' other hearts
Won't you come back again and break mine.'

Shane McGowan slouched in the front seat of his panel van, his right hand tapping on the sheepskin steering wheel cover, his left scratching an itch in his corduroy board shorts. The sun-bleached hair on his muscular thighs glistened in the light from an outdoor light at the back of the council hall. His fair locks, turned almost white by the sun's burning rays, the salt of the ocean and a bottle of Bettina's House of Beauty Blonde Bombshell lotion, hung limply on his bare broad shoulders. He gently kissed the soft suntanned hand that had been caressing the back of his neck. From where he was parked, he could make out the sounds of laughter, of dancing feet on a wooden floor, and what sounded to him like the plaintiff baying of a young goat.

'Jesus, Kaz, what's that shit they're listening to. Wog music?' he asked in disgust.

'I think it's country and western, Shazza. Me dad's got some records like that. You know, the bloke that sings that "Sounds of Goodbye". Whassisname?'

'Kamahl.'

'Yeh, that's 'im.'

'Another wog.'

So there they were raising money for their bullshit soccer club, Shane thought. Why somebody had stuck a flyer advertising their piss-up on the canteen wall at the footy club was beyond him. As if anybody would be interested. Why didn't these people just come here and play footy like Alex Jesualenko or Sergio Silvagni and leave all that soccer shit behind them? And they should, what's that word? Assimilate. The bastards should fuckin' well assimilate, and leave all that stinking food behind while they were at it. All that fuckin' garlic. The buggers put garlic in their Weetbix. Christ, he could smell it from here. They'd be in there munchin' away on it, that was for sure. Hoeing into the bloody salami as well. What was wrong with Australian food, like steak and eggs or chicken chow mein or a few slices of Stras?

Shane leaned across and stuck his tongue into Karen's mouth. He felt her breast under her thin cotton T-shirt. Jesus, she had great norgs. Even after an hour of solid rooting down at the beachfront before, he was still ready for another go at it, and judging by the appreciative sounds Kaz was making, so was she. He pulled her closer and ran his hand up her thigh to the frayed edge of her cut-off jeans. Jesus, her skin was so fuckin' soft, he thought, so fuckin' soft. The best thing that ever happened to him was the day he latched onto her at the Colindina pub, no bullshit. Well, that and being made captain of the footy team.

Karen undid the top button of his shorts and slid her hand down slowly like the old Baytown rattler pulling into Flinders Street Station. He adjusted his position to give her better access as he lifted up her T-shirt and licked her hard brown nipple. She dug her nails into his back and let her head rest against the top of the seat.

Valletta Vince and Aberdeen Angus stood outside the rear of the council hall, having ventured out into the night for a bit of fresh air and a cigarette.

'Bloody beautiful panel van, mate, eh? Look at the sunset painted on the back. It's a work of art, just like whashisname, bloody Canaletto!' Vince exclaimed, holding his cigarette between his thumb and his forefinger and taking short desperate puffs.

'Aye, it is very nice at that,' Angus agreed, the warm evening breeze wafting up his kilt. 'And so is the young lassie in the front seat.'

Vince moved slightly to the left and quickly made out a pair of slender legs pushed hard against the driver's side door. The car was rocking like a porch swing in a gale.

'Good shockers on that van,' Vince said, impressed. 'Jeez, they really goin' for it, eh mate? Bloody beauty.'

'Aye, when petticoats woo, breeks may come speed.'

Vince looked up in mullet-eyed confusion at his sagacious companion. 'What are you talkin' about, mate?'

'He said when the fair sex shows some interest, men come running,' Douglas explained as he quietly joined them. 'What's going on?'

'Twa youngsters having a bit of sexual congress in yon vehicle,' Angus said.

'Yeh, mate. And there's two surfies having a bloody big root in the front seat of that panel van over there.'

Douglas squinted and saw that the driver's side window had been lowered and two brown feet clad in maroon treads were protruding horizontally out of it. Douglas felt Kirstin take his arm and snuggle up against him. He noticed that a few others had left the party to get some fresh air.

Inside the car Shane was sweating hard; he felt as though he was going to explode as he tried to push himself further into his prostrate girlfriend. 'I love ya, Kaz,' he moaned.

'No, wait, wait,' Karen protested, placing a restraining hand on his shoulder. 'Put a franger on.'

Shane twisted his body sideways and executed some other Houdini-like contortions, searching the pockets of his shorts, which were wrapped around his ankles. He stretched forward and desperately rustled around the glove box.

'Fuck, no fuckin' frenchies. Fuck, fuck,' he groaned.

Karen let out a long sigh. 'Shit. Oh well. I'll be seein' ya tomorrow night anyway.'

'Kaz, fer fuck sake. It'll be all right, I promise. I'll pull out. It'll be all right.'

Karen shook her head, her back suddenly uncomfortable. 'Nah, better not. If I get pregnant me old man'll kill me, dead set.'

'Nah, Kaz, it'll be all right, it'll be all right. Trust me.'

Valletta Vince, Aberdeen Angus, Lively Ernie, Andrew, Douglas, Gina, Kirstin and Alfredo the goat watched in silent fascination as the panel van began undulating like a four-foot offshore swell. As Shane shot his full load of tenacious fifth-generation Irish seed into his spread-eagled and unsuspecting seventeen year old paramour, the spectators gathered by the front entrance to the hall erupted in loud cheers and fervent applause, as if Georgie Best had just scored another cracker for Manchester United after a mesmerising run down the left wing.

As Shane sank sleepily into his own little postcoital world of high marks, tall waves and long cool bottles of Melbourne Bitter,

Karen slowly became aware of the noise from outside. She shook her spent partner by the shoulders and pushed him off her.

'Jesus, what's that, what's that, Shaz?' The panic in her voice was palpable.

Shane yanked up his shorts, sat up straight and stuck his head out the window to be confronted with five men, two women and a small cloven-hoofed ruminant mammal cheering and waving at him.

'Fuckin' cunts!' he shouted, shaking the steering wheel with both hands and hurriedly starting the engine. 'Fuckin' bastards!'

The crowd watched them explode away in a squeal of rubber and a cloud of dust and exhaust fumes. While the others laughed and joked, Kirstin felt slightly guilty and intrusive.

'We shouldn't have watched, it's not right,' she said.

'Well, they should have taken a bit more care, Kirstin,' Andrew said. 'It's their own fault for doing it in public.'

'Aye, it is,' Angus interjected. 'But you know what they say, love's wan e'e and ower deef.'

'What?' Gina said, looking at Douglas for some sort of explanation.

'Love's almost blind and a bit deaf as well,' Douglas translated.

Valletta Vince shook his head and turned up the collar of his pink velvet jacket. 'Bloody Jesus, mate. Why don't you bloody Scottish buggers learn the Queen's bloody English? I'm not bloody jokin'.'

'Aye, right ye are, nae bother,' Andrew said, turning to Alfredo the goat and raising his glass in the wee animal's direction. 'Here's lookin' at you, kid. Here's lookin' at you.'

They finished their cigarettes and their laughter at what they'd just witnessed, some confessing that they wished they'd had a panel van like that when they were young, instead of having to freeze their bare arses off up the back of a close, then began to move inside. But the sound of running feet thumping on the concrete path stopped them in their tracks.

'I was just getting my ciggies from the car,' Perry McIntosh said breathlessly. He gulped at the cool late-night air. 'Some bastards let all the tyres down in the car park.'

'Look at my eyes, Douglas,' his father had said, gazing hard at the creased and brown-tinged photograph he'd taken from the old biscuit tin where he kept the records of his life that had not been lost or broken or just forgotten about. He stroked the small picture with his index finger as if to brush away the inexplicable passage of the years, a translucent glaze that allowed him an intuitive recognition of the young man presented in the image but still kept a thin film of uncertainty over whether it was indeed him. 'Would ye just look at them. The life in them.'

Douglas sat beside his father on the settee in the living room of his small flat near the centre of Glasgow. Outside it was wintry and wet and they could hear the wind howling up the close like a witch at Halloween. They were sitting close to the fire, rubbing their hands together and holding their palms up flat to catch the heat from the burning coal. With only one day until Douglas was due to take the train to London before boarding the long flight to Melbourne, he'd gone round to have a last talk with his father.

Of course they would write and there would the occasional telephone call, but as his father rightly pointed out, they might not see each other for a while. Indeed, they mightn't see each other again, his father had said in a stoic statement of fact. After all, there was his age and health to consider. In the preceding few weeks they'd had the reassuring possibility of making further times to get together, to delay the inevitable, for them both to pretend that the inevitable might never happen. So they'd yet to say goodbye or look after yerself or take care or any of the other platitudes of farewell that evoked nothing of what they really felt or wanted to say. These were just words to fill the spaces where words were expected, but they both knew they would regret what wasn't said. That regret would swell their stomachs with panic and fear and a longing for the past when their relationship as father and child was secure and uncomplicated and its intensity still undiluted by growing up, growing old, and in Douglas's case, knowing things about his father he wished he'd never known, seeing things he wished he had never seen.

Douglas smiled at the photo, shook his head. *February 1930, Largs*, it said in faint black ink on the back. His father astride a bicycle, one foot on a pedal, the other planted firmly on the ground. The bottoms of his baggy trousers were reined in by metal clips, his shirt sleeves rolled up to his elbows, his hair tousled by the wind. The top three buttons of his shirt were undone and there was a red v-shaped stencil of sunshine beneath his neck. It was Douglas's mother who had taken the photograph and there was a similar one of her in the tin somewhere. They had obviously taken it in turns to record their first holiday together. There weren't many pictures of them together except for a couple taken by a professional photographer who worked the foreshore in the summer. His name was stamped on the back. It was their honeymoon and they'd rented bicycles, big black muscular contraptions built to withstand even the most careless use by distracted holiday-makers, and they'd ridden along the foreshore and out into the countryside. There were pictures of them eating sandwiches and drinking tea from a tartan-patterned flask. They sat on a rug they'd placed on the long grass. In some of the pictures there were other people in the background enjoying the hot summer weather and having picnics as well, giving the scene the appearance of being a moment in time worth capturing because it might never come again. Why he'd asked his father to get the photograph tin out of the cupboard he didn't really know, but it seemed like the right thing to do, to review their lives before they were separated for who knew how long. As a child, it was one of his favourite games, to take that same tin out of the cupboard and arrange the photographs in neat rows according to size and shape. He would pore over them in an attempt to understand that his father and his mother had had a life together before he was born, but no matter how hard he tried he could not quite believe it, and it remained a fairytale in his mind.

As he scrutinised the photograph again Douglas could see himself in his father's moist dark brown eyes, he could feel himself in there behind them, waiting to burst out. He could feel what his father was feeling when the picture was taken. Can such moments be passed on from generation to generation? Although it didn't make any sense, he knew that they could. He had lost his faith in the Church, but a faith in the strange and inexplicable ways of human interaction had taken its place.

'You were a very handsome man, Da,' Douglas said, lifting his eyes from the photograph and smiling at his father.

'Aye, well, some of the lassies used tae think so anyway. I wisnae short of someone tae go tae the dancin' wi' on a Saturday night, that's for sure.'

'I bet you weren't,' Douglas laughed. 'Or any other night for that matter.'

'Naw, Saturday night, that was it for me. I always had my work in the mornin'.'

Douglas's earliest memories were of his father coming home from the pit, covered in coal dust, a black devil hungry for his breakfast. On a Saturday when his father sometimes worked a half-day, Douglas would be ready and waiting for him to get home so they could be away to the game. With his coat on and his Celtic scarf wrapped around his neck, he'd barely be able to contain himself in the chair and he'd be up and down looking out the living room window to watch for him hurrying up the street. When he couldn't stand the waiting any longer, he'd go down and sit at the bottom of the close in case that might make his father come home quicker. Then, when his father was finally washed and ready, they'd have a race to the bus stop and his father would always let him win. 'Christ Douglas, ye've got some legs on ye,' he'd say, puffing hard. And then they'd run up the stairs to the top deck so his father could smoke.

'Ye know, Douglas, I look at yon picture and I think that I'm still that young man, because that's what I feel inside. Then I look in the mirror and I see this auld bugger wi' a grey beard and these auld rheumy eyes. I cannae fuckin' believe it. S'cuse the language, son.'

'It's all right, Da, I'm no a priest any more. You can swear as much as you like.'

'Aye, but I should be careful, it wullnae be long till the day of reckoning and I need as much grace as I can get,' he laughed.

'Ach, I'm sure you'll be okay, just say the odd rosary and go to confession once a week.'

'Aye, and I'll put an extra bob or two in the plate on a Sunday as well.'

'Good idea, it's best to be on the safe side,' Douglas said, patting his father's arm and smiling to himself.

His father began rifling through the pictures in the tin, pushing some aside, extracting others, squinting at them through his spectacles and giving a little commentary about when and where they were taken and the other people in them. The past had become his present and he was more talkative and at ease than Douglas had seen him for a while. Since his mother had died, Douglas had often visited the house to find his father just sitting in his chair, making no sound but his eyes streaming with tears. Douglas wondered whether it was an aching remorse or just the absence of a body in the chair opposite him when he watched the television at night. Someone to talk to and share his dinner with. Did his father regret the way he had treated his wife for forty-two years, or the way they had treated each other? If he had his time over would he do things differently? But, thinking back to when he was a confused and frightened boy hiding under the bed, it seemed to Douglas that when his parents screamed and yelled at each other and scratched and bit and punched, there were outside forces at play, backing them into a corner so all they could do was come out fighting in the hope that it would make a difference to their lives, relieve the pressure of poverty just enough to let them breathe easy for a while. Maybe now, when he sat by himself in the half-light and wept, his father knew he had missed his chance for happiness and it was too late to do anything about it, that no matter how many times he looked at old pictures, there was no going back. His life had just got away from him without him noticing.

'Look at my eyes now, Douglas,' his father said, clasping his son's forearm with his thick, stumpy fingers, permanently swollen by a life's hard labour. 'They're a' pale and tired. There's no life in them. There's not even any fear of death in them, is there, son? They're eyes that cannae be bothered. They're buggered eyes.'

'Ach away, Da, you've still got a lot of life in you yet. And when you come and visit us in Australia, that'll put some colour in your cheeks.'

'I'm too old to be gaun a' the way tae Australia. Besides, I've only got the pension now. I'd have tae win the pools.'

'Don't worry about money. When Kirstin and I get settled in we'll send over a postal order and you can buy a ticket and before you know it you'll be lying in the sun and swimming in the sea.'

Douglas got up from the settee and turned on the standard lamp by the side of the fireplace. It wasn't even half past three, yet it was almost dark outside. He certainly wouldn't miss this daylight robbery that kept you inside and made you feel like a prisoner in your own home. He could see how the weather affected a person's view of the world and he was looking forward to waking up in the morning with the sun streaming through the windows, to sitting on the beach at night and watching it sink below the horizon, with everything around him bathed in a soft crimson light.

'Well, I'd better be away then, Da. I still haven't finished the packing.' Douglas held out his hand and his father shook it hard, looking his son in the eye and trying to smile. 'I'll telephone you to let you know we arrived all right, tell you if there's any kangaroos in the street, eh.'

'Aye, I'll be waiting for your call, son. Take care of yourself and don't worry about anythin'.'

Douglas moved towards the door. 'So Auntie Mary is still coming around to do for you then?' he asked, delaying the inevitable just a moment longer.

'Aye, two days a week. She does my washing and brings my tea as well.'

'That's grand. That's a big help. Right, I'm away then. I'll be seein' you then, Da.'

'Aye, see ye son, see ye. All the best.'

Douglas picked up the photograph album from the kitchen table. His father had insisted Douglas take the honeymoon pictures with him to Australia. He rarely looked at them, he'd said, and when he did they just made him depressed anyhow. When he got the time, Douglas thought he might get them framed.

Douglas was just beginning to feel almost human. He must have drunk more than he had thought last night. He shouldn't have gone back to Vince Vella's place after the dinner dance. It was already pretty late by the time they'd all pumped their own and each other's tyres up. He knew it was a mistake when Vince rolled out a huge barrel of home-made wine and started dancing to old Elvis Presley records with Teresa and most of their kids. Even Vince's old man Charlie came in from the sleep-out, and threw back a few. He started doing some strange Maltese dance on the kitchen table and then promptly fell off, landing on a squawking chicken that had wandered in from the backyard. Andrew fell asleep in one of the wrecked cars rusting away at the bottom of the garden. Lively Ernie made Vince a good offer for the car because he reckoned he could do it up and sell it for a tidy profit, but Vince said he'd promised it to his eldest boy, Joe, who was approaching his seventeenth birthday and would officially be able to take driving lessons, although Vince had been letting him drive to Werribee South to go fishing since he was twelve.

The telephone rang and gave Douglas a start. He took another gulp of orange juice and picked up the receiver.

'Sabotage! Bloody sabotage!' Andrew shouted down the phone. The sound of his excited voice reverberated around Douglas's head like a penny squib going off up a close.

'What? What are you talking about?' Douglas asked, trying to plug in the kettle with one hand. 'Speak slowly. You still sound drunk.'

'Some-bastard's-torn-up-the-ground,' Andrew slurred, each syllable like a periwinkle inching its way across the wet and slippery rocks by the sea's edge. 'It's a right mess, so it is.'

'Where are you the now?'

'I'm in a telephone box round the corner from the ground. Vince is here as well.'

'What are you doing there at this time of the morning?'

'Well, we haven't actually been to bed yet. We thought we'd just go for a wee walk to sober up a bit.

'I see,' Douglas said, taking a canister of tea from the cupboard. 'Right, I'll see you up at the ground in fifteen minutes.'

My God, Douglas thought, pouring the hot water into the teapot, Andrew must be steamin'. He sounded as though he was speaking from the bottom of Port Phillip Bay with his tongue welded to the roof of his mouth.

Kirstin slipped naked into the kitchen, rubbing her eyes and yawning, her hair vertical and alert as if it had woken in fright. He still couldn't get over how perfect she was, the way the bits all fitted together into a highly functional but exquisitely pleasing shape. He couldn't imagine how he'd managed to be celibate for so long, how he'd lived without that physical intimacy he so craved. But at the same time, he didn't understand why he held himself back, why he feared his attachment to her, why he kept her at bay. If he could only be a bit more open. He knew in his heart that Kirstin was right in complaining that she had to drag everything out of him.

'What's all the commotion? I could hear Andrew yelling down the phone from the bedroom,' Kirstin said, stretching her arms above her head. 'What's he done, found a new girlfriend?'

'No, somebody's torn up the soccer ground. Andrew says it's a right mess.'

'My God. Who's doing this, Douglas? First the fence, then the tyres and now this? Who's doing these things?'

'I don't know. But whoever it is, he's getting on my nerves,' Douglas said, grabbing his jacket from the back of the chair.

Andrew, Valletta Vince, Douglas, Lively Ernie, Ayrshire Archie and Aberdeen Angus stood in the middle of what they had hoped would be the main pitch of the Baytown Soccer Club and surveyed the damage in what a few days earlier would have been tearful disbelief. Now they wanted someone to blame, someone to have a quiet word with up a dark alley.

'I've seen fields that have nae been as well ploughed up as this,' Angus said in his lilting brogue, surveying the site like the farmer he was. 'All we need is some seed and we could get a fine crop of potatoes and tumshies.'

'What?' Vince asked.

'Tumshies. Turnips.'

'Aw right. No worries, mate.'

'Godssake,' Andrew interrupted. 'Forget the fuckin' turnips. Let's get on. I want to know who's responsible for this. We've put a lot of work into this place, and I for one am sick of doing it over and over again.'

Douglas placed a hand on Andrew's back. He was sure he could feel his cousin's heart beating. 'Okay, Andrew. We all feel the same way, but we have to stay calm and have a right good think about this.'

Vince knelt down on one knee and carefully examined the tyre tracks in the dirt. He let his fingers drift over each ridge and indentation, and he peered at the pattern left behind by the tread. He saw that the tracks were fairly deep. He stood up and dusted the soil from his trousers. He noticed that the crease was less than sharp.

'What is it, Vince?' Douglas said.

'Me trousers need ironing, mate.'

'No, what is it with the tyre marks?'

'Aw yeah. Did it rain last night?'

'No, I don't think so. I didn't hear any rain anyhow. Why do you ask?' Douglas said.

'These tracks, they pretty deep, mate. If it didn't rain, and the dirt, it wasn't wet, then maybe the car she must be pretty heavy. Maybe she have a lot of tools inside. Lots of bloody equipment or something.'

Douglas bent down, and examined the tracks closely.

Angus knelt down beside him, picked up a handful of soil and sniffed it.

'There's a definite rubbery aroma here wi' a light hint of sump oil on the nose,' he said.

Douglas stood up and rubbed the dirt from his hands. 'Anything else?'

'Aye,' Angus said, pointing to the edge of one track. 'See how the print is a bit faded on one side. The wheel alignment's probably off and the tyre's worn at the outer edge.'

'Well spotted, mate,' Vince said, patting him on the back. 'Bloody beauty.'

'So what do we do now?' Andrew asked as the men stood silently gazing at the wreckage before them.

'I don't know,' Douglas said 'But this doesn't make any sense. No sense at all. Is someone out to get us?'

'Och away, Douglas, you're being a bit dramatic here, son,' Ayrshire Archie, ever the optimist, said. 'It was probably just some stupid wee laddie wi' nothing better tae do on a Saturday night.'

'I'm not so sure. Something about this doesn't feel quite right, especially after everything else that's happened. Who do you think did this, Andrew?

'Could be anybody.'

Andrew was right, it could have been anybody. There were no obvious enemies, no old scores to settle. The country was a melting pot, with no place for religious bigotry or warmongering national pride beyond a vague sense of nostalgia for the old country based more on food, weather and football than on any fierce belief in the superiority of any particular race or creed. And indeed any thoughts of using violence to defend their perceived integrity came well behind having a barbecue on a Sunday afternoon or doing bombs off the end of the Baytown pier on a hot summer's day.

'What do you think, Archie?'

'I think there's a fox in the henhouse.'

'Ernie?'

'I think we have to keep our noses to the ground, son. I'll ask around. I know a few people.'

'Angus. What do you think's going on here? Do you think we should forget about this whole soccer club idea?' Douglas asked, slipping his hands in his pockets, suddenly feeling deflated.

Angus folded his arms across his broad farmer's chest and looked Douglas directly in the eye. 'Wet sheep don't shrink, Douglas, they shak aff the water.'

Vince shrugged and squinted and nodded in confusion, then looked to his friends for some explanation.

'Don't give in to misfortune,' Douglas said.

'Aye, Angus's right,' Andrew said. 'We'd just be a bunch of lassies if we gave it away now. Vince, it looks like we might be needing that grader of yours again, son.'

'No worries,' Vince said. 'She'll be the bloody apples, mate.'

Kirstin slipped back into bed with a cup of tea and the newspaper. Carlton were top of the ladder, everything was on schedule for the Apollo 11 moon landing and there were rumours that the Beatles were about to break up. She was more of a Stones fan herself, although she had to admit *Sgt Pepper's* was a very good album, nothing on *Let It Bleed*, mind, but not bad at all. If she weren't married, she'd give that Mick Jagger some satisfaction he'd never forget. She placed her cup on the bedside table, making a mental note to get rid of it and its twin when she and Douglas moved to the new house. They'd bought the tables from a second-hand shop, and they were as ugly as sin. She'd buy some new stuff when they shifted. Admittedly the house they'd just purchased was a bit tumbledown, but light did stream into the place. It had character, a sense of home about it.

Which was important because neither she nor Douglas were feeling at home right now, that was for sure. Douglas spent more time at that soccer club than he did with her, and she found herself working back a couple of nights a week and having a drink with Clive. He was a good dancer. Funny how people surprise you, because he didn't look like he would be a good dancer. Especially in that brown suit. Brown suits didn't augur well for skipping the light fantastic, that's what she thought, anyhow. She'd never seen a brown-suited man on *Come Dancing*. Someone had told her that men who were good dancers were likely to be good in bed as well. She wondered if that was true.

Kirstin pulled the blankets up over her breasts and laid her head on the pillow. There was nothing planned for today so she might as well have a lie-in; besides, Douglas had gone out to inspect the damage to the soccer pitch and she had a hangover.

The phone began to ring, and although she tried to think it away, it persisted, sounding even louder when she buried her head under the blankets. Eventually she gave in to its insistent burr.

'Hello,' she mumbled, her voice sounding as though it had bubbled to the surface from the bottom of the sea.

'Hello! Is that you, Kirstin?'

'Aye. Mum? Mum, is that you?'

'Yes, it's me darling.'

'Oh Mum, it's so good to hear your voice,' Kirstin said, suddenly bursting into tears.

'Darling, are you all right? What's the matter? I haven't reversed the charges or anything. Honest I haven't. Kirstin, sweetheart, what is it?'

Kirstin rubbed at her tears with the back of her hand. She noticed she was shivering. 'Mum, I'll have to go and get my dressing-gown, I haven't got any clothes on.'

'Och, you'll catch your death. Mind, you'll get a chill in your kidneys.'

Kirstin couldn't help but laugh. Getting a chill in your kidneys was a particular preoccupation of her mother's. As a child, Kirstin had been forced to wear two vests most of the time, although her mother allowed her to wear just one in the summer. She quickly fetched her dressing-gown and returned to the phone.

Kirstin heard her mother's voice soften, the voice she used when Kirstin and her sisters were little girls with scraped knees and sorry tales of bad boys in the playground.

'Tell me all about it, darling. Is it Australia? Do you not like it?'

Kirstin pulled her dressing gown tight around her. 'No, it's not that, Mum. It's fine. I'm getting used to it now. It's got lovely weather and there's a beach near where we live.'

'Yes, you've told me in your letters. And you've got a good job and a car and you've made some nice friends . . .'

'It's Douglas, Mum. I don't know what's going on with him. He's not the man I married. Something's happened to him. I don't know how to explain it. He's so, so . . . remote. And he never talks to me about his feelings. I mean, he's obviously not happy, but he won't tell me why. He just pretends everything is fine. He's all jokey with his pals; I know because Andrew told me. But as soon as he walks in the front door he retreats into this shell of his. I don't know what's going on, honest I don't, Mum.'

'Men are like that, dear. They save their feelings for some other person or some other thing. Usually it's a secretary or a yacht.'

'Not every man is like Dad, you know,' Kirstin said, her mouth fixed hard, like a crack in stone.

'I'm not so sure about that. Sometimes you just about have to hang yourself from the light fittings to get anything out of them, and even then they'll wait until you're turning blue.'

'But Douglas told me everything when we were in Scotland. We used to share all our feelings. Now he hardly ever tells me anything. He's always staying up late and getting up early and looking at old photies and writing things in books. We always seem to be awake or asleep at different times. We hardly ever even make . . . you know.'

'Oh, that. Perhaps he's having an affair, darling. It's a dead giveaway when they don't want to touch you. Your father was the same with me. He denied it, but I knew perfectly well he was spending his evenings with that harlot he called his secretary. Men will deny anything; remember that.'

'Oh, Mum. Douglas is not like that. He's different.'

'Well, I told you it wouldn't be smooth sailing, did I not?'

Kirstin had to admit that her mother had indeed told her it wouldn't always be a jolly little bus ride to Saltcoats with a few songs on the way and a picnic and a carefree stroll along the foreshore at the end of the day. Kirstin knew that in her heart, and from the warnings issued by others. But where was the comfort in that?

By the time they'd finally made the decision that Douglas couldn't live with the collar around his neck any more, like a yoke around a draught horse, and that life with Kirstin promised more than he could imagine ever redeeming from the Church, she'd already been in contact with the wives of some other refugees from the priesthood and knew that she was in for a difficult, if not tumultuous time. But she was ready for it; at least she'd thought she was. Indeed she'd wanted it more than anything she'd wanted for a long time, more even than the Stones' first album. Thinking about it now, it was more an ultimatum than a mutual decision. She'd been with men before, men she thought she'd loved, who couldn't quite decide whether they loved her enough in return to commit to spending, if not the rest of their lives with her, then at least as much of the future as they could foresee. But these men, in the end, never appeared to see very much ahead at all. She seemed to specialise in shortsighted buggers who fled from commitment like eager greyhounds bolting out the box at the dog track. Not this time, though. If Douglas couldn't make up his mind, then that was that. It wasn't that she wasn't sympathetic his dilemma—Christ, it was more than a dilemma wasn't it, it was a bloody nightmare—but you get to a stage where you have to look out for yourself, don't you? That's the cold truth of it; you can love someone till your pores ooze blood, but if they don't love you back enough to want to be with you, there's no point, is there? That's what her mother told her in the big granite house in Bearsden where she grew up. With its three floors of big airy rooms, carved wooden fireplaces and carpet that sunk like a sponge beneath your feet, it was a far cry and a coal sack full of money away from where Douglas had spent his formative years in the spitting skies and daily grime of the East End. No books, no music, no bath and a very small fridge, was how he liked to describe it himself. Kirstin recalled with a wry smile her mother's reaction to the news of her daughter's relationship with Douglas. It was over tea and scones and a bought Swiss roll that Kirstin admitted she'd been seeing someone for the previous year and half that she probably shouldn't have been seeing, and although she had meant to tell her mother before this, she somehow hadn't got around to it.

'A married man? You're seeing a married man, is that it?' her mother had speculated, her cup of tea suspended in midair, the saucer poised several inches below the fine china cup, like a thought before an uncertain action.

Kirstin shook her head in disgust. 'Of course not, you know what I think of married men who play around,' she said to her mother, who blinked involuntarily but chose to ignore her daughter's reference to her absent father.

'You never know, do you, this being the swinging sixties, the era of free love and all that,' she said haughtily.

'There's no free love as far as I'm concerned, Mother. You always end up paying for it in some way or another.'

'Well, thank God for that then,' her mother said with obvious relief.

Kirstin took a bite of her scone, some of it crumbling onto her top. She shooed the crumbs away with her fingers.

'No, actually, I'm seeing a Catholic priest. His name's Douglas,' she smiled. 'Father Douglas Fairbanks.'

Katherine McKenzie had often described her daughter to her friends as unorthodox, but this degree of nonconformity had taken her by surprise. She sipped at her tea, gulped down her trepidation and tried to remain calm.

'Douglas, that's a good Scottish name,' she said. 'What does his father do?'

And then, when her mother asked her if she'd had 'intimate relations' with him, she nearly fell off her chair. Amused, she explained that she hadn't yet but was planning to deflower him some time in the not too distant future.

Katherine could not subdue the smile that skipped across her lips. 'Well, I do think they look very handsome in those black suits they wear.' She looked concerned for a moment. 'But it would have been much simpler if you'd found yourself a nice vicar, dear.

The problem with the Catholic Church is that it's so unchristian. I think you're in for a very rough road ahead. More tea?'

But she knew that already. Life hadn't exactly been silky smooth during the previous twelve months as they'd snuck around the city, sitting in the darkest corners of pubs, creeping into cinemas after the film had started so they wouldn't be seen lurking in the foyer together. Kirstin had told Douglas they were just like fugitives, like yon Dr Richard Kimble. But one day they'd have to stop running and face the music.

'Fugitives for love,' Douglas had intoned like an amateur thespian at the local dramatic society. 'It would make a good movie, eh, starring Humphrey Bogart and Ingrid Bergman. They could set it in Glasgow. What do you think?' He flicked a cigarette into the corner of his mouth and squinted. 'Of aw the gin joints in aw the toons in aw the wurld, she walks intae mine. Ye know whit ah want tae hear. Play it. Ye played it fur her, ye can play it fur me. If ye dinnae I'll batter the shite oot ay ye. Ye ken?'

Kirstin couldn't help but laugh. Douglas could do them all. Bogart, Burt Lancaster, John Wayne, Cagney, James Mason. She knew it was his way of diffusing any tension in the air, of postponing decisions he found too overwhelming to confront, decisions that left him hollow in the pit of his stomach at the very thought of them. She had been told that it was not uncommon for a paralysing fear of the future to keep priests tottering uneasily towards the precipice of freedom from taking that final resurrecting leap into the unknown.

Kirstin had read somewhere that in the thirteenth century a priest could live with a woman as long as he paid a whore tax. Kirstin, however, had no intention of being anyone's whore. Bugger that. She wanted a proper life with Douglas, some children, a home, soft-boiled eggs with soldiers in the morning. But the problem with your priests who wanted to quit the game at half-time was that they were terrified of being released into a world they had not been prepared for. At least with the priesthood, a man knew what was what. But outside, with his collar in the bottom drawer and his heart in his mouth, he was rigid with the possibility of failure, of being left destitute and penniless, like some of their old parishioners. Maybe it was better to be a shepherd than a bleating sheep in a large indifferent flock. Kirstin didn't agree, but she was doing her best to be as sympathetic to Douglas's fears and uncertainties as she could. She'd told him that there'd be many opportunities awaiting him, just as there had been before he'd joined the priesthood and his choices had been cut off, cut off too soon as far as she was concerned. And he'd told her that despite sitting alone in the confessional box and weeping at the thought of being a priest for all his life, he was still afraid of losing the identity he had. Personally, she thought this was bordering on the melodramatic. When you are unhappy you move on and don't look back, that was her credo. Life was too short and, besides, too much retrospection just made you miserable and gave you a headache. Despite her own misgivings, she was prepared to accept Douglas's confession, knew for the sake of nurturing their relationship and helping it grow into something rich, sustainable and, with a bit of luck, pleasurably carnal.

But for the moment Douglas said he wasn't prepared to turn her into his 'concubine', which for some reason Kirstin had incorrectly assumed was some form of small spiny anteater. Douglas explained that in the old days the mistresses of priests and their children were burned at the stake. The priest himself was spared such diabolical agonies and dispatched back to his parish after being given a good ticking-off. He said the Vatican's hostility to women, while less physically vengeful these days, was still barely disguised and he wasn't going to perpetuate that by using Kirstin as an object for his sexual relief. She said she wouldn't mind now and again. It wasn't that he didn't want to, didn't need to—Christ some mornings he woke up with an erection the size of a Glasgow Cathedral candlestick—but he needed to sort his head out first before moving to any other part of his anatomy. He wanted to clear his mind of the abrasive and confusing presence of the Church, to scrub the inside of his head, to leave it as clean and stain-free as his mother's front step at Hogmanay. Then he would welcome anything.

Douglas said he had a lot of life to catch up on and he needed to take a few classes in the ways of the world. Kirstin didn't disagree. She laughed as she remembered the night he'd sneaked her into his house attached to the chapel. The eagle-eyed Mrs McDougall had gone for the night and Father Docherty was asleep in his chair, drunk and drooling, a half-empty bottle of Johnny Walker on the side table next to him. You could almost smell his breath and hear his rattling chest from the street. They crept up the stairs in their stockinged feet, a couple of thieves in the night, and tiptoed into Douglas's bedroom, holding their breath as if one wheeze would wake up the neighborhood, if not the Pope himself.

For a while they sat on his perfectly ordered bed, with its dark wooden cabinets on either side like ageing guardian angels doing one last job before they retired to sing hymns and play canasta, and held hands, talking in whispers. While Douglas went to the toilet, Kirstin slowly and quietly removed all her clothes. She sat naked on the side of the bed, her feet dangling over the edge and her hands folded primly across her lap. When he returned she calmly asked him if he would take her confession. He stood frozen by the door, as if his feet had been glued to the carpet, and hesitantly explained that she wasn't a Catholic and anyway she would need something to confess to.

'Come here,' she whispered. 'I'll think of something.'

He seemed to glide over to her as if in a trance. He told her he'd never seen a naked woman before. He was twenty-seven. She pulled him to her and held him tight. In the end the room was so cold and Douglas so nervous and uncertain and bloody well shaking that they didn't do anything. Her mother would have been proud of her. The Lord would have been proud of him.

'Kirstin, are you still there? Kirstin?'

Kirstin found herself staring at the wallpaper, an offensive pattern of brown and yellow rectangles. She would be glad to see the back of it.

'Yes Mother, I'm still here. I just wandered off for a wee minute.'

'Write me a letter, dear. Tell me everything. These long-distance telephone calls are horrendously expensive.'

'Yes, Mum. I'll write you a letter. I'll write to you tonight.'

Kirstin let the phone slip back onto the receiver and returned to her bed. She pulled the blankets tight around her and closed her eyes.

Malcolm Myers sat on the wooden benches outside the school canteen, his long socks draped sadly around his ankles. His slate grey shorts, the colour of a Glaswegian summer sky, hugged his massive thighs. His thick torso could have hung happily on a hook in the cool room of the Baytown slaughterhouse and few would have noticed the difference between it and a side of beef, except perhaps that it was wearing a pale blue short-sleeved shirt.

Malcolm had placed his lunchtime fare on each side of where he was seated. Liquids to the left, solids to the right. One chocolate malted milkshake, two small bottles of orange juice. Two Four & Twenty meat pies with sauce, two sausage rolls with sauce, six jam doughnuts in a narrow rectangular box, a cream puff, and a custard tart dusted with icing sugar. On the ground by his feet was a brown paper bag containing a cheese sandwich, an apple, an orange and a small box of Sunblest sultanas which his mother had packed for him. He did not eat methodically, item by calorie-drenched item, but rather chose to take bites out of each of piece of food in an order that only he could fathom, his very own eating etiquette. He looked happy, sitting in the sun, chomping away like a contented animal in the field, stopping only occasionally to breathe, belch and fart.

Douglas and Andrew stood by the handball courts watching the young man methodically ingest his food, their arms folded across their chests, their mouths agape in wonder.

'If only he attacked his homework the way he attacks his lunch,' Andrew said, unable to take his eyes off Malcolm's bulging cheeks and the piston-like motion of his jaw.

'He chews his food very well though, don't you think so?'

'Aye, he's a good chewer, right enough.'

As the two teachers assigned to lunchtime yard duty, it was their responsibility to ensure that the students ate some lunch and that they ate it in the designated areas, that they did not throw it at each other and that they did not smoke in the toilets or on the football oval. The delectable Mrs Konieczny had once gone for a quiet lunchtime stroll around the oval and had had to be rescued by Brother Donald who had wisely boarded the school tractor and herded the trailing tribe of salivating boys into the machinery shed. Even so, Mrs Konieczny had managed to lose the heel off one black-patent leather shoe. There were rumours that Frankie Disabato, a fourth former who had been shaving since grade five, kept it in the breast pocket of his Levi denim jacket as a sort of good-luck charm.

And, if he was to be believed, it worked. He claimed that at the drive-in one Saturday Isabelle Gianfranco came across twice in the one night while his older brother Mauro munched on a packet of Twisties in the front seat. But that was just schoolyard gossip and Douglas refused to believe it of a sixteen-year old boy whose father ran a fruit shop at the Victoria Market and was a pillar of the local Catholic church. Andrew, however, said it was well known that Frankie Disabato would fuck anything with a pulse and was particularly successful with teenage migrant girls who had enthusiastically abandoned the mores of the old country and lustfully embraced the more relaxed conventions of the new.

'He's not stupid, you know,' Douglas said, watching Malcolm bite a meat pie in half.

'Who?'

'Malcolm Myers. He's just lazy.'

Andrew laughed derisively. 'You're too kind, Douglas. If he could keep his mind off his stomach and his hands off his willie for a minute then there might be some hope for him, but other than that he's a lost cause.'

'Ach, I don't know about that,' Douglas replied, watching in astonishment at the speed at which a jam donut could disappear down his pupil's gullet. 'Do you know what he wants to do when he leaves school?'

'He wants to be a policeman.'

Douglas nodded at his cousin. 'Polis, eh?'

'Hello, sir,' Malcolm said as Douglas sat on the bench opposite him, taking care to avoid a half-melted icy pole that someone had abandoned in favour of a game of kick-to-kick.

'Hello, Malcolm. That's some lunch you've got there. I don't know how you can fit it all in.'

'Well, I forgot to have me dessert last night, sir, so I was starvin' this morning. Could've eaten the wool off a sheep's back.'

'And what caused you to make such a grievous omission?'

Malcolm squinted, his mouth half open revealing half a pound of mince meat and gravy.

'How come you forgot to eat your pudding, Malcolm?'

'Aw yeah. *The Beverly Hillbillies* was on. That Elly May Clampett has got the best tits on TV. I suppose I got distracted.'

Malcolm slurped the cream and raspberry ripple from the inside of his cream bun.

'Do you like her, sir?'

Douglas shrugged. 'I don't think I've ever thought about it, Malcolm.'

The young man looked incredulous, so much so that he stopped chewing for a moment. 'Yeah? Well I suppose Granny's Clampett's more your cup of tea, eh sir?' he chortled. 'But, Jeez, you're missing out, fair dinkum. Elly May, she's my ideal woman, sir. She's shit hot. She's got long blonde hair and big tits an' she's virgin as well.'

'That's good, is it?'

Malcolm looked blank. 'It's better if women are virgins, sir, before they get married an' that.'

'And if they're not?'

'Then they're slags. That's what me dad says anyway.'

Douglas appraised Malcolm's last sausage roll and thought that he wouldn't mind a bite of it himself. But when Malcolm picked it up and licked the tomato sauce clean off with one long trawl of his bullock-like tongue, Douglas thought better of it.

'Do you think that's fair? What about boys who aren't virgins when they get married? What do you call them?'

'Lucky bastards, sir,' Malcolm hooted, pieces of flaky pastry and masticated mince meat spraying out from the young man's mouth like beer from a shaken can.

Douglas decided to change the subject and asked Malcolm whether he had ever thought of trying out the health lunch that had been introduced by the sports teacher, Ronnie Richards, in an attempt to encourage the boys at the school to be more health conscious and to take better care of their growing bodies, bodies that he poetically described one sunny morning in the gymnasium as buds waiting to burst into full bloom.

Of course, this floral depiction of their pubescent sprouts of facial hair and pimples had immediately led to him being labelled a poofter by the students who were always on the lookout for someone to brand with this pejorative hot iron in the hope that it would confirm their own rampant heterosexuality. There was also a certain degree of self-interest in Ronnie's health food initiative. Being a former VFA centre-half forward whose body had simmered and congealed into a rectangular tub of suet, held together only by a pair of red groin-throttlingly tight nylon footy shorts and a Viva Zapata handlebar moustache, he was keen to curb his own ferocious appetite for potato chip rolls and Kentucky Fried Chicken. A new KFC outlet had recently opened up around the corner from the school, which had expanded Ronnie's, and indeed the entire western suburbs', opportunities for gastronomic adventure beyond Chiko rolls and hamburgers with the lot.

Unfortunately, the health lunches, which consisted of a stick of celery, one peeled carrot, an apple, an orange, a triangle of processed cheese and a salad sandwich, had not met with the success Mr Richards had hoped for. This confirmed the derision of the long-term *uberführer* of the school canteen, the matronly lawn bowling fanatic, Mrs Doris Wickstead. She had just laughed at the sports teacher's proposal, saying that growing boys needed more than rabbit food after a hard morning in the classroom. As she joyfully wrapped another steaming jam donughnut in a brown paper bag, she was often seen to smirk at the forlorn figure of Mr Richards standing by the bustling queues to the canteen counter and watching dolefully as not one student turned clutching a delicious box of health-inducing fruit and vegetables. Indeed, there were rumours that the sports teacher was seen one lunchtime at the Baytown Hotel guzzling a counter lunch of T-bone steak and chips with four slices of buttered white bread on the side.

Malcolm wiped the tomato sauce from the side of his mouth. 'Nah sir. I tried a health lunch once. But I had to have a pie and sauce after because I was still starvin'. I feed that stuff to me guinea pigs.'

'You'd probably feel better for it if you laid off the pies and cakes for a while and ate some fresh food,' Douglas said.

'But I always feel grouse anyway. Except on Sundee mornins.'

'Why is that?'

'On Satdee nights me and me mates go down the back beach and drink piss. Last Satdee I drank eight bottles of Melbourne Bitter.'

'No wonder you felt a bit under the weather.'

'Yeah, but I shouldna had that bottle of marsala. God, was I crook. I spewed six times.'

Douglas decided to change the subject once again. He always felt better as a teacher when he could connect on some level with his students, however minute. After all, that's what he was there for, to impart knowledge to them, to get them to think, to question, to be interested in the world around them and to refrain from spitting in the corridors.

'I hear you want to be a policeman, Malcolm.'

'Ah, not really. Well I s'pose so. Me old man reckons they're the only ones that'd have me. It wouldn't be too bad, drivin' around in a divvy van an' that.'

'Have you talked to your father about this, that you might no really want to be a policeman?'

'Nah,' Malcolm said, taking a gulp of his malted chocolate.

'You should, son. This is the rest of your life we're talking about here.'

'Yeah, but he's never home. He's on the council as well, you see. And he's president of the footy club.'

'What line of work is he in?'

'He's a builder.'

'There you go, why don't you get into the building game? You're a big strong lad, you'd be ideal.'

'Yeah, well I'm good at buildin' things, good with tools an' that, but me old man says I'm too stupid to be a builder. Says I'm too stupid to be even a brickie's labourer.'

Douglas shook his head in disagreement. 'That's no true, son, you just need to get motivated, do your homework, think about your future. You can't afford to make a mistake. You might end up doing something you hate, something you regret choosing.'

Douglas ran his eyes along the wooden bench and noticed that the boy was now free of food. There was nothing more to consume. It had taken approximately eight minutes to devour a lunch that could have fed half of Biafra for a week. He felt sorry for the boy, who was obviously unhappy. Fat and unhappy. Childhood was a bastard if you didn't enjoy it, because things only got harder as you got older. When you were young you were irrepressible, but the capacity for happiness seemed to diminish as people got older and greyer and more buggered by life bearing down on them, at least that was the impression he got from his own parents. The passing years seemed to squeeze the life right out of them, like juice from a lemon. The optimism of youth turned into a weary life of working overtime to pay the bills piling up behind the clock on the mantelpiece. Sometimes a thought-free snooze by the fire was the best you could expect.

'Listen Malcolm, Andrew Fairbanks and I are trying to start up a wee soccer club, you know, down at the old lake. Why don't you come along on Sunday? We're having a bit of a working bee. You being good with your hands you might enjoy it. What do you think?'

Malcolm shook his head. 'Jeez sir, I dunno. Me old man mightn't like it, him bein' the president of the footy club an' that. He doesn't like wogball.'

'Well, it's up to you. Have a think about it. You might enjoy it. You can do your homework later in the day after we've finished.'

Malcolm smiled, more to himself than to his teacher. 'Yeh sir, I'll have to study up for next week's HE class, eh. Chapter 15, 'Puberty and Sexual Awakening'. Wet Dreams and Dry Rooting we call it. Best to be prepared, that's right, isn't it, sir?'

Douglas couldn't help but laugh. The boy certainly had a sense of humour, even if it was firmly located at the bottom of the toilet. 'I suppose so, Malcolm, I suppose so.'

Douglas nodded as Malcolm rose heavily from the bench and, with a parting hike of his eyebrows, headed back into the canteen, his hands rifling through his taut pockets for some change.

'Pastie with sauce please, Mrs Wickstead,' Douglas heard him chirp when he reached the calorie-laden counter.

'My God, what do ye look like?' Douglas gasped as Andrew stepped into the hallway. He couldn't quite believe what he was seeing. Perhaps there'd been some sort of malfunction of his nervous system and the visual stimuli being processed by his eyes were being garbled as they travelled along the long and winding road to his brain. He gave his cousin the once-over again, from head to foot, eye to arse. Andrew Fairbanks, blue-eyed, blond-haired lady killer from Carntyne, was gift-wrapped in an orange terry towelling short-sleeved top with a ring-pull zipper, the collar and sleeves finished off with half an inch of blue and white striped elastic. 'Holy moly, Andrew, you look like a bottle of Fanta.'

Andrew scowled. 'Ach away, you don't know what you're talking about. This is the latest fashion. Yon lead singer from the Master's Apprentices has one. I saw him wearing it on *Uptight*. If it's good enough for him, it's good enough for me.'

Douglas moved south, taking in the bright purple flared trousers that hugged his cousin's groin so fiercely that his wedding tackle was lifted, separated and highlighted to such a degree that it looked like two coconuts hanging off a tree. A tropical todger. It also appeared to have been pushed at least six inches further up towards his stomach. Any tighter and his balls would be poking out his gob.

'Are you in pain, at all?' Douglas smirked.

'No, not all. Should I be?' Andrew asked, puzzled.

'Well, those trousers, I'm surprised you can walk in them. They're awfy wide at the bottom. They look like a couple of teepees from the knees down. You could fit a wee family of Red Indians in there, one in each trouser leg.' Douglas studied Andrew's feet. 'Where did you get those sandals from?'

Andrew appraised his new purchase. The sandals were attached to each foot by a thin leather strap and a leather ring though which he slipped his big toe. 'What do you mean? Jesus wore sandals like these.'

'No wonder he got crucified then,' Kirstin said, emerging from the kitchen with a tray of glasses and some crisps, biscuits and cheese. 'But at least you're making an effort to keep up with the times. Maybe you could take a leaf from Andrew's book, Douglas, and move out of the 1950s. You could buy a body shirt or something.'

'I bought one of those the other day,' Andrew said enthusiastically.

'What did you do, put the body on lay-by,' Douglas laughed, taking in his cousin's thin hipless frame, a stick with hair and lips.

'Douglas!' Kirstin exclaimed.

'Sorry Andrew, I don't know what's up with me the day. Usually I quite like purple on a man.'

'Thanks very much,' Andrew said grudgingly.

'Isn't it about time you moved into the sixties, Douglas, even though we've only got a few months left to go?' he added, punching his cousin playfully on the arm. 'Why don't you buy some flares, maybe a nice peach coloured shirt with a peaked collar. I'm no kidding, you'd look a treat in a pair of maroon flares with a nice thick white vinyl belt. Maybe you could even grow your hair a wee bit, at least over your ears.'

'What about a nice kaftan, Douglas,' Kirstin winked, taking a crisp from the bowl and biting into it. 'You would look quite Apostolic, don't you think.'

'Aye, that'd be me, the thirteenth Apostle.' Douglas made a show of smoothing down the wrinkles in his short-sleeved checked shirt and straight-legged trousers. 'No, I'm happy as I am, thanks.'

He began to chuckle as he suddenly recollected a scene from his childhood. 'Remember when you were wee, Andrew, and your mammy would take you out to Goldberg's and buy you a coat for the winter that was three sizes too big?'

'Aye, so it would last you a while and you could grow into it.'

'Except that for three years you looked like a right eejit with the bloody thing hanging off you like a tent on a pole. And by the time you did finally grow into it, it was all scabby and moth-eaten and full of holes anyhow.'

'You were lucky, you had sisters; but I was the youngest of three boys. After they'd passed theirs down to me I could end up wearing the same kind of bloody coat for nine years. It was diabolical, so it was.'

'It was great going shopping with my ma,' Douglas responded, shaking his head in wonder at how he and his sisters had managed to recover from the head-hanging humiliation of it all. Grinning, he acted out a parody of his mother, complete with her scalpel gaze and ferociously wagging finger. 'I don't care if you don't like it, you'll just bloody well dae as yer telt and wear it. There's some weans who dinnae have a coat. You don't know how lucky ye are, ye ungrateful wee shite. Some ae yon wee black babies would gie their eye teeth fur a jaikit like this. Now get oan that bus before ah lose ma rag wi' ye.'

'The magic of childhood, eh,' Andrew laughed. 'People talk about your first sexual experience as being the defining moment in your life, but being able to buy a coat that actually fits is far more significant as far as I'm concerned.'

Kirstin grimaced. 'I think you two poor wee tenement boys should move on to another subject before I break down and cry over your terrible deprived childhoods. I think you should both have a drink. What will it be? Beer or wine, a wee whisky maybe?' she asked, heading towards the fridge.

'A nice cold beer would be good.' Andrew replied.

'Aye, me too. Colder than his,' Douglas said.

Douglas took his drink and went over to the television, hunkered down and began fiddling with the knobs on the front. They'd bought it second-hand a couple of weeks after they'd arrived in Baytown. It looked like something John Logie Baird had built himself. It specialised in weather-affected transmission, the screen more often than not afflicted with snowflakes, pea-soup fogs, vertical and horizontal static, the occasional sandstorm and explosion of fiery sun spots. After a few minutes of being pushed, shoved, kicked, twisted, shaken and sworn at, the ancient appliance finally relented and presented a picture as clear as it was ever going to get.

'There y'are,' Douglas said, gesturing towards the television like a magician celebrating the successful completion of a difficult trick, 'a picture fit to watch a man landing on the moon.'

Andrew chuckled with excitement, rubbing his hands together in anticipation. 'This is a defining moment in history, you know that don't you?' he said. 'A defining moment.'

'Och, I don't know about that,' Kirstin scoffed. 'The invention of ready salted crisps is right up there, I think.'

She squinted at the blizzard underway again on the television screen. It looked like Sauchiehall Street on Christmas Eve. 'I think when we get a new TV that will be a cause for world-wide rejoicing.' She walked over to the television and gave it a good kick. The picture improved momentarily before reverting to its usual impersonation of a slush-bound Scottish winter's day with a storm approaching off the North Sea. Further consultations with adjustment dials both front and back were interrupted by two loud thumps on the door.

'That'll be Angus and Archie,' Douglas announced. 'They said they'd drop around and watch the moon-landing with us.'

Kirstin laughed. 'Valleta Vince thinks those two are from the moon themselves, so they should have no trouble relating to the whole experience.'

'Andrew, Douglas, Kirstin, this is my brother Richard,' Angus said, presenting the tall red-haired and ruddy-cheeked man next to him. There was certainly no doubting the resemblance between them, although Angus's eyebrows were twice as thick, a consequence perhaps of spending so much time in cold and windy country fields or having been swaddled in a cow pat. 'He's out here to see me and have a wee holiday.'

'That's lovely,' Kirstin said as they all shook hands. 'I'll get you a drink, Richard.'

Archie, resplendent in a black Stetson, jeans and a pair of snakeskin boots, took a seat on the settee and gladly accepted Douglas's offer of a bourbon and coke.

'You're looking awfy like Ben Cartwright there, Archie,' Andrew smiled. 'Taken the day off from the Ponderosa then? That's the game. It must be good to get away from the spread now and again, eh. Relax. Roundin' up all those steers all day must do yer head in. How's Little Joe by the way? He's a handful that yin, is he no?'

Ayrshire Archie sipped his drink, savouring the taste. He nodded, an almost imperceptible dip and lift. 'Did ye actually go and pay good money for that shirt, son? Perhaps they'll take it back if you beg nicely.' He smiled and began humming a few bars of 'San Antonio Rose' quietly to himself.

Andrew took no notice. 'Right, you lot, it's on in two minutes so sit yerselves down,' Andrew shouted, taking out a small notepad and a pencil from his shoulder bag, his trousers being too tight around the thighs to allow anything other than his natural attributes to be accommodated within them. 'So, who's for a wee bet then?'

Andrew licked the tip of his pencil and explained the odds: 5–1 the Eagle runs out of petrol and crashes; 9–2 Neil Armstrong falls off the ladder going down to the moon's surface; 6–1 Armstrong and Buzz Aldrin go for a wee walk and get lost and are never seen again; 7–2 they find a Mars Bar wrapper; 4–1 Armstrong does a shite in his spacesuit; 20–1 they run into the Loch Ness Monster; 25–1 they meet the Man in the Moon and he's from Inverness; 15–2 they find Harold Holt wandering around in his swimming trunks looking for his towel.

After some more, increasingly drunken discussion about the possibility of finding a fish and chip shop up there, money was produced, bets duly noted and they settled themselves in for the historic landing. Kirstin got some more saveloys from the kitchen and another packet of cheese and onion crisps, which she passed around as they sat watching the television with rapt attention.

'The Eagle has landed,' announced ground control as the lunar module touched down on the Sea of Tranquillity.

'There ye go,' Angus said, pointing to the screen. 'A perfect landing.'

They watched fascinated as Armstrong descended from the Eagle to the moon's dusty surface. 'It looks like a right midden,' Richard said. 'No like my village. In Pittenweem you could eat your dinner off the streets, so ye could.'

'Wheesht, Richard, Armstrong's gonnae say something,' Angus whispered.

'That's one small step for man, one giant leap for mankind.'

The group let out a collective moan of disappointment. 'Ach away, is that it?' Andrew grumbled. 'What a pathetic thing to say. So American. They're always saying things that sound pithy but in the end they're just a load of shite. One giant step for mankind my arse. What about providing enough jobs for the workers, eh?'

'And what would you have said, smarty-pants?' Kirstin demanded.

'Och, I don't know. What about, "Hello Ma, can you send on my green pullover, it's a bit nippy up here".'

'Or how about "Danger Will Robinson!"' Douglas interjected, roaring with laughter.

'What do you think, Archie?' Kirstin asked, passing him another bourbon and coke.

'I don't rightly know, but I might've been inclined to do a wee turn, ye know, a bit ae tap dancin' or sing a wee song. Somethin' by Sinatra maybe. Archie spread his arms wide, closed his eyes and took a deep breath. *Fly me to the moon-ah, let me play among the stars, let me see what spring is like on Joo-pee-ter and Mars . . .* '

'Very nice, Archie,' Kirstin said, patting him on the knee.

'What about, "Hello Jesus, it's all right, you can come out now. Those nasty Romans have all gone home," Andrew joked.

'Trust you,' Douglas said, giving him a withering look

'I don't know what you're all going on about,' Richard said, shaking his head in disbelief at the ingenuousness of the others in the room. As a policeman who'd been walking the beat for more than twenty years, he knew a set-up when he saw one. 'It's all nonsense. I don't think they've gone to the moon at all. They'll be in some Hollywood studio somewhere, having a right old laugh. Yon lunar surface looks awfy like the set from *The Treasure of Sierra Madre*, don't ye think?'

'What, the one with Humphrey Bogart in it?' Andrew asked, always excited by a good conspiracy theory.

'Aye, that's the one. Walter Huston, was he not in it as well?'

'Some film that, eh. Did you see it, Douglas?'

'Aye, I did,' he said, immediately launching into his best Bogie impersonation. '*Nobody puts one over on Fred C Dobbs!*'

'Ach, you're kidding yourselves, how could they fake that, eh?' Andrew demanded.

'No problem, son. They managed all right wi' the Thunderbirds. Fakin' the moon would be a doddle,' Richard said seriously.

'I'll tell you what but, eh, I'd take that Lady Penelope out for a fish supper any day,' Andrew drooled. 'Gie her one in the back seat of that big pink motor of hers.'

'You've got a one-track mind, Andrew Fairbanks, so you have,' Kirstin said, wagging her finger at him in mock admonishment. 'And what about the chauffeur, what was his name, Parker was it? What wid ye do wi' him?'

'Ach, he could watch.'

'You're sick, Andrew, so ye are,' Angus spat. 'The least ye could do is gie the man the afternoon off.'

'So Richard, what do you do back home?' Douglas asked, pulling up a chair next to the newcomer.

'Finest polis north of Hadrian's wall is our Richie,' Angus said before his brother could answer.' Nobody knows the workings of the criminal mind like this man, I can tell ye that for nothin.'

'Is that right?' Douglas said, impressed. 'Maybe you could help us with our wee problem.'

Douglas explained the strange goings-on at the soccer club site and how they were at a loss about where to start to discover who it was that had been vandalising their club.

'Aye, I'd be happy to have a wee sniff about for ye.'

'Thanks, that's grand,' Douglas said, shaking Richard's hand. He took another sip of his beer and leaned forward towards the policeman. 'Your brother happened to mention that you came here to get away for a while, that you had a bit of bother back home.'

Richard leaned forward and rubbed his hands together. Douglas noticed that his fingers were as thick as his brother's. 'Aye, things were not going so well back home. I'll admit that. I thought a wee rest and a bit of a change would be the best thing all round. It's as good as a holiday.'

GRAHAM REILLY

'Well, we'll make sure you have a holiday to remember, don't you worry about that,' Douglas said. 'And if you need someone to talk to, I'd be happy to lend an ear. I might be a failure as a priest, but I learned to be a good listener.'

'Well,' Richard said, sighing loudly and with what seemed like a deep well of regret. 'It's a long story, son. If ye don't mind I won't go into it the now. All I can say is that just a wee while ago my wife Annie left me.'

Douglas was suddenly lost for words and immediately regretted his intrusion into the man's private life. 'I'm very sorry to hear that,' he mumbled.

'Aye, me too. When sorrow sleeps, wake it not, eh. That's what they say, is it no?'

'Aye, some folk do. But others say that it helps to talk about your troubles, get them off your chest. It can be therapeutic.'

'Ther-a-peu-tic?' Richard savoured each syllable, as if by doing so he could convince himself that there might be some truth to what Douglas was saying. 'Do they now? Well, I'm no so sure about that.'

Richard picked up his whisky and, in a gesture of compromise, clinked his glass against Douglas's. 'Maybe later, but no the now, eh. Maybe later, I'll tell you about my troubles. But not for my benefit, mind.'

When the two policemen arrived at the door Douglas quickly led them into the living room. Once they were introduced to Andrew and Angus, and everybody was comfortably seated, he began to explain how the working bee had progressed.

Everyone had turned up, he said, and there were even a few surprising additions to the construction team, although he had to admit that people seemed to be functioning more like a blown head gasket than a well-oiled machine. Still, he supposed they'd get there in the end and the Baytown Soccer Club's changing facilities would be ready for the start of the season. Andrew had brought his latest girlfriend along, Minh Thanh, a Vietnamese student from Saigon, who'd won herself a scholarship to study in Australia. He wasn't quite sure what she was studying but Andrew was certainly spending a considerable amount of valuable working time studying the finer points of her anatomy. They seemed to be enjoying themselves at the working bee and Andrew was wearing a conical straw hat, which Minh Thanh insisted he wear to protect his fair complexion from the blazing Australian sun.

'Sun no good,' she warned, tying the red velvet straps around his freckled chin, much to the amusement of everybody else. 'You get very serious sick.'

If Douglas didn't know better, he'd swear they were in love. She'd brought along some Vietnamese morsels which she was handing out like sweeties at a children's party and which were being accepted by everybody with equally childlike enthusiasm.

Nodding towards her long, thick black hair which tumbled to the small of her back, Andrew declared to Douglas that she had a certain mystical quality about her. 'You can't go past South East Asian lassies,' he said, his previous infatuation with Italian, Turkish and French women apparently forgotten. 'They're unfathomable. Looking into their eyes is like looking into a thousand years of history. There's an understated elegance about them; ye know, the way they hold themselves. They walk tall, but without arrogance.'

'But aren't they generally quite short?' Douglas asked. 'Your Vietnamese.'

'They walk tall *inside*, Douglas.'

Douglas looked sceptical. 'Oh aye.'

'And they've got great arses.'

Douglas handed his cousin a length of timber. 'Tell me, Andrew, you're a professional man, a man of learning, a teacher of history, the history of this world for God's sake, and yet when it comes to women, you seem to exist in a fantasy land where women aren't real, where they're kind of otherworldly creatures with bosoms. Why is that? I mean what the hell are you thinking?'

Andrew removed a roofing nail from between his clenched teeth, folded his arms and thought hard. 'I don't really know, Douglas,' he sighed. 'It just seems easier that way.' He shrugged and nodded at the sun. 'Good day for it, eh?'

They had a good day for it, right enough. The sun was warm but not oppressive and glinted happily off the recently erected wire-mesh fence. Still, it was thirsty work and Kirstin had brought along a few gallons of lemon and orange cordial. Vince had supplied some home-made wine, salami, bread and cheese, and there was plenty of beer and a few pounds of snags and steak for a barbecue later on.

Douglas took a breather, wiped the sweat off his brow with his forearm. Jesus might have been a carpenter's son but Douglas had never been what you would call practical. He was focusing on supplying Andrew, Angus, Richard, Valletta Vince and the others with the necessary timber, nails, hammers and other essential equipment for getting the frame up and the roof on. They had all been banging away since early morning, with regular breaks for drinks, chatter and consultation with Vince's transistor radio to check the progress of the races at Flemington. Vince also checked the wellbeing of several of his children who appeared to be constructing what looked like some sort of enclosure for the family's fowl population. The second youngest Vella, Charlie, three, was having trouble stuffing a wriggling ferret into an old hessian bag but continued to push and shove and stab and poke at the poor wee animal in the way that only terminally cruel adults and innocent young children can do. Vince had tied Alfredo di Stefano, the goat he'd won at the fundraising dinner raffle, to a stake by the main pitch, where Angus was sprinkling grass seed with a confident swish and sway

129

of his experienced farmer's arm. Vince had intended to hoist the young beast over a spit some Sunday afternoon and invite a few friends over for a barbecue, but he had spared its short life after pleas from the children.

Some of the Coppola boys, who were still mates with Andrew even though Gina had dropped him for Carlo from Caltanmissetta, had laid the concrete foundations for the clubhouse earlier in the week with the help of several hundredweight of raw materials unknowingly supplied by the Baytown City Council thanks to a small donation from one of Vince's Maltese mates who worked in the depot. If they could get the frame up and the roof on by the end of the day, they'd be doing well. They were in good hands under the supervision of Alec Walker and his brother Dennis, both such fanatical fans of Leeds United that they'd named their various children after players in the team, even the girls, something six year-old Marjorie Billy Bremner Walker tended to keep to herself.

Ayrshire Archie's bass player, Arthur Kyriakpoulous, worked in a hardware shop in Footscray and was happy to supply corrugated iron at a heavy discount. So heavily discounted, in fact, it was free. Apart from being exceedingly generous, Arthur was a former semiprofessional soccer player in Athens and was keen to get a run with Baytown Soccer Club. He was short, wide and infested with hair, a small mangrove of a man with a natural talent for scoring goals. Douglas had already included him in his plans, free roofing material or not. Indeed, he had to admit the team was shaping up, much to his own surprise. Once word had got out that a new soccer club was starting in Baytown, a whole squad of potential Peles and the odd Nobby Stiles had come dribbling out of the woodwork. He never ceased to be amazed at the power sport held over your average male, even the ones whose brain activity stretched to thoughts other than their next beer, root or cigarette. If only Jesus had been a centre-forward, the Church would be in much better shape than it was today and pews all over the world would be crammed with devoted followers, cheering, singing along and waving flags in the air. If he could find a good goalkeeper, Douglas reckoned he'd have a fairly solid team to field for the club's first season in the state third division. The bottom rung of the ladder maybe, but that was where many of these people came from in the first place, so they should feel right at home.

Perry McIntosh, himself a fair right-back with a liking for the occasional bold dash down the wing on his long elegant legs, whistled loudly at Douglas and nodded in the direction of the makeshift entrance to the ground. It was as if a skyscraper and a single-roomed farmer's croft had decided to go for a stroll together. Malcolm Myers and Wullie Henderson were ambling their way across the pitch, Wullie leading with the Glasgow wee man's gallus walk, a confident challenge of swaying hips and shoulders, Malcolm following languidly in a John Waynesque rolling shuffle. Both were wearing overalls, Wullie's rolled up at the ankles, Malcolm's terminating abruptly halfway down his calves. They carried bags with various implements protruding from them like jemmies from a cartoon burglar's swag.

'Hello, sur,' Wullie said, squinting up at Douglas, who was halfway up a ladder handing a piece of four-by-two to Aberdeen Angus.

'Hello Wullie. What a pleasant surprise. You too, Malcolm. Nice to see you both. No old women or weans to terrorise the day then, Wullie?' Douglas said, making his way down the ladder.

Wullie looked disappointed, removed a cigarette from a packet of ten and lit up. 'I hope you're no takin' the piss, sur. I'd be right disappointed, so I wid. Me and Malcolm here thought we'd just come along tae gie yeez a hand, it bein' fur the fitba an' that. I have tae admit tae a certain degree of self-interest but, bein' that I cannae stand that Australian Rules shite, so a chance tae see a good game ae fitba would be a great help for the settling-in process, if ye know what I mean. My Auntie Betty, she lives doon by the beach, ye know. Well, she's fae Maryhill and she says it took her four years tae get settled in here. Fuck that, but. Sorry sur, I mean I plan tae get settled in quicker than that. So if ye cannae get a decent black puddin' or a fish supper in this country then ye might as well get the fitba if ye can, so I thought I might as well get doon here and pit the shooder in.'

'That's very good of you, Wullie,' Douglas replied, chastened. 'And you're very welcome. Both of you brought your own tools too, I see.'

'Yes sir, had me own tools since I was twelve,' Malcolm said, casting a critical eye over the frame. 'Some lovely joinery there, sir, if you don't mind me sayin'.'

'No, not at all, Malcolm, get wired in, son,' Douglas said encouragingly.

Malcolm dropped his bag, reached in and withdrew a professional-looking carpenter's leather tool belt, which he proudly, if self-consciously, buckled around his waist. Douglas watched as the lad carefully inspected the frame; he thought Malcolm looked more comfortable with his hammer and nails and work boots than he'd ever seen him before. Douglas smiled warmly at him and gave him the thumbs-up. The boy wasn't as bad as some folk made him out to be. Malcolm smiled back and nodded conspiratorially.

'Hey sir, that red-headed sheila over there, wouldn't ya love to give her one, eh?'

'That's my wife, Myers,' Douglas growled, nonetheless admiring Kirstin's svelte form in her T-shirt and thigh-hugging cut-off denim shorts. She and Vince's wife Teresa were setting up a table for lunch.

'Shit, sorry sir. Didn't mean anythin' by it.'

'No, I'm sure you didn't, son. Just keep your mind out of your trousers and on the work at hand.'

Douglas turned to see Wullie squinting at him in what seemed to be a reassessment of his place in Wullie's world and the scheme of things in general.

'Ma mammy says she knows you sur, by the way.'

'Is that right?'

'Aye. She says you were the priest at the chapel she used tae clean in the mornins, ye know, back in Easterhouse. Is that right, sir, did ye used tae be a priest?'

'Aye, that's right, Wullie. I used to be, and in some ways I still am, I suppose.'

'Aye, I can see that, sur. You've still got a priest's haircut and your hands still look a bit white and clammy an' that.'

'Thanks, Wullie. You've got a big mouth for a wee man. Did anybody ever tell you that?'

'Aye, a few. But most of them regretted it afterwards, sur.'

'I bet they did,' Douglas grinned. 'So your Agnes's boy then. I should've put two and two thegither. You do look a bit like your mother.'

'Aye. Same teeth.'

'Is that right?' Douglas said, confused.

'Aye, sur. False yins.'

Douglas laughed, nonetheless noting the gleaming and perfect uniformity of Wullie's National Health gnashers.

'You're a bit young to have false teeth, Wullie, are you no?'

'Ach, they got a' smashed up in a fight wi' Eddie Murdoch. Mind ae him, sur? Big fat cunt wi' a squint.' Wullie almost blushed then, in his own understated version of contrition. 'S'cuse the language, sur.'

Douglas was well aware that as a boy from the schemes Wullie would have been reared on a diet of teenage gang warfare, a compulsion to look and sound tough for the sake of survival, and no language other than bad language. Young Wullie couldn't help himself. He was a victim of circumstance if ever there was one.

Douglas made a mental note to have a quiet word with the boy on Monday about the necessity to water down his use of expletives while in conversation with his elders or anybody in a position of authority. Douglas smiled to himself. He'd fuckin' well gie it tae um straight. Nae mair fuckin' swearin or he'd be in fur it.

'How is your mother, by the way?'

'Ach, no bad. She says she's gonnae come up here eftir. She says she wants tae see ye. Say hello an' that.'

'I'll look forward to it,' Douglas lied. Agnes Henderson was as voluble as her talkative son, a graduate cum laude of the University of Glasgow Patter, majoring in the lexicon of physiological infirmities. 'And your father, how's he getting on?'

'Ach, no sae well.'

'And why's that?'

'He's deid, sur.'

Douglas hadn't expected this, a double hernia or a bad case of catarrh maybe, but not death.

'I'm sorry to hear that, Wullie, very sorry. My deepest condolences.'

'Thanks, sur. But in all honesty I cannae say I'm sorry he's kicked it. He wis a right auld bas—bugger. Always let his fists dae the talkin', especially wi' ma mother.'

'How did he die, Wullie, if you don't mind me asking?' Douglas inquired with genuine sympathy.

'Stoatered oot the pub, and he wis well on, ye know. He took the short cut hame and fell intae the canal. The polis said the gypsies found him and dragged him oot.'

'That's very sad, Wullie. I'm sorry. But he's with his maker now, eh.'

'Aye well, whoever made him will probably chuck um back. I can tell ye that for nuthin',' Wullie said, shaking his head before surveying the scene around him, taking it all in. He spat on his palms and vigorously rubbed them together as if he wanted to make a spark. 'Right then, better get intae it, eh. Time waits fur nae cunt.'

Douglas dropped his head and rubbed his nose. The schemes, they spat out some characters, no doubt about it. A mad expectoration of drunks and poets, psychopaths and dreamers, geniuses and tap dancers. You wouldn't credit it, Agnes and Wullie Henderson from Easterhouse, out here in Sunny Australia. The world was getting smaller by the minute.

Thinking back, he'd nearly died when he'd been sent out to the eastern edge of the city once he'd finally made it out of the seminary. He'd grown up in poverty, but at least it was poverty in the heart of the city where there were shops and cinemas and a community of close-knit neighbours and even family members who'd arranged it with the landlord so they could live in the same street. But out there in the schemes it was a case of countryside meets pebble-dash tenements meets hard bastards meets folk with no choices trying to keep their heads above water as the place tumbled into mayhem around them. Gangs trying to kill each other for something to break the monotony of it all; nowhere to go, nothing to do but drink or beat the wife, screams in the night, women weeping at the bus stop of a morning. My God, when he'd first arrived there, Easterhouse had only been a few years old but already it had reeked of trouble to come. You can't stick thousands of people in a dank, cheerless place with nothing but houses and a few shops, some schools and bugger all else and expect them to be content with their lot. Something has to break, a few heads being the most likely contenders. No wonder folk were doing anything to get out on a ten-pound ticket to Canada or Australia. Desperate to get on that plane to some sort of future, they were prepared to leave everything they'd ever known behind them—fathers, mothers, wee sisters, football teams, singsongs on a Saturday night, Irn Bru and potato scones. Everything that helped them belong.

The problem with the schemes and being skint in general was that you could only look back for some sort of comfort. The best part of your life was behind you, that's how it had seemed to him as he'd listened to people going on about the past and the supposedly grand old days when they were young. But even though there was all that uncertainty about the future in another place, at least there was hope that things might get better. And here was the manifestation of that, Douglas realised, all these buggers banging away to put up the clubhouse for what would one day be the Baytown Soccer Club. Either that or they were buttering, chopping and slicing to get some dinner ready. If someone were to ask how Douglas felt at that moment, the sun warm on his back, the comforting grate of a saw cutting through timber, the tantalising smell of rump steak and onions sizzling on the barbecue, he would have said proud. Aye proud. Douglas felt himself coming on all emotional, as his Auntie Jesse would have said after throwing back five vodka and oranges.

'Hello faither! Is it really you? My God, wonders never cease, eh. Ye widnae credit it!'

Douglas's quiet reflection was shattered by the piercing shriek of Agnes Henderson, a wail that could strip the fur off an alkie's tongue. He couldn't help but smile at her in her floral calf-length apron and her hairnet. She looked like a young Ena Sharples on her way out for a half a pint of stout and a packet of crisps.

'Hello there, Agnes. What a surprise.'

'Aye faither,' she said, breathing heavily after her brisk walk across the field and pulling a pack of cigarettes from her apron pocket. 'Who would have thought, eh? You and me here in Australia. Thousands of miles away from Glasgow. Life's full of surprises, is it no?'

'Aye it is, no doubt about that.'

Agnes blew cigarette smoke drawn from somewhere in the region of her lower intestine. 'I hear yer no a priest anymair. Is that right, faither?'

'Aye, that's right.'

'Ye loast the faith then?'

'Look, Agnes, to be honest, I don't know if I lost the faith exactly, but I know I lost something.'

'Och well, these things happen, eh. Ye just hiv tae get oan wi' it.'

Douglas took Agnes' hand and held it. 'Wullie told me about Alec. I'm sorry.'

'Aw, thanks, faither, very kind ae ye,' she said, quietly withdrawing her hand from his. 'But God forgive me, he was a terrible man, so he wis. That canal did us aw a favour, I'm tellin' ye. I wis near ready tae kill um masel. He goat awfy punchy when he had a drink in um, faither, if ye know whit I mean.'

'Aye, I think I do, Agnes, I think I do.'

'Ach well, it's a' history now, eh, and best forgotten. It's just me and the boys now.'

'Do they like Australia then?' Douglas asked, trying to lighten the conversation.

'Ach, they're gettin' along no bad. They hiv a bit ae trouble because they don't ay ken whit people say tae thum, because ae yon funny accent the people hiv goat here an' that, but ye know they're getting' used tae it. They don't like the sausages here, but. They say they taste funny. And the bacon's shite.'

'Well, they'll just have to eat more chips then,' Douglas laughed.

'Aye faither, I don't think they'd have any problems wi' that!'

Douglas saw that Agnes looked worn out, as if more life was being drawn out of her than was being put back in.

'And how about you, Agnes, are you managing all right?'

'Ach aye. We're wi' my sister and her man. They've been oot here fur years. Goat a big weatherboard hoose doon near the water. They've goat a lovely bungalow oot the back. We'll stay wi' them till we can save up a deposit fur oor ain wee hoose.' She paused and lit another cigarette. 'Ahm workin' at a place on the Geelong Road, the road that goes tae Geelong, ye know, unless yer gaun the other way, then it disnae. They make plastic coats an' that. It's no a bad wee joab but a bit hard oan the back. I dae a bit ae cleanin' at the council offices at night and on a Sunday morn as well. That's why I'm dressed like this,' she said, running her hands across her apron.

'Ach aye, things are gaun just fine. I hid a wee bit ae trouble last week, but. Ah wisne feelin' well, ye know, so I went tae the doaktir and he says he'd better gie me a few wee tests because I wis hivin' tae go tae the toilet a lot an' that. So he did the tests, a yoorhine sample and a few wee other things, and I hid tae ring up the next day, ye know, tae get the results. So I rings up and spoke tae the receptionist, nice wee lassie, and I says I'm just ringin' up tae get ma results ae ma tests and she says wait a minute and she pits me oan tae the doaktir. He says hello Mrs Henderson and I went hello doaktir and I says call me Agnes. He goes right, Agnes it is. He says I'm afraid you've got a kidney malfunction. Christ, whit a fright I goat, faither! So I says oh my God hiv I goat the cancer then? And he went naw, it's just a wee yoorinerry tract infection. And I goes then why the fuck did ye no just say so? I thought I wis gonnae die. Some doaktirs, I'm tellin' ye, they need hingin', so they dae.'

'Aye you're right there, Agnes. But at least it's not the cancer, eh.'

'Aye, that's right enough. Somethin' tae be thankful fur. Here, but that cancer's a terrible thing, is it no? Ye know, in the auld days when we were wee it wis the TB an' the typhoid and the scarlet fever an' that, but noo it's the cancer. Ye think ye're making' progress wi' the diseases but then another yin just pops up. An' that fuckin' cancer's a terrible yin, so it is. It sneaks right up on ye.'

'It seems that way. Still, John Wayne had the cancer and he's still ridin' the range. He beat the big C!' Douglas exclaimed.

'Aye, that's true enough. Maybe there's hope for us after a'.' Agnes fumbled in her apron pocket for her cigarettes. 'Fag, faither?'

'Och, why not,' he sniffed. 'Life's short, eh.'

'Aye, it is that.'

Douglas paused and poured the policemen a cup of tea. He offered them some digestive biscuits and continued explaining what had happened during the remainder of that Sunday at the soccer club.

They had, he said, achieved much more than he had expected, even though Andrew had felt it necessary to take regular breaks to gaze into Minh Thanh's dark and mysterious eyes as if they held the very secret of existence itself. The frame had been mostly completed and the corrugated iron roof was on, even if it wasn't exactly symmetrical. They probably would have got a couple of windows in if Valletta Vince hadn't been regularly required to adjudicate in disputes between his children, who had organised themselves into two five-a-side soccer teams, although with one child short of the full complement they had found it necessary to recruit Alfredo the goat to act as goalkeeper for one of the sides. This had proven unsatisfactory as Alfredo, when not wandering off to graze, either tried to eat the ball or lance it with his tiny horns. Tired of climbing on and off the roof, Vince eventually sent Alfredo off for foul play, pointing towards the flaming barbecue as he admonished him, and delighting his children by joining the game himself. He was the Captain Von Trapp of Maltese parenthood who would lead them across the mountains to freedom and good jobs as motor mechanics.

Wullie turned out to be as agile as a monkey up a tree and managed to make a sizeable contribution to the roofing process in between cigarettes. But his mother, nervous that he would fall and break his scrawny neck, kept urging him to climb down to the safety of terra firma and tea with three sugars.

'Fucksake Wullie, wull ye get aff that roof this minute or ye'll fa' aff and break yer neck, so ye wull,' she implored.

But Wullie was not to be convinced by his mother's heartfelt pleas. 'Ach away wi' ye, ye auld bag.'

Agnes turned to Kirstin and Teresa, her lips a thin smile of resignation. 'Whit can ye dae? I know he loves me but, the wee bugger. Has trouble expressing affection, though. Typical man, eh.'

At about half past four they all downed tools and headed for the barbecue and the cold beer. It was a feast, no doubt about that. Rump steak, sausages, two different salads, some pastizzi Teresa had made that very morning and some red wine Vince had made the night before. The women marvelled at the vigour of Malcolm's appetite but urged him to eat more salad as the meat seemed to be disappearing rather more quickly than they had expected and they were worried it would run out altogether. He seemed happy to make the change when Kirstin took a personal interest in his dietary habits and Agnes gave him a stern warning.

'If ye dinnae eat yer vegetables ye'll get the cancer, I'm tellin' ye.' She turned to her determinedly carnivorous son. 'You an a', Wullie. Wan death in the family is enough for the noo. If ye go an' die oan me just see whit ye get. Eat wan ae yon fuckin' carrots, wull ye, eh.'

They ate and drank happily until the sun set over the petroleum refineries. They had a lively debate about who was the best band of the sixties, a decade which Andrew pronounced to be the greatest in the history of mankind and the likes of which would never be seen again. Andrew would brook no suggestion that it was anyone other than the Beatles and dismissed rumours that Paul McCartney was dead. Kirstin said you couldn't go past the Stones and was certain that Brian Jones was definitely dead.

Angus sang the praises of Jimmy Shand and the Clansmen. Archie liked Kenny Rogers's new record. Joyce said the Ronettes were the top of her list and she sang a few bars of 'Be My Baby' to support her claim. Malcolm nominated Dave, Dee, Dozy, Beaky, Mick and Titch, declaring that 'The Legend of Xanadu' was the stuff of pop mythology.

'Och away tae fuck, ya bampot,' Wullie shouted dismissively. 'Load ae shite, them. Whit aboot Manfred Mann? Doo-wah-diddy, diddy-dum-diddy-doo an' a' that. Magic.'

This suggestion was met with howls of derision, particularly from Agnes, who, having drunk several glasses too many of Vince's fruity little drop, was feeling particularly confident about her own standards of musical appreciation.

'Is that right?' Wullie challenged her. 'Who dae you think then, eh? Moan, tell us the noo, if yoor sae clever.'

Agnes didn't hesitate. 'Whitsese name? Yon Richard Harris.'

Wullie's laugh verged on a sneer. 'Away ye go. He's no a group, he's a person.'

'Disanae matter. It was still some fuckin' song that MacArthur Park, wis it no, eh?' Agnes flicked her cigarette from her mouth and began to croon.

'Sumwhun left the cah . . . hake out in thuh huh rain
I ah don't think tha . . . hat I can tay . . . hake it,
Cause it took soh . . . hoh long to beh . . . hake it,
And I'll ah never have that reh see pee again!
Oh . . . hoh no!'

As the argument threatened to get out of hand, Archie fortuitously pulled out his guitar. At his wife's request he sang a lilting version of 'Are You Lonesome Tonight' and they all agreed Ayrshire Archie and the Vandellas were the best band of the sixties. They packed up their tools and the leftovers from their dinner, and Vince and Teresa piled their menagerie of dozing kids and their buggered wee goat into their huge old Chev. Wullie and Agnes marched off down the road, smoking like two lums in a Glasgow factory, and everybody else headed off in their separate directions, the evening sea breeze cooling their faces, the wine and beer warming their insides.

'So the plan was to go back tomorrow night after work and get a couple of more hours in, but that was before all this happened, ye know,' Douglas explained, pouring himself another cup of tea and offering more biscuits to the note-taking policemen. 'We'd only been back here an hour or so when we got a telephone call from Perry McIntosh that the clubhouse was on fire. He lives across the street. We couldn't believe it, could we, Andrew?'

'No, we could not, no.'

'Do you have any idea who would want to try and burn down your clubhouse?' the taller policemen asked, placing his empty teacup on the coffee table and wiping biscuit crumbs from his trousers.

'Well, we don't know who, exactly,' Douglas said. 'But there's some folk out there who are doing everything they can to stop our wee club getting started.'

'Aye,' Andrew interrupted. 'They've pulled down our fence, torn up the ground and set fire to the clubhouse.'

'And let down our tyres,' Douglas added.

'There's not necessarily a link between these events,' the shorter policeman said.

'Ach away, of course there is,' Andrew said, his voice singed with anger.

'The laddie's right,' Angus said. 'Why are they doing this? We're doing nae harm tae nabody. He that ill does, never guid weens,' he sighed.

The two constables looked at each other, mystified.

'There is nothing good to be gained from badness,' Douglas explained.

The taller policeman laughed. 'Tell that to some of the people we know.'

Tuesday night was the night of the council meeting and the post-meeting drinks and sandwiches in the big room next to the town clerk's office. For Councillor Brian Myers, this was the best part of the evening. After the seemingly endless and exhausting debates about road maintenance, the schedule for the introduction of the new sewerage system (no more dunny carts, thank Christ for that) and his proposal that the reclaimed land by the old swamp be sold for further housing development, he welcomed the chance to relax with his fellow councillors and have a few beers and a bite to eat before heading home to the house he'd built himself. His first project as a developer and building contractor, it was still an impressive structure. But he had plans for something bigger, more modern, with spacious rooms, open plan, that sort of thing. A stone fireplace that would accommodate not just a fire but a roaring bloody blaze. A conversation pit maybe, and a den for him. A three-car garage. Nobody in Baytown had a three-car garage.

He had just the site in mind. His place would be the showcase in a new development to be called Baytown Meadows. It would be the proverbial house on the hill to which all eyes would turn in awe and reverence. King of the castle, that was Brian 'Bulldog' Myers, and he wasn't about to let anyone forget it. He'd acquired his nickname during his footballing days with the Baytown Football Club. Tenacious, that's what people remembered about him. Never gave up, and once he got hold of a bloke in a tackle, they would have to drag him off before the poor bastard suffocated to death or rigor mortis set in. He'd won the best and fairest in '53, '54 and '56, and his photograph still hung on the clubroom wall, his thick arms folded across his barrel chest, his hair slicked back, one ear permanently swollen from too many whacks to the side of the head. He had a look of victory about him. Perhaps it was the steel in his eyes, the suggestion of a smile (or was it a sneer?) on his lips. He captained the club to three premierships in five years. After he'd retired from the footy and things started to go well in the building game with all these new migrants wanting a place to live, he built a new clubroom and bloody well donated it. Gave it to them free of charge. How was that? Of course, he was given life membership and made club president. Although it was his due, he appreciated the gesture and was proud to hold the position. It had benefits beyond the public profile it gave him. A lot of important people in the area liked to go to the football on a Saturday afternoon.

So it was a busy life for Brian Myers. The building, the footy, the council, the family. As the man said, who could ask for anything more? Well, there were just one or two more things, he laughed to himself as he bit into a curried egg sandwich.

'Evening Brian, how are you?'

Brian momentarily raised his eyes from his sandwich, half of which was still protruding from his mouth, to see Frank O'Connell, the editor, writer and owner of the *Baytown Star*. Frank had been on the dailies for years and made a bit of a name for himself as a police roundsman but had decided to give it away after the *Argus* had closed down. He couldn't face the thought of starting again at another paper, so with the bit of money he hadn't drunk away he bought the *Star* and opted for the quieter life by the sea. A journalistic backwater maybe, but it had its moments beyond the golden wedding anniversaries, little athletics and occasional weekly beat-ups about internecine warfare in the lushly carpeted halls of the council offices. And advertising was picking up nicely as the local population began to swell. Pretty soon he'd have to take the *Star* up to sixteen pages.

Brian Myers rubbed at some curried egg that had spilled onto his new suit, and succeeded only in rubbing the sandwich filling further into the navy blue pure wool with just a hint of pinstripe.

'Ah, fuck it! Look at that, me new bloody suit. First time I wore it too.'

'Curried egg does it every time, councillor. You should stick to the ham and cheese.'

Brian ran his eyes over Frank O'Connell's greasy suit which, he noted, fitted him like a sack of soggy potatoes, some of which had begun to sprout. He laughed. 'Yeah, you would know, mate.'

Frank smiled to himself. Myers always had an answer for everything. 'It's not what I know, Brian, but what you know that interests me.'

'Aw, yeah. About what in particular?'

'About this new soccer club that's starting up, for example.'

'Whaddya mean? Could you be a bit more specific, maybe focus your brain for a minute. I know that's not easy for you, Frank.'

The newspaperman let this pass. For the moment at least. 'Well, there's been a few mishaps up there by the old swamp, I understand. Bit of vandalism, I hear. A little bonfire the other night. Anything you can fill me in on, Brian?'

The councillor finished the last bite of his sandwich and wiped his hands vigorously with a paper napkin.

'You've got a little bit of egg on your cheek, Brian,' Frank obligingly pointed out.

Councillor Brian Myers pretended not to hear but dabbed at his face anyway.

'Sorry, mate, can't help you on that. First I heard about it.'

Frank O'Connell scoffed and managed to spit a few scraps of soggy white bread and tasty cheese onto Brian's pristine white shirt. 'I thought you knew everything in this town, Brian. Especially about building, you being the chairman of the planning and development committee and all.'

'As you know, Frank, the committee only meets once a fortnight. Maybe it'll come up at the next meeting. Talk to me then, eh? I'll see what I can find out.'

'Yeah, thanks. I'd appreciate it.'

Brian nodded it the direction of the town clerk. 'Must go and have a word with Albert. I'll be in touch.' He paused as he turned away. 'So what's the big story this week, Frank?'

'Can't say too much, you know that, Brian.'

'Come on, Frank, we're all friends here.'

Frank laughed. 'What's the old saying? With friends like you I don't need enemies.'

'Aw, Frank,' Brian whined, 'you'll hurt my feelings.'

'COUNCILLORS EMBROILED IN EXPENSES SCAM!' Frank said slowly, locking the man's eyes with his own.

The colour drained out of Brian Myers's face like dishwater down the plughole. He seemed to lose control of his eyelids and kept blinking, like a defective shutter on a cheap camera. The seconds ticked by like minutes until his lips defrosted in sudden realisation. 'You're joking, aren't you?'

Frank smiled, his eyes bright with pleasure.

'You're a bastard, Frank.'

'Thanks, Brian, so are you. Two peas in a pod, eh?'

As he made his way from the council building to his car, Frank flicked his cigarette onto the winding concrete path. Floodlights placed strategically on the expansive lawns illuminated the building in all its ultramodern glory. With its circular eucharistic construction, the whitewashed concrete walls, the copper-plated roof and spire climbing to the heavens, it could easily have been a church. He spat a bitter brew of beer, tobacco juice and phlegm onto the grass. The poor ratepayers. Instead of a house of God they got a house full of self-serving pricks. Butchers and fishmongers who wanted their pictures in the paper and a municipal reserve named after them, and builders and real estate agents who felt it was their civic duty to offer the benefit of their advice when it came to matters of rezoning council-owned land, especially if it was along the foreshore.

Frank sighed to himself as he shoved the key into the lock. Maybe he should have stayed on the dailies. At least you met a better class of arsehole.

'So, do you think you'll have weans then, Douglas?' Andrew inquired, placing the thick sole of his boot on the blade of the shovel and pushing hard. He let out a grunt of satisfaction as he felt it slice into the soft earth, like a spoon into a bowl of ice cream. He loved digging; it was so simple but so rewarding. You pushed, you dug, you grunted, you turned the soil over, and there you had it, a garden bed. A beautiful woman waiting to be kissed. In with some seedlings, a few daisy bushes, and in a couple of months, the bloody Garden of Eden. It was great to be doing something so physical; it felt right, as if that was what nature had intended his body to be doing. Digging, running, jumping, climbing trees, that's what bodies were made for. Not teaching. Teachers sat around on their arses a lot or pointed at blackboards or scribbled on them with coloured chalk. Perhaps in three thousand years time, when archaeologists unearthed the remains of an ancient civilisation, they would be able to identify teachers by their specially padded bums, muscular forearms dusted with chalk and the eyes in the backs of their heads.

Andrew looked over at Douglas in his old wellies and baggy navy blue shorts and saw that he was enjoying the work as well. He thought back to when they were boys in Glasgow, cousins, best pals, a couple of six year olds with their tin buckets and spades, making castles and forts out of dirt and bits of wood, adding a few pints of water to transform the dirt into muck of just the right consistency. Perfect muck. The delicious slapping sound it made when you moulded it into a castle wall or a crenellated tower. Running up the stairs hungry for your dinner, only to be given a good skelp by your mother for being covered in shite from head to toe. This was his first realisation that mothers regarded it as part of their duty to keep their children as far away from dirt as possible, while children were programmed to enthusiastically pursue it. But as a grown-up, you could get as filthy as you liked and there was no one to slap your arse for it. There was definitely something to be said for adulthood.

Douglas bent down, wrenched a weed from the ground and threw it into the growing mound of rubbish. He'd already spent a fair few hours in the garden since he and Kirstin moved into the new house just over a week ago. They'd used Archie's van for the flitting. Douglas arched his back and felt his vertebrae shift and loosen as he placed his hands behind his head and pushed. 'Nothing like gardening to remind you that you're a human being with muscles that ache and bones that crack, eh.' He wiped the sweat off his face with a towel and squinted at the sun. 'I can't believe we managed to get by in Glasgow, you know, without a garden. Nobody I knew had a garden when we were growing up. Can you imagine what a difference it would have made to folk's lives if they'd had a bit of green of their own to potter about in. I'm sure it would have done wonders for our granny. Mind her house in Dennistoun? That wee pokey place where the light only managed to sneak in for a few minutes a day, as if it were afraid of being caught. All that house needed was some bars on the windows and it could've been an annexe for Barlinnie Prison. She could have done with a garden, that's for sure.'

Andrew thrust his spade into the turned soil until it stood like a soldier to attention. 'She could have done with a shovel up the arse,' he scoffed. 'Mean old bag, she was. You know she once took my sweetie money off me. Said she needed it to buy cigarettes. And I knew full well she had plenty of money in her purse. Every penny was a prisoner.'

'Ach, well she grew up in hard times. Two world wars and a depression. That can bugger you up. No wonder she counted her every penny.'

'Aye, and other people's as well.'

Andrew paused to catch his breath and make a quick assessment of their progress. It had a big garden, this new house of Douglas and Kirstin's. Big garden, big tin roof, big house full of bedrooms, and just the two of them. 'You didn't answer my question, Douglas.'

Douglas swigged at a jug of water. Some of it spilled down his throat and he rubbed it into his bare chest. 'Aye, and what question was that?'

'You know bloody well what question it was. Don't come all innocent with me, Douglas Fairbanks. I've known you since you were still in nappies, don't forget.'

Douglas laughed. 'Am I going to have weans? That's a big question.'

'But there's only two answers, and they're both very short. Yes or no.'

Douglas threw his shovel on the ground and sat on the warm grass. 'Look Andrew, I don't know. I just don't know if I'm ready for it.'

'People say you're never ready, that it's a bit like leaping into the water from the high diving board. You just take a deep breath, close your eyes and jump.'

'I had my eyes closed for years and I'm not about to close them again. If I do it, I want to do it with my eyes wide open.'

'What about Kirstin?'

'Aye, she would like some weans. You know, six or seven.'

'My God!' Andrew exclaimed, punching his cousin on the shoulder. 'You're going to be busy, eh.'

'I didn't say I wanted that many. I didn't say I wanted any. I don't know if I'd be a good father. Christ, I don't even know if I'm a good husband.'

'What are you talking about? Anyone can see you two belong together.' Andrew paused, kicked at the dirt. 'Isn't Kirstin happy?'

Douglas plucked at some grass. 'Aye. No. Sometimes.'

'I'm not with you, Douglas. She is, or she isn't.'

'Look, you know what Kirstin's like. She's more inclined to be happy than most folk. She has to have a very good reason not to be. But I know—she knows, too, in her heart—that there's something not right.'

'Is it sex? If you don't mind me asking, that is. Things no good in the bedroom, like?'

'That's a bit personal, Andrew. What sort of Scot are you asking questions like that?'

'I'm Australian now, Douglas. I've been liberated from my repressed Caledonian Catholic background.' He waited for Douglas to respond but his cousin just stared at the grass, as if the answer might be found within the blades of couch. 'Is that the problem then?'

'No. Well yes. Yes and no.'

'Here we go again,' Andrew sighed, exasperated.

'No, it's not, Andrew,' Douglas said, shaking his head. 'It's not sex per se, but more the way I am, the way I've turned out to be since I've left the bloody Church. It's just that in my head, when I'm with Kirstin, I can be somewhere else as well. There's other stuff going on in there, things I'm trying to sort out. Things that hold me back.'

'Hold you back from what, Douglas?'

'From loving her enough.'

'Och, that's bullshit, Douglas. I know you love her. You left the Church for her, didn't you?'

'Well, yes and no.'

'Godssake, Douglas.'

'I left the Church for her, that's true. But I left it for me as well. But it hasn't gone away yet. It's still hanging about and I need to get rid of it or make some arrangement with it that allows me to be myself, be the person I want to be. Until I can do that, I can't have weans, because I won't be able to give them, or Kirstin for that matter, the thing I want to give them, the thing they deserve.'

'And what's that when it's at home?'

'The real me, the real bloody me.'

Andrew scoffed. 'The real you? The real you is what you make yourself, son. Everything else is just pissing in the wind.'

'Is that right?'

'Aye, it is. Look, I know you think I'm some sort of playboy romantic who never thinks about what he's doing with his life. But it's not like that. I know what I want at this time in my life and what I don't want. And the things I want I go after. The other stuff can come later. I can wait for them, or her, or it, whatever it is. I try and make my life how I want it to be. I try and make myself the person I want to be. It's a matter of choice.'

Douglas laughed, taking his cigarettes from the back pocket of his shorts and lighting one up. 'Ach away, it's not that simple. You are the way you are for a lot of reasons. Your childhood, for one. Whether your parents loved each other or whether they were always at each other's throats, whether you had a few books in the house or just bottles of whisky and gin. Maybe your uncle read poetry to you or just tried to feel you up on the sly. Maybe you had no money or maybe you were stinking rich. You see what I'm saying, Andrew? You're not born fully formed, a perfectly content, well-balanced person. There's a lot of stuff on the way that can bugger you up, and you've got to work through that, get your head sorted out.'

Andrew sighed. 'Look, I know what you mean. And I suppose God can fuck you up more than most things. But you have to get over it, Douglas. Otherwise you'll never be happy, and happiness is what we all want, isn't it? We're all the same in that respect, even if some of us didn't have an inside toilet when we were wee. Get your priorities sorted, Douglas. I know Kirstin has.'

'Oh aye. If you know so much, what is her priority then?'

'You, you idiot. Douglas bloody Fairbanks.'

'Shaz, I'm up the duff.'

It was as if the telephone had frozen to Shane McGowan's right ear. His stomach decamped up his alimentary canal in a northerly direction before skidding to a halt at the base of his throat. His tongue turned to coarse-grained sandpaper that would take the paint off a garden fence in a couple of seconds flat. His legs, legs that had born him through three glorious seasons with the Baytown firsts, wobbled like his mum's Sunday jelly. Suddenly his head felt detached, as if it belonged to somebody else. He couldn't focus; he couldn't think. He felt faint.

'Shane! Shane! Are you there? What's goin' on?'

'Yeah, sorry Karen, I'm here,' he said, as if awaking from a dream. 'Just tryin' to think. Work out what to do an' that.'

'You do that, Shaz, you do that.'

'How do ya know?'

'Know what?'

'That you're up the duff?'

The pitch of Karen's voice almost burst her boyfriend's eardrum. 'What do you mean, how do I know? I just bloody well know, all right.'

They were both lost for words, the only sounds being those inside their heads.

'What *are* we gonna do?' Karen asked, her voice falling to a whispered plea for reassurance.

Shaz pulled at his left ear and bit his lip. 'We'll have to think of somethin'.'

'Like what?' Kaz's voice abruptly became shrill and anxious and it bore into Shane's vice-clamped head like an electric drill on high speed.

'Dunno. I just dunno. Couldn't you drink a bottle of gin and sit in the bath for an hour or somethin'?'

'Jesus Shaz, I knew you were a bit thick but I didn't know you were that stupid.' Karen was weeping softly down the line. She sounded like a small child crying in the night. 'I wanted to finish matric, go to uni, get out of this bloody place. I don't wanna end up workin' as a checkout chick and I don't wanna be somebody's bloody secretary.' She began sobbing, small cries of desolation from deep within her. 'And I don't want to end up like that Christine Dodds, pushin' her kid down the street in a pram when she's still a bloody kid herself.'

'Come on, Kaz. It'll be all right. We'll think of somethin', no worries.'

'You told me you'd pull out. You shoulda pulled out.'

'I did, I did.'

'Well, not bloody quick enough.'

'It's not as easy as it looks.'

Karen screamed down the line, finally losing her patience.

'Not easy! Not easy! I bet it's easier than givin' birth to a bloody seven pound baby!'

Shane scrambled for a quick retort but couldn't think of one. 'Anyway, I didn't hear you complainin' at the time.'

'You're a bastard, you know that, a bloody bastard,' she shrieked.

'I'm a bastard? I'm a bastard? What about you? How could you do this to me? I've got enough on me plate as it is.'

'Whaddya mean?'

'Nuthin. Forget about it.'

'Nah, nah, just say what's on yer mind,' Kaz said, trying to calm herself.

'I said nuthin'. All right?'

'Typical, bloody typical. You're a bloody bastard, that's what you are.'

'I'm a bastard? I'm a bastard. I tell ya, that kid'll be a bastard if ya don't smarten up, girl, and calm down.' Shaz rubbed the back of his hand across his mouth. 'Anyway, how do I know it's mine?'

Never before had Shaz heard such an unearthly wail. It would have aroused every mummy in Egypt, sent witches scuttling to their broomsticks to flee.

It was as if Kaz was beyond words, as though they'd been wrung out of her. All she could do was screech and moan. Finally, they flowed; lava from a volcano.

'Don't you bloody well move, Shane McGowan. I'm comin' round there and I'm gonna kill you. I'm gonna ram that fuckin' surfboard up your arse till it's stickin' out your stupid gob. And then I'm gonna take you down the coast and I'm gonna throw you and that fuckin' stinkin' panel van of yours to the bloody sharks. And then I'm gonna get in the water meself and make sure you're fuckin' well dead and if there's any sign of life in you

I'm gonna get my spear gun and shoot you in the guts. And then . . . '

'Kaz! Kaz! Hold on. Hold on!' Shaz yelled, trying to get a word in. 'It's a fair question.'

'Fair question? Fair question?' she screeched.

'Yeah. I know what you sheilas are like, once yous get a taste for it. You could've rooted Wozza. I wouldn't put it past ya.'

'Wozza? Wozza? Bloody Wozza's stupider than you are!'

Karen began to moan, deep and inconsolable. 'I was a virgin when I met you, Shaz. I was a virgin.'

Shaz rubbed at his nose. He was feeling something he rarely felt. He guessed it was guilt. 'Look, have you told your old man yet?'

'Nah. He's gonna kill me, deadset.' She was slowly calming down, her tears just a sniffle now.

'Well, don't say anythin' yet. Let me talk to Brian, okay?'

'He'll kill me, he'll bloody well kill me.'

'Kill you! Kill you! What about me?'

Karen couldn't help but laugh. 'He'll kill you twice.'

The wind drifted gently down Bay Street, sweet and warm, like cherub's breath. Sergeant Richard McDonald was glad to be out and about, particularly on such a glorious day. He couldn't remember the last time he'd seen so much blue sky or so many consecutive hours of sunshine. He thought back to one day during the war when he was playing with Angus in a field near their mother's village of Crail. It was a day like this, he recalled, and it seemed to go on forever. They had spent hours in that field, the two of them, just weans with so many games to play with stones and long grass and bushes. There were potatoes lying in the furrows, abandoned and forgotten. They'd carried them home in their pockets like treasure. They peeled them at the sink and their mother said they tasted better than anything from the shops. Sometimes they'd pick wild raspberries to make jam. Their mother's biggest pot, burned black by years over the flame, would spit and bubble on the fire and they'd have jam on their piece for weeks after.

Richard tilted his head back and gazed up. Look at that sky, not a cloud in sight. He could bloody well kiss it, so he could. And the shoppers were obviously enjoying it, taking their time, blethering away outside the shops, or relaxing on nice wooden benches with potted plants on either side of them, smelling the sea breeze or just quietly enjoying the touch of the sun on their faces. There were four different banks in the street. Four! It must be doing all right, this place. There must be a lot of money kicking about to keep them all in business. Aye, it was a lovely street, no doubt about it. If you stood at one end, up by Penfold's hardware shop, and gazed straight down its length, you could see the sea, bright blue on a day like this and calm as your granny's afternoon nap. It wasn't that the sea was a novelty, far from it. In Aberdeen, where he grew up, in Crail where his mother's people were, and in Pittenweem where he lived and worked, there was more sea than you could poke a lobster pot at, but it was sea with the pallor of a dead man. Grey, cold and unwelcoming. It made you wary of going in, as if it might never let you leave its shadowy grip. Here, it was positively begging you to jump into its blue-green warmth. Dive, leap, do a bomb off the pier, but for fucksake get in here, man! Richard was definitely tempted but didn't have his trunks with him and it wouldn't do for a member of the Scottish constabulary to be found skinny-dipping in a foreign country. It just wouldn't do at all. Best to keep your willie covered up in public at all times.

Besides, he had other things on his mind. He'd promised Angus he'd make a few discreet inquiries about the business at the soccer club. He'd spoken to a young sergeant at the Baytown Police Station, polis to polis, and he said the two constables who'd called at Douglas's house the other day were on the case. But there had been a rash of burglaries and they had a lot on their plate.

Something wasn't right, Richard could feel it in his bones. Call it a hunch, call it instinct, call it paranoia. Whatever it was, it came in handy sometimes when you were polis. There was something going on here that smelled of fish, and if anyone knew about fish, it was him. All you had to do was cast out a line and reel them in.

Douglas sat on the low beach wall, arranging the sand with his toes into a little mound. If he had a couple of lollipop sticks he could make a cross and stick it on the top. Kirstin had gone out shopping, so he'd decided to go for a walk. It gave him a chance to think. Why did he have trouble saying the things he knew were inside him, behave the way he wanted to behave? Why was he so distant, when all he really wanted was to be close? It was as if someone had stuck a plug in his guts and he didn't know how to get it out. He knew he had a responsibility to Kirstin to say what he felt, she needed to know so that she could know him. Otherwise what was the point of them being together? He knew that. But knowing was different from doing. Funny thing was he'd spent so many years waiting for the chance to let his true feelings emerge. But they were still bound up, like string around a parcel.

'I have to know that you love me. You need to tell me,' Kirstin had told him last night as they lay in bed. 'You have to remind me. Maybe you need to remind yourself.'

There were times in the dark and fearful hours in the middle of the night when he lay awake listening to the whisper of the breeze through the trees by the bedroom window, a muffled bark from a dog roused by the throaty acceleration of a passing car. He grasped at straws, anything to give him a better grip on how to be in this different life.

Sometimes he'd wake up in the morning feeling stronger, more certain of direction and armed with a new determination to find his way.

Other times, it would take him an hour to get out of bed, to tentatively place that first bare foot on the carpet. Father Docherty told him that when he left his vocation it would be like a death, as if he had no past and no future. Some days, it certainly felt like that.

Kirstin was forever telling him to lighten up and embrace his new life and she'd told him again last night. It wasn't that she lacked sympathy, it was just that she was running out of patience. She was happy and she wanted him to be happy too. Maybe he didn't have it in him.

Douglas shivered involuntarily and gazed out to the horizon, looking for something to take his mind off himself. There was the club, of course, plenty going on there, what with the fence being pulled down and the fire and time marching on if they wanted to be ready for next season. But that was just moving from one problem to another. If it doesn't rain it bloody well buckets down. He didn't leave Scotland for this. He thought he would have been able to leave his troubles behind him, not pick up a few new ones. If he were in a more fanciful frame of mind he could spend some time admiring those girls lounging about in their bikinis on the sand in front of him. They weren't bad to look at and would take your mind off most things. Sport and women. What more could a man want?

'Fish and chips,' he murmured to himself, as he stomped on his mound of sand and headed off down the Pier Street to Jimmy Staccato's takeaway.

Andrew looked at his watch. Christ was that the time? He'd better get a move on or Minh Thanh would be left standing outside the picture hall by herself. She wanted to see *Butch Cassidy And The Sundance Kid*, with Paul Newman and Robert Redford. They were the two sexiest men in the world, she said. Next to him, of course. He didn't understand it. If she found him so sexy, why wouldn't she express that sexual electricity in the way that two people did when they were truly attracted to each other? She said she was saving herself for when she got married and just wanted a few indications from Robert and Paul of what she might be saving herself for. He had offered to show her first hand, but to no avail.

He studied his watch again. The next train wasn't for twenty minutes so he had just enough time for a bite to eat from Simpson's bakery. He might even sit down and have a cup of tea as well. If he hadn't spent so long shopping he would have had plenty of time to have a relaxed lunch. He'd ended up putting a deposit on a mauve safari suit from Mel's Menswear that Mel himself had sworn would be in fashion for years to come.

'Timeless,' he'd said. 'Classic.'

Andrew had had his doubts but handed over the money anyway. Mel had pointed to a chocolate brown tie the same colour and width as the Yarra and said he'd throw that in as well. 'Don't say I don't look after ya,' he'd laughed, slapping him on the back with a hand unexpectedly large for a retailer of male attire. When Minh Thanh saw him in that get-up she'd have her knickers off before you could say Ho Chi Minh.

Andrew crossed the road to the baker's. The problem with Simpson's was that it catered to most of Andrew's culinary tastes. With his naturally slender frame he had never had to worry about watching his diet and so therefore didn't. And his Glasgow upbringing was no disincentive either, encouraging, as it did, a taste for all things cream, fat and pastry laden. Indeed, Douglas had once caught him trying to furtively dispose of one of Ronnie Richards's school health lunches. Douglas had been watching from the second floor staffroom window and had seen him nonchalantly dropping the lunch in one of the large metal bins by the canteen. A minute later he emerged the proud purchaser of what looked like two of Mrs Wickstead's finest sausage rolls. Douglas was happy to remind him of this whenever he lectured his students about the importance of a healthy diet.

Andrew gazed into Simpson's window like a toddler at a toyshop. The doily-decorated glass shelves sighed with cream buns dolloped with jam and dusted with sugar, apple pies as big as plates, Swiss rolls, custard tarts swollen with sin, vanilla slices, scones as fluffy as clouds, freshly baked bread and meat pies and Cornish pasties not long out of the oven. There were long buns smothered with coconut, and round buns decorated with a splash of chocolate icing. Or he could have a sandwich or a roll filled with ham and cheese. Corned beef and pickle. He could lash out and have chicken. Actually, what he fancied was a piece an' sausage from the Italian cafe in Duke Street in Glasgow. But that was a long way to go for your lunch. Minh Thanh said they did a lovely baguette in Saigon, a legacy from the French. They were a pain in the arse the French, but they did a good loaf, he'd give them that.

What to choose? A coffee scroll, maybe? He pressed his face against the glass. Through a gap between the shelves, he saw Kirstin take a bite from her sandwich. A shopping bag from Sonia's Lingerie lay at her feet. She laughed as Clive Peterson took her hand in his and stroked it with his index finger. Andrew waited for her to withdraw from his touch. When she didn't, he decided he wasn't hungry after all.

Douglas couldn't quite get used to eating shark. It was more the idea of shark than the actual taste of it, because as sea-going creatures went, it wasn't that bad. Certainly he'd tasted worse fish in his life. Kippers for a start. Why folk went on about kippers for breakfast was beyond him. As far as he was concerned he couldn't think of a worse way to start the day, except maybe being bludgeoned to death in your bed. Of course, there was the fish pie they served on Fridays at his old primary school when he was wee. It would have been a sin to eat meat on a Friday, but not as much of a sin as the pie itself. It was definitely the fish John West rejected, and some of the weans who'd just started school would start crying when the teachers made them eat it all up. The pastry wasn't so bad but inside it looked like the cat had been sick. Fish pie certainly made you wonder whether being a Catholic was worth it. Surely, there would be no fish pie in heaven. But this shark, flake they called it here, wasn't anywhere as bad as that. But it wasn't cod or haddock either. What he'd give for a cod supper from Costello's in Shettleston Road. Loads of salt and vinegar. Mrs McDougall could do a good fish and chips on a Friday night for him and Father Docherty. But if she was on one of her economy drives it used to be all batter and no fish and the chips would be sliced thin and mean. She was one person he didn't miss from Glasgow. Hard shell and not soft inside either.

Douglas rubbed a chip into the salt that had accumulated at the bottom of the wrapping paper, then bit it in half, a clean break down the middle. As he chewed, he held the rest of the chip in front of his face and stared at it. He'd watched other people do this, and he did it himself, but he wasn't sure why. He put it down to ritual. Ritual made you do a lot of things you didn't necessarily understand or question. A bit of HP sauce wouldn't go astray, he thought, taking another chip. Seagulls squealed and stalked the green wooden beach where he sat at the edge of the park eating his lunch. It was a lovely park, this. Built at the turn of the century when Baytown was a quiet seaside village, it was dotted with pine trees that were sturdy and broad and provided welcome shade from the blinding brightness and intense heat of high summer. The original bandstand still stood in the middle, now offering only a refuge for couples with hearts full of love, or drunks with bellies full of beer. It looked defeated, resigned to its fate. It was if it knew its time had passed and that the bleat of brass and the boom of drums would be unlikely to resonate from there again.

Douglas closed his eyes and offered his face to the sun. Take me, I'm yours. The meanest looking gull, its beady eyes glaring with unadulterated evil, hissed and snapped at any other bird that tried to usurp his position at the front of the queue. Douglas made a mental note not to give Godzilla the Gull any leftover fish.

Suddenly the birds scattered as a large rock hurtled into their midst. Douglas turned to see Richard McDonald strolling towards him with what appeared to be his own lunch in a brown paper bag.

'Richie! What a nice surprise.'

'Mind if I join ye, Douglas?'

'Of course not, my bench is your bench,' Douglas said, gesturing to the space beside him.

Richard removed a meat pie from his bag. He nodded towards Douglas's lunch. You've got a fish supper, I see. Cod?'

'No, shark.'

'My God! I wonder what they've put in this pie then,' Richard said, looking anxious and poking at the pastry.

'Best not to think about it. Just make sure you put lots of tomato sauce on.'

Douglas broke off a bit of his fish and bit into it. Richard took a gulp from a small bottle of orange juice. The seagulls had regrouped and, emboldened by the seeming lack of interest shown in them by the two men contentedly eating their lunch, were edging closer to the bench through a series of small guerrilla-like manoeuvres punctuated by raucous and squabbling retreats. Douglas threw the birds a cold chip and immediately regretted it as they launched into a frenzied attack on it and each other. Several of the birds looked like they'd been in the wars before and had eyes or bits of leg missing. Another had no tail feathers. Godzilla looked like a possible serial killer. He attacked some of his fellow gulls, snapping and screeching, secured the chip and guzzled it down.

'Birds don't chew their food, have you noticed that?' Richard said.

'Aye, and they don't pee either.'

'No, but they shite a lot.'

'It's a strange world, no doubt about it.'

Richard finished the last of his pie and wiped his hands on the back of his trousers. 'Listen Douglas, I've been doing a wee bit of poking around, ye know, just asking a few questions about yon trouble up at the football ground. A strange business right enough. But I think I might have found something. In fact, I know I've found something.'

'Is that right?' Douglas said. 'Well, you'd better tell me everything ye know.' He scrunched up his fish and chip wrapper into a ball and chucked it at the killer gull. 'Everything.'

'So do ye keep the butter in the fridge or on the kitchen bench?' Angus asked, staring intently into Douglas's eyes. 'Because I find that if ye put it in the fridge, it gets too hard. But if ye keep it on the bench in this weather, it melts.' He frowned. 'I'm no quite sure what to do about it.'

Douglas patted the big man on the forearm. 'Pray for guidance, Angus, and thy prayers shall be answered.'

Ayrshire Archie had offered to hold the meeting at his place this time and everyone was there. Joyce had made a few plates of sandwiches since most folk had come straight from their work and were hungry. There were a couple of bowls of crisps for people to be getting on with as well. Archie had made sure everyone had a drink and a chair to sit in. He'd got Johnny Cash on the record player. The Man in Black was stuck in Folsom Prison and time kept moving on. As it is wont to do, Archie thought. It wasn't so long ago that he was a young man himself, and now here he was, grey haired with one rheumy eye, a gammy leg and a wall full of memories. Photographs of him and Joyce in their younger days, winning yet another music competition, their hats tall, their boot heels high, their smiles broad, and their future limitless. Everyone from Jedburgh to John O'Groats had heard of Ayrshire Archie, Scotland's own country music king, and Joyce Dalrymple, queen of hearts. But things hadn't quite been the same since the Beatles. Everything had suddenly changed and there had no longer been much demand for his kind of music. 'What've Freddie and the Dreamers got that I haven't?' he'd once asked Joyce in a moment of despair. But Australia still had a little bit of country in it and had served them well ever since they'd made the move. They were rarely out of work these days. One door closes, another opens.

Aberdeen Angus sipped at his whisky and grasped Douglas's arm. 'Now, do ye know how Americans got to be known as gringos?'

'Aye, I do.'

'What? Ye do?' Angus said, surprised.

'Aye. At the Battle of the Alamo, the Yankees—and there were a lot of Scots among them, mind—used to sing "Green Grow the Rashes O" of a night-time. And yon Mexicans could only make out what they thought was Gr . . . een . . . go.'

'Aye, that's right, Douglas. No wonder you're a teacher. You've got it up here,' Angus said, tapping his temple with his forefinger. 'No doubt about that, son.'

'Did you see the film, Angus?'

'Aye, I did . . . Yon John Wayne and Richard Widmark were in it. Davy Crockett and Jim Bowie they played. Some film, eh?'

'Aye. What was it? Oh aye. The mission that became a fortress, the fortress that became a shrine!'

'That's it. Some memory ye've got there. Here, the woman in it, Linda Cristal, she's in the *High Chaparral* now, ye know. It's on the telly tomorrow night. Did ye know that?'

'No, I didn't know that, Angus. Is that right?'

'Aye, it is,' Angus said, beaming.

'Okay!' Andrew's raised voice broke though the hubbub like a gunshot in the crowd. 'Let's get on wi' it. It's getting late and I know everyone wants to get home.'

'Not me, mate.'

Everyone turned to Valletta Vince, who was laughing and nudging Alec Walker in the ribs. 'Too many childrens at my place. Noisy as buggery. Every time I look there's a new children. I dunno what's goin' on. I'm not kiddin' you, mate.'

'I think you need to go to Douglas's Health Education classes, Vince. He'll explain it all to you,' Andrew said.

'No worries,' Vince laughed, raising his glass of red wine.

'Right, settle down, we haven't got all night,' Douglas said, calling the meeting to order. 'Now, we called this meeting because Richard here has been doing a wee bit of investigation into these mishaps at the soccer club and he thinks he might have found something. You want to explain to everybody, Richard?'

Richard McDonald nodded and raised himself from the kitchen chair he'd been glued to for the last half-hour. He coughed to clear his throat, took his glasses from his shirt pocket and a small black notebook from his new trousers. 'As Andrew was saying, I thought I might do a wee bit of poking around and ask a few questions about the troubles at the club. I left Angus's house at approximately 10.15 a.m. on Tuesday and headed on foot in an easterly direction towards Bay Street. It was a bright sunny day and visibility was excellent . . .'

Richard explained, slowly and in the kind of detail that had made him a legend in Pittenweem, how he had first made a visit to the Baytown Police Station to make a few routine inquires about the progress of their investigation into the damage at the ground. A young officer, Detective Constable Bruce Gilmour, whose mother turned out to be from Anstruther, a village not far from his own, explained that as yet they hadn't managed to turn anything up but that it was early days yet. Richard confided that he was on the case himself, a longstanding member of the Fife constabulary, and as one polis to another, what were his thoughts about the possible culprits and their motives?

'No motives, mate. Just a bunch of cunts goin' off.'

Richard disagreed but didn't say so, not wanting to get the young man offside. The constable promised to do his best anyway and would get back to him or Douglas as soon as he had anything to report.

Richard had then decided to take a walk around the streets and see if he could recognise any vehicle that matched the characteristics of the car that may have been responsible for the villainous acts in question. 'It was a long shot, but what did I have to lose?' he said.

Perry McIntosh leaned forward in his chair. 'And did ye find anythin', Richie?'

'Aye, I did.' he nodded gravely.

Douglas took up from where Richard left off. 'Richie found a panel van in the car park behind Paddy Penfold's hardware shop. Do you want to describe it, pal?'

'Aye, it was a cream-coloured panel van, something called a Holden.'

'Were the tyres worn a bit on one side?' Vince, asked excitedly.

'Aye, they were. And they were very wide as well.'

'Fats, mate,' Vince broke in. 'They're called fats.'

'Aye, fats. They were fat, no doubt about that.'

'Anything else?' Archie said.

'Aye. I had a peek through the window. I couldn't see much, but there were some tools on the front seat. A hammer and a big spirit level. And there was a big ladder in the back and some scaffolding. Oh, and there was half of something called a Chiko roll on the floor. It didn't look that appetising, I can tell you.'

'Did ye get the registration number, Richie?' Angus asked.

Richard gave him a look that could have split a caber. 'What do ye think?'

Angus raised his glass to his brother and turned to Ayrshire Archie. 'Will ye no give us a song, son?'

Archie took a nip of his whisky, picked up his guitar and began to strum.

'Green grow the rashes, O,
Green grow the rashes, O,
The sweetest hours that e'er I spend,
Are spent amang the lasses, O.'

Kirstin sat limply at the kitchen table, a cup of tea cradled in her hands, her long hair draped in front of her face like a veil.

'Hello, I'm back,' Douglas announced, making his way straight to the fridge. 'The meeting went quite well. Richie's on to something.' He pulled open the door and stood, hands on hips, gazing into it as if he were searching for the meaning of life. He finally settled on a bottle of orange juice. 'What is it with fridges? There's always something not there that you think should be, or if it is there you can't find it anyway.'

Kirstin tried to force a laugh but could only manage a choked sob, a small chink in a dam wall waiting to burst.

'You all right? Sounds like you're getting a wee bit of a cold there,' Douglas said, pouring his juice into a glass. He took a long gulp and winced. 'They put too much sugar in this stuff.'

He pulled up a chair beside Kirstin. Her hands covered her face, tears squeezing out from between her splayed fingers.

Douglas slipped his fingers behind hers and gently prised them back. Her eyes were red and watery.

'What is it? What's the matter?' Douglas whispered, the softness of his voice disguising his alarm. Her tears frightened him.

'What's the matter?' Kirstin searched her pockets for a handkerchief but, not finding one, wiped her eyes with the back of her hands. 'What's the matter?' she sighed heavily, staring at the tabletop. 'I'm lonely, Douglas. I miss my mother, my sisters. I miss being able to talk to them on the telephone when I want to. I miss being able to drop in for a cup of tea and a blether. I miss the sound of their voices.' Her voice broke. 'I miss you, Douglas.'

'Miss me? Miss me? How can you miss me? I'm here, here with you,' Douglas said, taking her hand in his. Not sure whether to rub it or squeeze it, he held it like a nervous father held his newborn baby.

'Are you, Douglas? It doesn't seem like you're here with me.'

'Well, the meeting did go on a bit longer than expected. You know Archie, once he gets that guitar in his hand . . . '

'Stop it, Douglas, just stop it,' she shouted, releasing her hand from his grip. 'Stop pretending. You know what I mean.' Kirstin rubbed at her nose with her shirt sleeve. 'You know what I mean,' she said again, as quiet as a solitary prayer in an empty church.

Douglas sat, saying nothing, not sure what to say, or at least to admit to himself that she knew he was being less than honest.

'Where are you, Douglas?' She looked into his eyes. 'You never talk to me. I think married people are supposed to talk to each other, aren't they? I talk to you. Why don't you talk to me? I don't understand. Even when you're with me I can tell that half the time you're away somewhere else. Do you think I don't know, Douglas? Do you think I'm stupid?'

Kirstin stood and looked out into the still darkness of their garden. She could just make out the mounds of earth and bits of broken old water pipe and concrete where Andrew and Douglas had been digging. 'You talk to me in between other things, in between other thoughts. You don't talk to me for the sake of it. What's happened to you? You weren't like this when we first met. You used to talk to me all the time. Sometimes I couldn't shut you up, always quoting those stupid westerns of yours. Now talking to me, being with me, is an afterthought. It's like you're just doing your duty. Am I that boring?' She slumped back into her chair. 'God, you hardly ever even fuck me any more.'

Douglas stared at the wall. Just give me a minute, a minute, he thought, and I can look at you.

'I know you're right, Kirstin, I know that. But I don't know what's going on. I didn't expect this. But I just seemed to have lost my way a bit. I thought I was doing well, that I had shaken off my past, or at least shaken it off enough to allow me to get on with my life. But it doesn't seem to go away, Kirstin, no it doesn't. I wanted a divorce from Rome but it keeps coming back to pester me. They say that once you are a priest you are a priest forever. Maybe that's right. Maybe there's no escape.'

Douglas took both Kirstin's hands in his and squeezed them. 'You know, Kirstin, sometimes when I look in the bathroom mirror in the morning, I can't see myself. I can see an image in the mirror, but it's not me. It looks like me, but it's like there's someone else inside my face. I press my face against the mirror, but I can't get in. I'm locked out of myself. I don't know what to do about it. Sometimes I don't know where I am and I touch my neck and I am surprised that I have no collar on. I don't know why. Then I remember and my heart beats too fast. It beats in my stomach. It pounds away in my head.'

Kirstin said nothing.

'I feel like the whole world is slippery and I can't get a grip on any of it. I grasp at things and they slip away. I'm barely making it through the day at school. Sometimes I have to stop halfway through the lesson because I've forgotten what I was supposed to be talking about.'

Kirstin looked up at him. 'So what's all that got to do with me? I'm not part of that. I'm not part of your school or your stupid bloody football club or your bloody awful God. I'm your wife. I'm the person you're supposed to love, to confide in. Why haven't you told me all this before? You've had the opportunity, so you have. But you sit there correcting your papers or fiddling with the television or looking out the bloody window. I see you laughing and joking with everybody but I know you're pretending because when you get home you change. You drop this happy face as if were a facade. I see it before my eyes.' She stroked his cheek and he leaned into her hand. 'Where have you gone, Douglas?'

Douglas ran his fingers through his hair, digging his nails in deep in a pathetic purge. If he had a birch at hand he would have beat himself till his skin burst and bled. 'I don't know.'

'Is that it? Is that all you can say?'

Thoughts of the day he'd left the priesthood came rushing into his head, of shaking hands with Father Docherty. He'd barely been able to hold back the tears, even though he'd felt liberated, about to embark on a great journey of discovery. They'd held each other's grip and promised to keep in touch. Kirstin was waiting in the car. It looked smaller all of a sudden, too small for all the baggage he carried. Kirstin had gripped his knee as she started the engine. They'd driven away from the kerb and he'd waved at his friend till he had receded into the distance. He'd fiddled with the radio until he'd found his favourite station then he'd stared at the road ahead.

He thought back to his uncertain goodbye to his father, how controlled and dishonest it was. There were so many things to say and yet they said nothing.

'I love you, Kirstin. I know that.'

'Is that right? Well, I'd hardly know it these days. I want more than your version of love. I want happiness; I want you to be happy. I want children. I want some sweetness between us. I want good times. I want sweet times, Douglas.' She slumped back in her chair and met his eyes with hers. 'Otherwise there's no point.'

Kirstin took a sip of her tea. It had gone cold and tasted bitter. 'I'm away to my bed.'

Shane McGowan drove slowly through the entrance to the Pines. It was dark and the old trees were scary shadows looming over him. Christ, it wasn't that long ago that he'd been here as a kid, a Boy Scout learning how to tie knots and build makeshift shelters. Humpies and wigwams, bark huts and lean-tos. This was the place the troop would come, the First Baytown Scouts, shorts pressed, shoes shined, toggles polished. Always polish your toggle, that's what he would say to his mate, Charlie 'Chook' Quinn, and they would laugh because they both knew what he really meant. He hadn't been here for years but from what he could make out, it seemed just the same. The same tracks through the trees, the same clearings for camping, the same breeze blowing in from the bay, no more than twenty yards away through the sandy scrub. Sometimes at night, he and Chook would sit there in the dark and count the stars.

They were both born and raised in Baytown, before it was a bona fide city, before the petroleum refineries and the slaughterhouses, before the migrants, way before Chook came back from Vietnam with only one leg. He'd left the other one somewhere near Cu Chi, after a landmine forced him to part company with it. There were more stars in the sky then, and there wasn't so much shit in the air in Baytown. All those fumes. And garlic. Fumes and bloody garlic. It was quiet now and deserted. Maybe he should bring Kaz down here one night. Then again, maybe not, they were in enough trouble already. Christ, it was every bloke's nightmare—parenthood when you were not that far from being a kid yourself. And everyone would know that it was a shotgun wedding and it would hang over them, a skeleton in the cupboard. Nothing would be said but everything would be known.

But hey, maybe it wouldn't be that bad. It had to happen sometime, didn't it? He could work overtime, break away and set up his own business. His own fuckin' business! McGowan and Son. Imagine that. He'd buy the kid his own kelpie or blue heeler and they'd sit up there in the cabin of the work truck like king fuckin' dicks. He'd learned a lot working for Brian Myers. The cunt knew more about the building game than the fuckin' Egyptians. If you wanted a pyramid, he'd be the man to build it. He might cut a few corners, but doesn't everybody? He could even build his own house right here in Baytown; it wasn't such a bad place. It was a bloody good place. He could never understand these people who itched to get away and hit the road the first chance they got. Didn't make any sense. You had all these Australians who couldn't wait to get to bloody England and all these Poms who couldn't wait to get to Australia. Look at that Rolf bloody Harris, or those bloody Easybeats. Sometimes life just didn't make any sense.

He'd have to stop this bullshit though, this would have to be the last deal. If he was gonna be a father then he'd better get his shit together. Christ, if he hadn't been stoned he would never have got Kaz up the duff in the first place. That was the trouble with the weed. It might go to your head first, but then it rushed straight to your dick. Then, what was the expression? That was right—you threw caution to the wind. That was also the trouble with being a bloke, you were ruled by your knob. Whatever it wanted, it got. People who talked about self-control didn't know what they were talking about. Either that or they had no balls. God made a huge fuckin' mistake when he put men's brains in their heads. He should've put a second one in their old fellas, you know, like twin carbies. The world would be a wiser place. And there'd be fewer sheilas getting into trouble, that was for sure. If he'd used a Johnny he wouldn't be in this mess. But they were just like cops—when you wanted one they were never around.

Shane turned on the radio. 'Purple Haze' by Jimi Hendrix. Fuckin' beauty. Where was that bugger? How could Kaz be so hot and her brother be such a deadshit. Jesus, if Brian knew he was selling dope to his son, and rooting his daughter, he could find himself in a bit of trouble. Shit, this was definitely the last deal, absolutely fuckin' definitely.

He finished rolling his joint and lit up. He sucked in hard and held the sweet smoke in his lungs for as long as he could, then slowly let it waft out of his mouth and his nostrils, as if the world might end tomorrow and this was his final scoob. Before you could say spliff he was drifting across a calm sea in a small wooden boat, the stars in his eyes, the breeze toying with his hair, his dreams all coming true. On second thought, maybe he'd do a couple more deals, you know, just to get a bit of dough together for the kid. Two or three more deals, and that was it.

Fuckin' definitely. He lay back and sang along with the radio. Jesus, he could handle a bit of a dance. He began madly rocking his head back and forth and side to side. He loved the swish and sway of his long hair. Shit, he hoped it never went out of fashion. You couldn't surf with short hair, everybody knew that.

'That must be bloody good pot you've got there, mate. You should see yourself. I thought you might've had Karen in the back, the car was rockin' that much.'

Malcolm Myers's boulder of a head poked through the open side window of Shane McGowan's panel van, his substantial bulk almost obliterating the diminutive frame of Wullie Henderson, who was loitering behind him, his hands deep in his pockets, a cigarette dripping from his mouth.

'Who's your little mate?' Shane asked, too ripped to be startled by the unexpected appearance of a basketball with a crewcut.

'This is me mate Wullie. He's from Scotland.'

'Christ, another wog, they're fuckin' everywhere. Does he speak English?'

'Aye, I dae speak fuckin' English, ye cunt ye. Don't ye be takin' the pish wi' me, pal, or yer heed wull be stickin' right oot yer erse, nae bother.'

Shane held out his hands in a gesture of peace and reconciliation. 'You've got a big mouth for such a little fella, eh. But just take it easy, mate, ya don't wanna be gettin' yourself in any trouble. You're just a kid.'

Wullie said nothing. He removed his cigarette from his mouth, chewed on a couple of wayward fag flakes and spat a chewy gob of phlegm and tobacco juice onto the sandy soil.

Shane laughed, a grin that felt wider than his face. 'Right then, let's get this over with, I've got things to do.'

186

He stuck his hand under the seat and pulled out a plastic bag bulging with dried green foliage. 'A mate of mine grows it in Werribee South. Top stuff. And since you and me go back, Malcolm, it's yours for five bucks an ounce. You won't get a better deal than that anywhere, not even from that dopey Italian cunt at your school, whatsisname?'

'Frankie Disabato.'

'That's right. Frankie fuckin' Disabato. He'd better watch himself as well. He's been sniffin' around Chook's girlfriend and Chook's about to smash his head in. You tell the little Italian prick that for me.'

'Yeh, well maybe Corinna wants a bloke with two legs for a change,' Malcolm said, nudging Wullie in the ribs.

'Is that right? Well, he's still got the leg that matters, mate. The one that gets him over, all right.'

'Yeah, but he's as ugly as a hatful of arseholes.'

'Listen, enough of this shit, Mal. Do you want this stuff or not? I've got things to do. I've got to pick up Kaz for a start.'

Malcolm shook his head. 'I don't think she'll be goin' anywhere tonight, mate.'

Shane looked perplexed. 'Oh yeah, why's that?'

'Well, when I left my place she was in the dunny chuckin' her guts out. And she's been cryin' in her room at night. You know what I reckon?'

'What do you reckon, Mal?' Shane said, feigning indifference and taking another toke on his joint.

'I reckon she's in the club.'

Shane exploded in a burst of nervous laughter. 'What would you know about it, Mal? Malcolm the little fourth former.'

'Plenty. Health Education, mate. Chapter Twelve, 'The Miracle of Conception and The Joys of Parenthood'. The Bun in the Oven chapter. We know all about it, isn't that right, Wullie?'

Wullie nodded, stubbed his cigarette against the side of the van. 'Everything there is tae know, we fuckin' well know it, pal. And in case yer interested, it disnae come oot her erse, either, despite whit ye may huv been telt previously.'

Shane shook his head, disappointed and disbelieving. Kids these days, thought they knew it at all. 'Maybe she's just crook in the guts, too many dim sims or something like that.'

'Aye, and pigs fuckin' fly,' Wullie said, drizzling a smile.

Shane sniffed. 'So what is it then, one ounce or two?'

'Actually mate, I've changed me mind,' Malcolm said, spreading his arms on the roof of the van. 'It fucks your head up, that stuff.'

Shane couldn't believe what he was hearing. Malcolm had asked him to come down here and bring some dope with him and now he was changing his mind like some half-arsed sheila at the drive-in.

'What are you playin' at, Mal? Eh? Just what are you fuckin' playin at?'

Before Malcolm could answer, the Pines were suddenly floodlit by two sets of headlights. The painted sunset on the back of Shane's panel van came to life under the glare. From the front seat of Valletta Vince's car, Douglas could have sworn he saw the sun sink over the horizon and the weary surfer pick up his board and wander off down to the shop for a milkshake and a toasted ham and cheese sandwich.

'Aye, that's the car,' Richard said as the Chevy growled up beside Shane's work of art. Ayrshire Archie, Aberdeen Angus and Andrew drew up next to them in Andrew's Mini.

Vince climbed out of the Chevy and made a beeline for the back of the van, runing his fingers over a beautiful painting of a surfer at sunset. He whistled in awe at the quality of the workmanship, like Pope Julius II getting his first look at Michelangelo's frescoes on the Sistine Chapel ceiling. Angus and Andrew were deep in muffled discussion as they examined the tread on Shane's tyres. They glanced up at Richard and gave him an affirmative nod. Richard pulled open the driver's door of the van and couldn't help but notice the bag of marijuana snug in his lap.

'Who the fuck are you? What do you want?' Shane demanded, his antagonism suddenly losing its ferocious edge as he felt the strong arm of the Pittenweem constabulary firm around his neck.

'A quiet word, son, a quiet word is all,' Richard whispered, hauling him out of his rootmobile.

'I don't know nuthin' about no fire.'

'Anything,' Douglas said, raising his eyebrows in admonishment. 'I don't know nothing is a double negative which makes it a positive, which means you're saying you do know something about it.'

Shane looked blank. 'What are you? Some sort of smart-arse or somethin'?'

'Aye, he's a teacher,' Wullie explained.

'Aw yeh. Well you'd better teach this little prick to speak English, hadn't ya.'

Wullie leapt at Shane like a feral cat attacking some wee boy's pet mouse. Before anyone could do anything about it he had McGowan's testicles in his right hand and was squeezing them like they were ripe plums. He would have had a bite at them as well if Vince hadn't dragged him off.

'You don't wanna do that, mate. I'm not jokin', these surfies, they don't like to wash, mate. You don't know what's goin' on down there. Infections or somethin', mate,' Vince warned. Wullie, nonethless, managed to nut him on the forehead when Vince momentarily turned away to admire the mag wheels on Shane's van for the umpteenth time.

'See you, ya bastart ye, ye widnae last five minutes in Glesga. Ye'd be carried oot in a box, so ye wid,' Wullie shouted at the pale-faced figure, now bent over double against the side of his painted wagon. 'Yer lookin' a bit peely-wally there, son,' he smirked. 'Ye all right?'

'You won't be doin' much shaggin' in that wagon for a while, eh Shaz,' Malcolm laughed. 'Bloody good thing too, given what you've done to me sister.'

'What's that?' Andrew inquired, his interest suddenly perking up.

'Kaz's in the club and he's the man responsible for givin' her her membership,' Malcolm replied, nodding in Shane's direction.

'Well done, mate. Bloody beauty,' Vince said, slapping the expectant father on the back. 'You are not a real man until you have the babies, no bullshit. Me, I got nine; two more and I got a soccer team, mate.'

'Speaking of which,' Douglas interrupted, 'let's get back to this business at the club, Shane, or should we go and see Brian Myers, have a word about the little parcel that his one and only daughter is about to bring into the world. How'd that be?'

Shane sighed. Suddenly the halcyon Boy Scout days at the Pines roasting sausages over an open fire, drinking billy tea and sneaking fags behind the tent had evaporated. How things changed in the blink of a black eye. One minute you're the King of Baytown, the next you're being beaten up by a fifteen-year-old maniacal midget from Scotland and being given parental advice from a hairy Maltese council worker. Just what the fuck was goin' on in this country?

Shane was placatory. 'Look, don't say nuthin' to Brian, yet, okay. Kaz and I have to work this out. Maybe we can make a go if it. If you don't wanna do it for me, think of Kaz. She's just a kid. Her old man'll kill her. We'll tell him when she's ready, eh.'

'And why should we do that, Shane?' Douglas asked.

'Because I'm gonna tell ya somethin'. I'm the one who tore up your, what do you call it, your pitch.' He thought for a moment. 'Anyway, why don't you people just call it an oval like we do here?'

'We don't call it an oval, pal, because it's a fuckin' rectangle,' Wullie pointed out.

Shane blinked. 'Yeh, right. So anyway, it was me.'

'And why did ye do that?' Richard inquired, folding his arms across his chest in a typical police sergeant manner. He rocked slightly on the back of his heels.

Shane gently touched his swollen forehead, gave Wullie a filthy look. 'Because . . . I . . . I . . . dunno. Look, why don't you soccer chocs just play Australian football, like real Australians. If youse wanna play soccer you should stay in your own country. This is our country and you should live by our rules, mate, and that's Australian Bloody Rules. Why don't you go back where youse belong, eh, wherever the fuck that is. There's enough wogs in this country.'

Again Wullie leapt at him, like a psychotic jack out of the box, but was quickly restrained by Andrew and Richie.

'You do that again, son, and I'm gonnae have to batter ye,' Richard said, grabbing the wee man by the scruff of the neck and shaking him senseless. 'Violence doesn't solve anything.'

'Wullie, just calm down, son,' Douglas said, turning back to Shane. 'Look Shaz, can I call you Shaz? We put a lot of time and effort into that pitch and you don't think we're going to put up with someone like you destroying all that work because you felt like it, do you? You can't get away with that sort of behaviour. One thing I know is that you always pay for your sins. There's always a man faster on the draw than you are, and the more you use a gun, the sooner you're gonna run into that man.'

Shane's face was a question mark. 'What?'

'Burt Lancaster,' Andrew explained. '*Gunfight at the OK Corral*. Douglas's favourite picture.'

'Never head of it. *Easy Rider*, mate. Now there's a fuckin' flick.' Shane attempted the languid drawl of a young Jack Nicholson, but failed miserably, '*This used to be a helluva good country. I can't understand what's gone wrong with it.*'

'Aye, well that's very good, Shaz, but that doesn't help us decide what we are going tae do with you, does it? What do you think, Richie? A wee word with Brian Myers? The polis? Stick his head down the cludgie?' Angus said.

Richard rubbed his fingers across the stubble on his chin and looked hard at Shane McGowan who was looking as anxious as a yellow canary being sized up by a salivating ginger tom.

'Well, it is a polis matter, now, is it no? And the young constable at the Baytown Polis Station said I was to give him a wee telephone if I stumbled across anything.'

Wullie chipped in. 'If ye don't mind me sayin', sur, I think we should give the cunt a right good kickin'.'

Douglas glared at him. 'For God's sake, Wullie, what have I been telling you about your language?'

'Sorry, sur. Fuckin' cannae help it, ye know. But I'll dae my best sur, aye I will, nae bother.'

'Wait, just wait a minute,' Shane interjected, suddenly looking worried. 'Look, I'm sorry, all right. I'll admit that I was a bit pissed off when I read about your wogball club startin' up and I thought, you know, I might have a word with a few people an' that, maybe write to the local rag, talk to that prick of an editor Frank O'Connell, but that's it. But then I got so shat off when you blokes all took the piss that night outside the council hall, I went off an' took some revenge.'

'Yeh, youse was really goin' for it,' Vince chuckled.

Shane was unable to contain the smile that flickered across his face.

'You might get twins,' Vince added.

Shane's smile suddenly evaporated and he looked panic-stricken. 'But I didn't have nuthin' to do with no fire,' he said, his raised hands protesting his innocence. 'I'm not bullshittin' you. And I didn't wreck your fence either. I just read about it in the paper.'

'What about the tyres?' Douglas asked.

'Tyres?'

'You didn't let them down at the fundraiser?'

'Nah, of course not,' Shane replied, incredulous. 'I was tearing around your soccer field then. I couldn't be in two places at once, could I? Fair go.' Shane became conciliatory, if not penitent. 'It was a stupid thing to do, I know that now. But I'd drunk six bottles of Melbourne Bitter and had a couple of spliffs, you know how it is. Sometimes you just act like a dickhead and then you regret it afterwards, eh. Me old man says I'm a bit reckless and he's probably right. But look, you know, as long as you migrants don't take all our jobs and root our women, we should all get along okay. And if you can play footy like Jezza then that's a bloody bonus, isn't it? One big happy fuckin' family. Look, I got wog mates, mate. A bloke that works with me in the buildin' game. He looks like a greasy little bastard but Christ can he lay those bricks. I met his mum an' all and can she cook grouse chips. She says he uses olly oil. That's the secret, she says.'

'You mean olive oil,' Vince said, thinking he might join Wullie and give the idiot a good kick in the guts after all.

'Yeah, whatever it is, it tastes fuckin' great. She's a great cook for a—'

'I think you'd better stop there, son,' Douglas said, placing a restraining hand on Shane's chest. 'Before you hang yourself.'

'Nothing like a good hanging, eh Douglas,' Archie said, smiling and tipping his Stetson.

'No, nothing at all. But let's find forgiveness in our hearts. Besides, I think Mr McGowan here might be able to help us out a wee bit. Call it his penance, if you like. What do you think, Shaz?'

Shane looked relieved, as if he'd woken up from a nightmare where a bunch of rampaging Apache were about to scalp him with a blunt knife. 'Yeah, whatever mate, no worries.'

Malcolm and Wullie watched the tail-lights fade as the men headed through the Pines and out the gate onto the quiet beach road.

'Fancy a game of pool, mate?' Malcolm asked.

'Naw thanks, pal. I've got tae finish ma English homework. That Fairbanks fair piles it on, ye know. Fuckin' poh-ye-try, fuckin' com-po-zish-ons. I've got a wee story tae write.'

'Fancy a bit of this then?'

Wullie stared at what had been Shaz's joint, only half smoked. 'I thought ye said ye'd gied it away.'

'Yeah, well I lied, didn't I.'

Wullie beamed a wicked grin and took a long slow drag. 'I think this is the beginning of a beautiful relationship, Malky, son. Aye, a bee-yoo–tee-fool friendship.'

Kirstin Fairbanks rubbed at the teak-veneered coffee table with a dry cloth and gave it another blast with the Mr Sheen. Why was it always women who ended up doing the housework, even when they bloody well worked all week? Maybe it was because their men were always at the pub or kicking a ball around a field on a Saturday afternoon. Sport was invented by men so they could avoid mopping floors and cleaning toilets. One day things would change and it would be the men who'd be wearing the aprons and watching their skin go all soggy and wrinkled as they washed up a week's dirty dishes. And there'd be robots for the ironing and little trained animals for cleaning out the cupboards. It couldn't come quickly enough as far as she was concerned. Get those little helpers into the darkest corners of the cupboards to give them a good scrub. You never knew what you were going to find in there, did you? Your auld granny, a half-eaten leg of lamb, a wee furry creature previously thought to be extinct.

Christ, the rubbish you thought about while you were doing the housework. You had to think about something or you'd go insane. What was Clive doing today? They'd worked back at the office last night and had had a few drinks. He was as good a talker as he was a dancer. Christ, could he talk. His tongue had muscles. He was one of those men who charmed their way into women's bedrooms. Kirstin was sure of it. He wasn't particularly attractive, but he was persistent, and enthusiastic. There was something to be said for that.

Kirstin rubbed at the table some more and spat on it. She wasn't sure whether that was because she wanted it to positively gleam, because she hated it so much, or because she just felt like a bloody good hawk. But she did loathe that table, no doubt about it. She and Douglas had bought a pile of furniture from a second-hand shop just round the corner from Bay Street when they first arrived. Andrew, who had taken them there, said the shop belonged to the father of one of the boys from school and that they'd get a discount. They'd bought a three piece suite, the horrible coffee table, a bed, a green formica kitchen table and six chairs, that stupid old television with the screen hidden behind two veneer mahogany doors, two bedside tables and an ugly standard lamp that lurked in the corner of the room like an axe murderer waiting to pounce. Why did starting afresh in a new country always mean starting with other people's cast-offs which made you wince each time you looked at them or sprayed them with polish? Archie's wife Joyce said it was all part of the migrant experience. Kirstin made it clear that it was a part of the migrant experience she could well do without. Douglas said he didn't mind the furniture, but then admitted he didn't have much to compare it to. He grew up in a house with wallpaper that followed you around the room and only a few sticks of stuff that barely passed as firewood, never mind tables and chairs. Kirstin, on the other hand, had been raised in a fully detached house with furniture that had been in the family for generations. Solid antiques and not a hint of veneer in sight. They had so much furniture they had to store some of it in the basement. Chippendale-rich great aunts kept dying and leaving it to her mother. She should have brought some of it with her so she could look around her living room with pleasure rather than embarrassment and distaste. Ach well, she'd inherit some of it one day, and then she'd be able spit on it and polish it with delight. Or maybe she'd get Douglas to do it.

That was if they were still together. God, what was wrong with men? It was as if they spent most of their time imprisoned in padlocked chests at the bottom of the sea, completely in-accessible to everyone and everything around them. Occasionally they managed to escape and float to the surface long enough to laugh and joke and talk about their feelings and their hopes and dreams and make love like beasts before they were recalled to their lives of darkness with the other bottom dwellers on the ocean floor. 'Douglas, Douglas, come back,' she murmured to herself. 'Stay on the surface with me.' But how long could she hold on? When she'd first told her mother about Douglas, her mother had warned her to look after herself. Women love more than men, she'd said, they love harder, they love deeper, they love till their insides shrivel. But when it begins to hurt too much, it is time to go, to leave it behind.

'You'll get over it and you'll be happier in the long run. It takes so long for men to work out what they want. But they sure figure out quick smart what it was when it's gone,' Katherine had laughed.

Kirstin pictured her mother running around Glasgow, attending this meeting and that, playing bowls, rushing to the theatre, always slightly late. She'd really come out of herself since she'd expelled her husband from the comforts of the family home. After all, he had been seeking his comforts elsewhere for some years. The man had run through girlfriends and secretaries and friends' wives like rain through a hole in the roof. Her mother had meant to leave him for some time, but had never quite got around to it. She wasn't poor, she had her own money, but she was afraid of being on her own, of being lonely. But now that she was by herself, she had never been happier. Strange, romance, wasn't it?

No matter how many tales of misery Kirstin heard, or acts of treachery she witnessed, she still clung to the idea of it like the fairy tales she revelled in as a child, curled up in bed in her warm pyjamas, snug and cosy with her favourite soft toys around her. Romance could be like believing in Santa Claus or the Tooth Fairy, but without the free gifts. But still she didn't want to let it go. It was so reassuring, so protective, it made your heart jump and your armpits itch. If you didn't believe in God, what else was there to believe in?

The doorbell rang, an annoying version of 'I Love To Go Awandering'. That bell had to go awandering too, and the sooner the better. Kirstin peered though the fly-wire screen and studied the man in front of her. Tall, thin, with hair that hitchhiked to faraway places, he seemed to be wearing someone else's suit, someone else's stained suit. Cigarette ash flecked his lapel and there were remnants of a previous meal on his waistcoat. His shirt collar was frayed and his tie slightly askew, a live man in a dead man's clothes. But she noticed that despite his shambolic appearance his eyes were bright and clear and sharp.

'Yes?'

He coughed and flicked his cigarette onto the lawn behind him. He saw that Kirstin watched its flight and landing. 'Oh, excuse me. I should give up these things. They'll kill me in the end,' he laughed.

Kirstin said nothing.

Frank coughed again. 'Mrs Fairbanks?'

'Aye,' Kirstin said, warily.

'My name's Frank O'Connell. I run the *Baytown Star*—you know, the local newspaper. Look, I was wondering if I could have a word, if you've got a minute or two. It won't take long.'

'It depends,' she said, still suspicious. 'It's not about anything scandalous I hope.'

'No, not at all. I get all the scandal I need from the local council. In fact, that's what I want to talk to you about.'

'The local council?'

'Well, a local councillor to be more exact.'

Kirstin shook her head. 'I don't know any councillors.'

'What about Brian Myers?'

'The builder? He's on the council?'

'That's right, and I understand he's employed your firm to buy up as much land as you can around the old swamp.'

'No, I didn't know that. I do know he's a friend of my boss, Clive. But look, I'm sorry, I can't talk about the firm's business. I'd lose my job.'

'Not even if it might explain why your husband's soccer club burned down?'

Kirstin stared at him through the wire. He didn't look like a murderer or a bank manager. She flicked the snib on the lock and pushed open the door. 'You'd better come in then. Sorry about the furniture.'

'What I don't like about yon opera buffs is that if you only like the good bits, they get all sniffy. They look down their noses and say that it's just your plebs that listen to the arias and no the whole bloody three or four hours of shite. They think if you don't sit through the entire thing you're no doing the opera justice and you don't deserve to listen to the couple of good tunes you get in your average opera. But the problem is that they only take up about ten minutes of the whole fuckin' thing, know what I mean? It's no much of a return on your investment, is it?'

'No, Andrew, I suppose it's not,' Douglas said, watching the passing traffic. It never ceased to amaze him that people driving in cars at night always looked as if they were in their own private little cocoon, lost in their thoughts. He used to feel like that in his father's car driving home after a long night at their Auntie Mary's house in Springburn or their granny's in Bridgeton. His sisters asleep in the back seat, wrapped in blankets, faces like angels. Nothing could touch them. It felt as though the world had taken the night off. Him beside them, squeezed into a corner with his head resting against the door, dozing and dreaming, not wanting to go home but to stay safe and close like that forever.

'But can you do that?' Andrew continued, warming to his theme. 'Can you just sit down and listen to the good bits and jump the needle when it gets too boring and they're a' up there on the stage singing away about what they're going to eat for their dinner or whose turn it is to take out the rubbish? Can you? No, you bloody well can't. That's your opera purists for you.'

'It certainly sounds a bit unjust, when you put it like that,' Douglas agreed. Andrew's Mini was so close to the ground that you felt like you were gliding through the road, not on it. Not like his father's car, an old Hillman that he couldn't really afford but managed to keep on the road thanks to some creative automotive engineering and bits of wire. It sat high on the road, stately and tired like a crumbling old country house. His father always smiled on the rare occasions when he pushed the ignition button and the engine started first time. His mother was embarrassed by the car and sometimes refused to get in it, saying she would rather take the bus.

'Like, if you go to the theatre to listen to the opera, can you go for a pee or have a wee nap and snore a bit, or head off to the pub for half an hour until the next good song comes up? You know, get a few pints in just to soothe your nerves and your sore arse from all that sitting. No. Can you get up and dance? No way. Can you sing along? Absolutely not. What sort of music is that, Douglas, I ask you?'

'Well, you've definitely got a point there. It's good to be able to sing along and have a wee dance. Get out of yerself.' Douglas placed his right hand against the dashboard. 'Slow down a bit, the parent-teacher night is not worth dying for.'

'I mean, you don't see Robert Plant wearing a dinner suit when he's on stage, do you, and he can sing the arse off most of these opera buggers.'

'Who's Robert Plant?'

'Fucksake, Douglas. He's the lead singer wi' Led Zeppelin.'

'Ach, that's right. I thought they'd broken up, people didn't like the name or something.'

'No, you must be getting them mixed up with somebody else.'

'Aye, maybe it was the 1910 Fruitgum Company that broke up.'

'You're no really much of a music fan, are you, Douglas,' Andrew said, taking one hand off the steering wheel and patting his cousin on the arm.

'No, I suppose not. I like Ayrshire Archie and Joyce. Tom Jones, I like him. When I was in the seminary I think music just passed me by.'

'I think a lot of things passed you by in there, Douglas,' Andrew laughed.

Aye, you're right there, pal, Douglas thought to himself. Bloody well took a detour more like it. 'So, how's the lovely Minh Thanh then? I tell you I could go a few of those spring rolls and those fried chicken wings, the ones she brought to the working bee at the club.'

'Aw aye, very tasty.'

'What, her or the chicken?'

Andrew laughed 'Both.'

'Are you still seeing her or have you moved on to another country. South America maybe. Have you had any South American girlfriends, by the way?'

Andrew shifted down to second gear as they approached a roundabout. 'No, I haven't actually. But I read about an island off the coast of Chile where the girls prefer to receive the male member in their—how would you put it—back close, so they can protect their virginity and not be sinners in the eyes of the local church.'

Douglas shook his head. 'Is that right? Doesn't surprise me. The Church makes people do strange things in the name of fidelity to its teachings. Men that don't have sex, women that take it up their backside. You know, this old Irish priest told me about a woman who came to see him back in Cork. She already had nine kids and her husband would beat her if she didn't have sex with him, and then he'd go and do it with a chicken. She wouldn't take the pill because the Church had banned it.'

'And what did the priest say?'

'He told her to take the pill, that it would be all right, that she wouldn't go to hell.'

'I would hope not. The husband might though, eh?' he said, pausing for thought. 'You'd think a sheep would be better than a chicken, but.' Andrew drove silently for a moment, his thoughts treading warily across the sodden dung-filled fields of Arcadian sexual practices.

'Minh Thanh's no on the pill. She's got this secret recipe of mysterious herbs and spices that she uses.'

'Like Kentucky Fried Chicken?'

'No, not quite Douglas,' Andrew laughed. 'It's some Buddhist Vietnamese thing. Seems to work though. And it beats using condoms, eh.'

'Aye, I suppose it does,' Douglas said quietly.

'The problem with condoms is that there's not much sensation, is there? I mean, you know someone's having sex but you're not quite sure if it's you or not.'

'Here, you told me Minh Thanh was saving herself for marriage.'

Andrew smiled. 'Well, I asked her to marry me, didn't I? And she reckoned that was good enough.'

'You certainly have the power of persuasion, Andrew.' Douglas gave his cousin a congratulatory punch on the shoulder and Andrew narrowly avoided colliding with the trees at the side of the road.

'Easy, son. I want to make it to the altar before I end up in a coffin.'

Douglas sat back in his seat, as far as a tall man can sit back in a Mini Minor. 'I'm in love,' Andrew told him. No more waitresses or air hostesses, no more Greek goddesses, Italian madonnas or Turkish heartbreakers. Minh Thanh was the one for him. When she wasn't there he missed her. There was a small hole in the pit of his stomach that ached with her absence. When he was with her his heart pounded. He couldn't concentrate on his work, he had trouble sleeping, he'd gone off lasagna. It must be love.

Douglas closed his eyes and suddenly Kirstin's thighs appeared in front of him, as white as glory box sheets. They glowed, a luminous invitation. He must have nodded off for a moment. Yes, he was still in the car. People talked about taking control of their lives. But how was that possible when you couldn't control your thoughts for more than a few seconds at time. They had a mind of their own.

Andrew turned on the radio. Led Zeppelin singing 'Dazed and Confused'. 'Here's a song for us, son. That's how we'll be by the end of the night.'

Douglas laughed. 'I'm feeling that way already and we haven't even started yet.'

Douglas watched the world glide by, quiet and chimeric. They passed the last of the houses and sped by the old swamp. He could just make out the charred skeleton of their clubhouse through the wire-mesh fence. The carbon works and the oil refineries with their hulking storage containers glowed and flickered and smoked away, sudden bursts of flame illuminating the night sky. Baytown was becoming wealthy, at least the council was, with all those factories and works paying their rates into the council coffers. The roads were wide and flat, the footpaths tree-lined and clean.

A few more minutes and they'd be at the school, scrubbed up for the twice-yearly parent-teacher interviews where teachers discussed the students' progress or lack thereof. The school building would be unnaturally hushed, as if it were waiting for a hearse to crawl by. The corridors would be filled with anxious parents lurking by classroom doors and sneaking a sly cigarette, or sitting on benches, their arms folded across their chests, emitting the occasional snore. Any of the students who had been dragged along by their parents because there was no one to look after them at home would keep an urgent eye out for the sound or smell of Mrs Konieczny swishing and swaying across the tiles, her arse like two ripe peaches on a tree. A few of the fathers would pretend to be examining the noticeboard while sneaking a mouth-watering look themselves.

The missionary brothers who had established the school a few years earlier would smile and shake the hands of everybody in sight. In their black suits and white shirts with little silver crucifixes on the collar, they were like a tribe from another planet. Soon after his arrival at the school Douglas had realised that many of the brothers were refugees from their own particular and undesirable circumstances, who sought the neutrality of another land to deal with their insecurities, unusual physical infirmities or irregular sexual tendencies. There were brothers who were way too tall or way too short, much too thin or much too fat. There were brothers who squawked like ducks when they spoke, brothers who could barely speak at all. There were those who were timid as mice or those who could barely contain their rage and who would beat their students on any pretext. There were brothers who went bald in their teens, brothers who were as hairy as yeti. Some spent too much time supervising their young charges in the showers, others liked to take them on intimate trips to the Dandenongs or to the Williamstown back beach. Among them was an occasional well-balanced and loving human being who possessed a true vocation as a religious and a teacher. But if it weren't for the lay staff, the place would have fallen apart, Douglas thought to himself as he got out of the car.

The school stood to attention before him, proud and a touch threatening. Schools at night had a sense of foreboding about them, as if you were trespassing. You felt you weren't supposed to be there, that your presence would upset the natural order of things and put the world all out of whack.

'Godssake Andrew, what have you got on your feet?' Douglas asked as his cousin loped round to his side of the car.

Andrew looked down at his sumptuous footwear. 'Ugg boots. They're called ugg boots.'

'Are they dead?'

Andrew stared at his cousin in disbelief. 'Of course they're fuckin' dead. They're dead sheep. Dead sheepskins to be exact.'

'It looks like you've got two merinos attached to your legs. You're not going to wear them to the interviews, are you? Brother Charlie will have a fit. He might even try and eat them.'

'Ach, don't be stupid. I've got my shoes in the boot of the car. I just wear these because they're comfortable to drive in.'

The two men skipped up the stairs, playing a game of cowboys and Indians like they used to do when they were weans in Glasgow. Andrew took a bullet in the leg and stumbled to the floor, while Douglas's heart was pierced by a flaming arrow and he died an agonising death outside the sick bay. Unfortunately Sister O'Donnell wouldn't be in this evening as she had no educative responsibilities. Her only contact with the students was to treat their cuts and abrasions and now and again check that their testes had dropped, a task she looked forward to with considerable relish.

Brother Paul, six feet eleven inches tall with a nose that acted as an advance party for his forthcoming arrival, stared at the two teachers now singing a mournful rendition of 'The Streets Of Laredo'. He blinked like a television with a defective horizontal hold, scowled momentarily and marched on.

In his classroom Douglas sat by his desk, pulled another couple of chairs up close to it and consulted his schedule. It would be a full night. He smiled to himself. First up was Wullie's mother, Agnes. No father, of course, the father having gone to the great detention class in the sky.

'Hello faither!' Agnes purred as she slunk into the classroom, taking it all in and running a finger across the surface of Douglas's desk. 'Nice wee classroom, dusty but. Needs a good polish.'

'Hello Agnes. I'm not a priest any more, by the way, so you don't have to call me father.'

'Ach, sorry faither, I forgot. Memory like a sieve these days. Gettin' auld, eh,' she laughed, touching his cheek with her surprisingly slender and newly manicured fingers.

Douglas was startled by Agnes's appearance. He had never really seen her body before, its fleshy contours, its enticing topography. But tonight, liberated from her usual shroud of enveloping apron, rolled-down stockings, sensible shoes and hair in a bun, she looked, well, attractive. With a tight black skirt, high heels, a towering beehive hairdo and a pink top ruffled at the cuffs and neck which offered a glimpse of two pale and succulent melons, she reminded him of Cilla Black, Diana Dors and Dusty Springfield all rolled into one. She'd clearly paid a visit to Bettina's House of Beauty and it had paid off.

Agnes caught Douglas taking a sly peek at her breasts and she smiled to herself, her upper dental plate shifting ever so slightly.

'You're looking very well the night, Agnes.'

'Thank you, faither,' she smiled, crossing her legs and patting her hair. 'Sometimes it's nice tae get oot ae yer pinny, ye know.'

'Aye, I'm sure it is. So how have you been keeping then?' Douglas asked, immediately regretting the question, like a man who had jumped off a tall building and changed his mind halfway down.

'Och, no sae well, now that you're askin', no sae well at a'. See me this mornin', I woke up wi' this heid oan me. Honest tae God I thought it was gonnae burst right open, so I did. It was that painful that I couldnae see. Naw, I couldnae. So I rang up the doaktir and I says hello doaktir and he went hello Mrs Henderson. So I says call me Agnes and he says right ye are then, Agnes it is. So I told him aboot ma heid an' that and ye know whit he says tae me? Ye widnae believe it.'

'What did he say, Agnes?'

'He says take a wee aspirin and have a wee lie-doon and if yer no better the morra come intae the surgery. Eh? And me wi' ma heed throbbin' like a prick in a hoor hoose. So ah says tae um, it could be the cancer and I might be deid the morn. But he says, naw, it would be highly unlikely. Highly unlikely my erse. Look at Jimmy Neill, I says tae um. So he says who the fuck's Jimmy Neill and I says ye must know Jimmy Neill fer fucksake, used tae work in the boiler room at the school and he says whit fuckin' school? I says fuckin' Saint Leonard's in Glesga and he says but I'm fae fuckin' Islamabad. So ah says well fuckin' forget it then, ya bampot. But ye know, fair point 'cause I minded that I was in a different country noo, ye know. Whit an eejit, eh? So I wanted tae tell um aboot my uterus, ye know, it bein' a bit prolapsed an' that, but the bastard hung up. Ye cannae talk tae these Paki doaktirs, ne'er ye can.'

'Ach, I'm sure you can, Agnes, even if they don't know much about Glasgow housing schemes and the people who live there.'

Agnes sniffed and lit a cigarette. It stuck to her thickly rouged lips like a wellie in wet concrete. She tilted her head back and exhaled with a breathy sigh. She and Douglas were surprised to see a head appear around the doorway and mumble something in a voice that seemed to be passing through a loudhailer inside a light aircraft some miles away.

Agnes looked at Douglas. 'Whit?'

'No smoking in the classroom.'

Agnes looked towards the doorway but the head had gone. 'Whit the fuck?'

'Brother Donald. He's got some sort of chronic nasal cavity problem. He's been to see a lot of doctors but they say they can't fix it.'

'He sounds like yon Donald Duck. It's a shame, so it is. Probably the cancer, eh? He could go an' see that Paki doaktir ae mine. They might no understand whit each other's sayin' but. He might well be died before he goat a diagnosis, like.'

Douglas spent the next ten minutes talking about Wullie and his progress at the school during the term. Despite his late entry he had established himself as a valued member of the class and had won the friendship and esteem of his classmates by virtue of his natural gregariousness, keen intelligence and the occasional use of force, which Douglas emphasised he had to try and curb in the future as it would only be an obstacle to his future prospects. He had a broad grasp of all subjects and if he maintained his current standard of work there was no reason why he couldn't go on all the way to university.

'You should be very proud of Wullie, Agnes. He's doing remarkably well considering he comes from such an underprivileged background.'

'Whit? You mean him bein' a Catholic an' that?'

Douglas laughed. 'No, I meant coming from a housing scheme in the East End of Glasgow.'

'Och away. Or hoose had an inside toilet. It wis fine.'

'But Wullie has to watch his language, Agnes,' Douglas said gravely.

Agnes nodded her head in agreement. 'Aye, don't I fuckin' know it. He can be a foul-mouthed wee bastard, so he can. If I've telt um wance I've telt um a million fuckin' times, so I have.'

The night proceeded, long and intense, punctuated by occasional snatches of jocularity and life-saving cigarettes outside in the cool evening, much to the displeasure of Brother Chuck, an ex-United States marine whose job it was to patrol the school grounds at lunchtime in search of student smokers, and who also felt it was part of his duty to maintain his vigilance at night. His intense piety, which oozed out of his every pore like spring water out of a fissure in a rock, coupled with an implied threat of extreme retribution, had slashed the incidence of smoking at the school in the last couple of years.

Parents came and went, pleased or displeased with their sons' progress or lack thereof. Douglas found it difficult to tell them that their little hopes for the future were lazy or badly behaved or, in some cases, just plain stupid. Some of these couples were hoping that their child would be the first in the family to go on to higher education and they worked long hours to that end. Some children felt the weight of this expectation to be too heavy to bear. Most of the boys were fair to middling and worked as best they could. Others were passing time until they could take up their appointed place in the family butcher shop or plumbing business, buy a '64 EH Holden with fats and have sexual intercourse in the back seat with as many high school girls as possible.

Then there were some, like Jeremy Spencer, who seemed not quite ready for the world and its challenges and complications, as if he could have done with a few more months in the womb just to get used to the idea of venturing out. Indeed, it came as no surprise to Douglas when Jeremy's parents told him during their interview that their son was considering a religious life and thinking of joining the very order of brothers that ran the school. They became quite heated and blamed each other. Still, he was their only child and they were concerned that such a move may not be the right one for him. Douglas wanted to scream at them, to tell them that it certainly wasn't, that he should not consider entering into such a life before he had a chance to grow up and experience the world as an adult, otherwise he might never become one. But something held him back. Sometimes he felt that he didn't know enough about the world himself to legitimately offer his thoughts about it to others. Still, he would talk to the boy, try to explain as best he could what he would be getting into.

Then there were those like Malcolm Myers who believed themselves to be without a functioning brain cell in their heads, but badly needed encouragement and the occasional parental expression of faith in their ability.

Maybe if Malcolm ate less, Douglas pondered, crossing another set of parents off his list. But then, maybe not.

'Mr Fairbanks?'

Douglas turned to see a thickset, well-dressed man bounding towards him, his hand outstretched. Douglas took it and heard the bones in his hand crackling like milk poured on breakfast cereal. The man looked familiar.

'Brian Myers, Malcolm's old man,' he said, still pumping Douglas's hand like a manic seesaw. 'Pleased to meet you. Can I call you Douglas?'

'Aye, of course, Mr Myers,' Douglas replied, feeling slightly overwhelmed. The man seemed to fill up the room, corner to corner, floor to ceiling.

'Call me Brian. I'm sorry, but the missus couldn't make it, she's feelin' a bit crook. Women's business, you know,' he winked.

Douglas sat at his desk, rearranging his papers. Brian Myers undid a button on his suit jacket, pushed his thick hair back and sat down, his legs spread wide. He leaned forward, smiled and attacked Douglas's eyes with his own.

'So, what's the bad news? What's Malcolm been up to, or not up to, should I say,' he laughed.

'Actually, Brian, Malcolm's done very well this term, very well indeed.'

Brian laughed. 'Aw yeh. Been cheating, has he?'

'Not as far I can tell.'

'Well, maybe you'd better look a bit closer,' he smiled coldly. 'I don't want to tell you how to do your job, mate, but Malcolm's never been exactly what you might call a bright spark.'

'Perhaps he's brighter than you think.'

'Look Fairbanks, I've known the boy for sixteen years, you've known him for what, six months, so don't tell me what to think, eh.'

'But—'

'Anyway, it's all academic,' Myers said, chuckling at his own joke. 'The boy'll be leaving at the end of the year. It's all fixed up, he's gonna join the police force, be a copper. Best thing for him. He's big and there's not much up top, so he'll fit in nicely.'

Douglas sighed. 'Look, Mr Myers—'

'Brian, the name's Brian.'

'Look, Mr Myers, just let me read to you the comments from some of Malcolm's other teachers. You'll be surprised. He's making real progress. He's doing very well, particularly in Health Education.'

Brian Myers abruptly stood up and smiled broadly, as if to a room full of constituents before an election. 'Have to go, mate, got a meeting in ten minutes. Bloody council. Nothing but meetings.'

He turned and marched towards the door, buttoning up his jacket as he went. 'One more thing,' he said, turning to Douglas, his bulky frame filling the doorway. 'I don't want the boy up at that soccer club of yours. We're a footballing family, always have been, always will be. I've told Malcolm that and now I'm telling you.' He looked at his watch. 'Christ, is that the time?' he said, shaking his head as his leather-soled shoes clacked across the tiles.

Douglas sat motionless and listened to the sound of Brian Myers well-shod feet echoing down the corridor. Poor Malcolm, poor bloody Malcolm.

'Douglas, you all right?' Andrew's head suddenly appeared around the doorway. 'Phone call, by the way. It's Kirstin.'

'No, he'd just walked out the door when Kirstin rang. It was only a matter of seconds,' Douglas said.

Aberdeen Angus shook his head, which hung low with disappointment. 'The things folk do. Ye widnae believe it. Why would he do such a thing? He's already a rich man. A greedy e'e ne'er gat a fou wame.'

Richard nodded. 'Never a truer word was said, Angus.'

'Aye,' Douglas concurred.

'What?' Valletta Vince raised his palms upwards and looked to his friends for elucidation.

'Greedy folk are never satisfied,' Douglas explained.

Douglas shifted his arse. As boulders went, this was not the most comfortable he had ever sat on. The other men did the same and the five of them sat listening to the sounds of the darkness and watching the flickering lights of the nearby petroleum refineries through the broken and charred remains of the Baytown City Soccer Club changing rooms and bar.

It smelled like history. Perhaps, Douglas thought, that idiot Shaz McGowan was right. Maybe they should be playing Aussie Rules, wearing those little tiny shorts that crushed your nuts and raised the tone of your voice half an octave. Maybe they should leave their past behind them. But what did Shaz know? The lad was a few chips short of a fish supper. What did he know about the world, about dreams and memory, about carving out a new life for yourself without abandoning the treasures of the old? About belonging? To tell the truth, he'd had McGowan down for the lot, pulling down the fence, tearing up the ground, setting fire to the clubroom. But he should have known better. The boy was stupid but not malicious. But Brian Myers? He wouldn't have picked him in a million years. When Kirstin had told him about her conversation with Frank O'Connell, he could hardly believe what he was hearing.

O'Connell had thought there was something untoward about the troubles at the soccer ground and had been making his own inquiries. Investigative journalism, he called it. He said it was just like the old days on the *Argus*, when he was chief crime reporter. He felt like a real journo again, stories about golden wedding anniversaries and complaints about dog shite on the footpaths became distant memories as he trawled through council reports and poured over financial records at Companies House in the city. It was painstaking work, but he got there. All right, he might have slipped a few bucks to a couple of blokes down at Myers's yard so he could tie up a few loose ends, but there was no real harm in that, even if it wasn't strictly ethical according the Journalists Association. But what the hell, ethics were for Sundays. And when it all came together he was speechless. For years, Brian Myers had been using a whole range of two-dollar companies to buy up hundreds of acres of land around the old swamp. Nowhere in the company records did his name appear. Mr Myers was a clever bugger, no doubt about it. He had brains enough for two and no one had a clue that it was him accumulating all this land, even though as a councillor he was required to declare his interests where council tenders were concerned. Brian Myers, chairman and managing director of Bulldog Building, had spent years on his plans for the ultimate housing estate. He dreamed of a series of small islands with a few select properties on them. The islands would be surrounded by man-made canals that would be filled by the water he drained from the swamp. And, get this, the main canal, the Grand Canal he liked to call it, would lead to the sea. How brilliant was that?

But then, like many a well-laid plan, sometimes it goes bloody well astray. As Shane McGowan would have put it, wouldn't ya fuckin' know it, just when big Brian was about to realise his dream and build the biggest and best housing estate in Melbourne, fuck, in Australia even, some upstart wog bastards come in and convince the council to give them a long-term lease on the land he badly needed if his painstakingly drafted plans were to work. Painstaking and expensive plans. It would cost him a fortune to redo them and his dream would fall short. And why should he wear that? No way, there was just no way.

'So, it was Brian Myers who did this,' Douglas said, waving an arm towards what was left of the clubroom.

'That must have been him lurking around the council hall on the night of the fundraiser,' Andrew said.

'Bastard,' Angus swore. 'Just wait till I get ma hands on him. I'll squash him like a thistle in the field.'

'Wait a minute,' Richard said, placing a steadying arm on his brother's shoulder. 'We don't want to be rushing in and doing anything stupid, ye ken. We're no criminals. A scabbit sheep will smit a hail herself. So we have to be careful.'

'One evil person can infect everybody,' Douglas said before Vince could open his mouth. 'So what do you suggest, Richie?'

Sergeant Richard McDonald rubbed the bristles on his chin, pursed his lips and looked Douglas hard in the eye. 'I might have a wee idea.'

Frank O'Connell was going to enjoy this. He was looking forward to it, like a Sunday roast with gravy, like a front page exclusive with his byline in eighteen point bold, like a night out with a sure thing with big tits. He could bloody well taste it. It was nectar on his lips. Shit, he'd even polished his shoes, he was that excited. There was something in the air tonight, he could feel it. A buzz, like electricity. He was in no way spiritual, but there was definitely something in the air. Then again, maybe it was just in his head.

It was only another council meeting after all, another Tuesday night with the councillors or, as that crazy Scotsman Aberdeen Angus called them, those crabbit wee cunts. Mad as a cut snake, that man. He'd met him the other night at Douglas's place with all those other New Australians. Barely spoke English. Funny bastards they were, but the country could do with a few more like them. It could certainly do with a bit of life in the place. God, after a walk down Swanston Street on a Sunday afternoon, you felt like topping yourself. Like a graveyard, it was. A graveyard where the corpses had buggered off because it was too dull a place to be seen dead in. Get a few of these new migrants on the council as well. That would put a rocket up the arses of all those smug butchers, builders and bicycle shop owners and other small-time, small-minded businessmen and Justices of the Peace who'd sell their grannies to get their name or their picture in the *Baytown Star* even though they slagged the paper off any chance they got. Especially on Tuesday nights with their little snide asides about the 'gentleman of the press' having arrived and that they'd better watch what they said. They sat there around their u-shaped, hand-crafted conference table with their plastic name plaques in front of them like victory monuments and, consumed with their own self-importance, disappeared up their own and each other's well-padded arses for four and a half mind-numbing, soul-crunching, stomach-sinking hours once a week, forty weeks a year, four hundred times a decade. And they loved every group-wanking minute of it.

But not tonight, Bulldog. Not tonight, you absolute fucking jumped up, limp dicked, self-satisfied, pissant pube of a has-been centre-half forward. No more holding back on information, no more telling Dodgy Albert the town clerk to 'forget' to give him the council meeting agenda, no more giving the regional weekly all the best stories, no more sixty days before you pay for your advertisements. In short, no more fucking me about, Brian. No more. Non, niente, fucking nada. No fun for you tonight. Tonight you are mine. Completely. And will you love me tomorrow? Absofuckinglutely, because I will have your balls in a vice, son. In a vice and squeezing.

Frank O'Connell smiled to himself, floating gently in his sea of dreams, and sucked the last breath of nicotine and carcinogens into his scorched lungs, flicking his cigarette onto the car park bitumen. He leaned against the door of his old bomb and quietly observed the people wandering into the council building: councillors with their cheap leather briefcases and bundles of papers stuffed under their arms; the municipal officers, the poor buggers who actually did all the work; and finally interested observers, who either had a permit application under consideration, wanted to complain that stray dogs were peeing on their begonias, or had bugger all better to do on a Tuesday night.

There were, of course, others who were psychologically disturbed and, given a slab of beer, a full moon and an AK-47, could quite happily wipe out the lot of them before quietly going home and sanding down the front fence then applying a new coat of full gloss weatherproof.

Watching all this, Frank was reminded of Academy Awards night in Hollywood, what with all the people making their entrance and smiling and going in to take their seats before the proceedings got underway, excited about the prospect of a reward at the end of it. But then he'd had a couple of drinks at the office and was smart enough to know that when he sobered up he'd realise any such comparisons were founded on nothing other than three fingers of whisky. But hey, he was a journo and occasionally entitled to extrapolate and embellish. Christ, if you didn't do that on the *Baytown Star*, there wouldn't be much worth reading.

There they went now into the foyer. Good on ya, Frank chuckled to himself and lit up another cigarette. Douglas and Kirstin, Andrew (what *is* he wearing?) and Minh Thanh, Aberdeen Angus and Richie, Ayrshire Archie and Joyce, the

Walker brothers, Jimmy and Connie Staccato, Carlo from Caltanmissetta, the Coppola boys and Gina (look a those breasts—what is she *not* wearing?). 'Lively' Ernie Lovett, Arthur Kyriakopoulous, Agnes Henderson and that little bugger Wullie, the lovely Bettina, Baytown's Queen of Beauty and Deportment (he laughed as she ducked to get her hairdo in the door), the Svensens and the Ericssons, Perry McIntosh, and finally Vince and Teresa Vella and their nine kids, one of whom was leading what appeared to be a small black and white goat with a pink ribbon around its neck.

Brian Bulldog Myers didn't know what the hell was going on. Who were all these people and what were they doing here? Christ, it'd be standing room only in the chamber tonight. Didn't they have anything better to do? A couple of faces looked familiar but he couldn't quite place them. And why was that bloke wearing a lime green body shirt waving at him? Brian smiled and waved back, taking the opportunity to perve at the sheila he was with. What was she, a Chink? That little bloke, Vince something or other, he'd seen him around the council yard. What was he doing here? Probably got some jerry-built extension on the back of his house and the planning boys have told him to pull it down. Tough shit, wog boy, Brian laughed to himself. He had a quick glance at the night's agenda, but couldn't see anything particularly controversial that would attract such a crowd. Motley-looking lot too. The guy in the Stetson needed to take a good look at himself. No bugger wore ten-gallon hats any more, except for big Hoss Cartwright, and he always took it off when he went indoors at the Ponderosa.

Brian Myers was waving to a small dark man in a woollen cap who looked like he'd spent his life in intimate contact with sheep or goats or some other grazing animal, when he winced at the unfortunately familiar sound of Frank O'Connell's cigarette-cured rumble.

'Evening, Brian. How are you?'

The councillor turned, his smile at once a snigger and a dismissal.

'Ah, it's you. The gentleman of the press. Come here tonight looking for a story, eh? Why don't you just stay home and make it up? You usually do. Save you the trouble of changing into that crappy suit of yours.'

He ran his eyes up and down the full length of Frank O'Connell's faded pinstripe. Frank followed the progress of Myers's gaze with his own. Purchased in 1952 at Henry Buck's after a rollicking win at the horses, it had been a faithful servant for the last seventeen years, but with its broad lapels and wide-bottomed strides, Frank had to admit that maybe it was time it was retired to a box under the bed.

'A good suit maketh the man, didn't you know that, Frank?'

Frank laughed. 'Oh yeah, whoever said that was a dickhead. Wasn't you by any chance, was it, Brian?'

Brian sniggered. 'Nasty, Frank, nasty. You'll hurt my feelings. You don't want to hurt my feelings, do you, Frank? That could have undesirable consequences for you.'

The journalist remained silent. But in his mind's eye he saw Brian Myers's head tumble into a wooden bucket as he, the masked executioner, felt his axe slice through flesh and bone, gristle and artery. He revelled in the thought of tying him to a tree deep in the Amazon jungle as millions of ravenous red ants began to devour him bit by very little bit. He saw himself force-feeding the bastard six dozen hard-boiled eggs and watching him fart himself to death. He could see himself clearly, the sniper hidden in the tree, the one bullet in the forehead, the trickle of dark thick blood as Brian Myers slumped in the back seat of his new Jag at the Pines with his dick in the less than willing mouth of his secretary Denise. Oral sex can kill you, Brian.

Brian Myers waited for the newspaperman to say something and smiled to himself when he didn't. 'I thought not, Frank.' He beamed suddenly. 'So what do you know?'

Frank sighed inwardly. The same old routine. 'It's what you know that interests me, Brian, you know that.'

'Aw yeh. And what might that be? I'm just a humble builder, Frank, I don't know that much.'

'I admire your modesty, but it's a bit misplaced. What about the goings on at the soccer club? Heard anything about that yet?'

'You still going on about that? As I told you last time, I don't know anything. Talk to the sport and recreation blokes. Tell you what I'll do,' he said, slapping Frank on the shoulder, 'I'll get Albert to give you the gen on what's going on up there, eh?'

He winked and poked Frank in the stomach. 'You should do some exercise, mate. You're getting fat. Anyway, gotta go. Important municipal matters to attend to. See you round, Frank. But not too soon I hope, eh.'

Frank let him move off towards the chamber before he called out, a warning bell from a Bourke Street tram. 'Hey Brian, you forgot to ask me what the big story is this week.'

Brian Myers waved him off. 'I don't give a rat's arse, Frank. As I said, you make it all up anyway.'

'Is that right? Well, what about "BAYTOWN COUNCILLOR IN ILLEGAL LAND GRAB SCAM" Or how about "FOOTY LEGEND BURNS WITH ANGER OVER SOCCER CLUB PLANS"? How about "WHOSE BEEN A NAUGHTY BOY

THEN?"' eh, Brian. How about those in ninety-six point bold across the front page of the *Baytown Star*?'

Brian Myers left his stomach two paces behind him. His heart skipped a beat, and then another. His chest felt tight. But his was only a momentary indisposition. When you drop the ball you pick it up again and boot it down the flank and that's what he did. He wasn't known as Bulldog Brian for nothing. He took a deep breath, turned and smiled, the smile of a man who refused to contemplate anything other than victory and, when necessary, annihilation of the enemy.

'You're full of shit, Frank, just like that rag of yours. So why don't you fuck off home and have a few more drinks and fall asleep in front of the telly?'

Frank grinned, taking a cigarette from the pack and lighting up. 'I'd really like to, Brian. A quiet night in would do me good. But I can't. Pressing matters to attend to, just like you.'

'Of course you can. You just turn around, put one leg in front of the other and bugger off.'

'You'd like that, wouldn't you, Brian? But if I went I'd be letting down my mates in the public gallery there, all thirty-seven of them.'

Brian scoffed. 'You're joking. At least ten of them are kids.'

'Yes, well, I'll admit that two of them aren't old enough to talk yet and one is admittedly a goat. But I can assure you the rest of them are ready to stand up and ask you some embarrassing questions about your business dealings, Brian. About how you managed to acquire all that council land without informing your fellow councillors. I'm sure they would be interested in hearing about that. Nothing like missing out on the gravy train to get their backs up, eh mate? And I'm sure they'd be fascinated by all the dodgy companies you've set up to throw people off the scent. I've checked it all out Frank, and the more I looked into it the smellier it got, I can tell you. And there's plenty more, plenty more.'

Brian marched ten feet and poked his head into the council chamber. There they were, up there in the public gallery. He bristled as Ayrshire Archie tipped his hat in his direction, Bettina rattled her jewellery and blew him a kiss, and one of Vince's brood poked his tongue out at him, stuck his thumbs in his ears and wiggled his fingers.

'You're not allowed to ask questions during a council meeting, you know that, Frank.'

'Well, that's true, Brian, very true. But you see, these people are very pissed off and they want to enlighten the council about who was responsible for tearing up their ground, burning down their clubhouse, ripping down their fence and generally frustrating their every move to add a little extra enjoyment to their lives. And you know what, Frank, they don't care what the fuckin' rules are. I mean, what are you going to do? Tell the council, tell the police, tell the screws at Pentridge that they're all fuckin' liars. One of those people up there is an ex-priest, for God's sake. Another's a member of the Scottish constabulary. Who do you think they are going to believe, eh? Them or you? I know who I would put my money on.'

'I didn't tear up their bloody soccer ground,' Brian said, pursing his lips.

'Yeh, but you let their tyres down. That was a dog's act, Brian. I didn't think you could stoop that low.'

'A man will stoop as low as he has to, Frank. But, you're right, it was a bit low for me. I had one of my boys do it. Told him I'd give him a few extra bucks in his pay packet. It was worth it just to see the look on all those soccer chocs' faces.'

'And cheap at the price when there's a shitload of money at stake, eh?'

The councillor said nothing. He tapped his feet frenetically on the floor tiles like a coked-up woodpecker banging its beak against a tree. He looked at the walls. He stared at the ceiling. He scratched the top of his head, where a little bald spot had recently began to assert itself. He sucked on his teeth and sniffed. He slouched back to the chamber and snuck his head round the corner of the door for another look. Sergeant Richard McDonald, proudly clad in the impressive navy blue uniform of the Royal Fife Constabulary, stared back at him. Wullie Henderson, much to the consternation of Dodgy Albert, jabbed his finger at him and shouted, 'Yer deid, ya bassa! Yer deid!' while one of the Coppola boys slowly drew an imaginary blade across his throat.

Brian turned, deflated and pale-faced. 'So what is it that you want, Frank?'

Frank O'Connell smiled, glanced across at the No Smoking sign on the wall and lit up another Craven A. 'Well, I'll have that suit you're wearing for a start.'

'Work was my religion, Douglas. It was what I worshipped and sometimes ye can be devoted to the wrong thing, the wrong person and, when sometimes you realise that, it can be too late to do anything about it. Aye, well, it was for me anyhow. I loved that uniform more than I loved my Annie. I look back at myself and all I can see is a right bampot wi' dreams of glory and promotion to chief inspector of all the polis in Fife. Imagine that, Richie McDonald, just a wee village boy, running the show. That was my dream, Douglas, and I forgot about everything else.'

'Angus says you are a very good policeman,' Douglas said. 'He's always singing your praises.'

Douglas took another sip of drink. He looked around and realised he hadn't been in this pub for quite a few months, not since the first few weeks of his and Kirstin's life here. Those blokes at the pool table looked like the same ones that were playing eight ball the last time. Same shorts, same work boots, same checked shirts and stubbled cheeks, same brown legs with their bleached hairs like down on a newborn baby's head. Ach, but it'd no be them, it'd be other folk. That was the trouble with Australians, they all looked alike. Richard seemed tired the night, Douglas thought. You'd have thought he'd be happy after the good work he'd done helping to solve the mystery of the strange events at the soccer club. But it was his last night and perhaps he was a bit glum about the idea of leaving his brother and going home to Scotland. Still, Angus would be here soon and so would the others and no doubt they'd cheer him with their banter, or if that failed, a few rounds of single malt and a few more after that.

'Aye,' Richard sighed, pushing his glass of whisky around the table. 'No tomorrow but the day after I'll be back in Pittenweem. You know it's still a wonder to me how you can be on one side of the world one minute with the sunshine and all yon mosquitoes and be on the other side the next with the sleet on the pavement and the cold waves crashing over the seawall. The wonders of modern travel. Pretty soon they'll be getting a man on the moon.'

Douglas smiled. 'But they have already, Richie, don't you remember? One giant leap for mankind and all that.'

Richard tapped the side of his nose with his forefinger. 'Aye well, mirrors gae us what we want.'

'Ach away. It's no a question of what we want to see, Richie. It's a fact.'

'Time will tell. Back in my village I never saw anything, Douglas. I only saw things as I wanted to see them. I was all caught up in my own wee place in the world. I saw myself through my work and my uniform and no through the one person who really loved me. Ach, I should've known better. When you're deid and buried your work will no remember ye. I'll be just another deid polis that once solved a few crimes in

Pittenweem. The only person that would've remembered me I let slip away. I knew in my heart that it would happen. Aye, and I did nothing about it. I was never in the house enough tae do anything about it. I just wasn't *there*. And when I came home from work that night I knew as soon as I walked in the door that she'd gone. I could feel her absence. I could touch it. And you know what, there was no note, nothing. But she'd got the fire blazing in the hearth and she'd left my dinner on a plate for me by the flames tae keep it warm.'

Douglas wanted to touch Richard's trembling hand but found himself unable to wrench his from around his glass, nor free his gaze from the tabletop with its circular stains and random scratches. 'What did you do, Richie?'

For a few long moments the big policeman said nothing. He reached for Douglas's cigarettes, took one from the packet and lit it up. He took two puffs and butted it out in the ashtray.

'I walked around the house and went intae every room and I looked in all the cupboards and the wardrobes and under the beds. I even looked in the bath and the old stables out the back. Then I sat down in her chair by the fire and began tae eat my dinner. The kitchen was all cosy wi' the firelight. I took a few mouthfuls and got up and had another look about the house. Then I finished my dinner, because she would have wanted me tae. It was a shepherd's pie. She'd made it from the lamb that was leftover from Sunday. Then I walked down tae the pub and I drank myself stupid. There was a wee ceilidh going on and for some reason, I dinnae know why, I started clapping and dancing away. Then I got up on tae the bar and I was dancing and leaping about and I felt myself getting all hot and sweaty and everything was spinning round in my head. I don't remember anything after that.'

Richard pointed at Douglas's empty glass. 'Another yin, Douglas?'

Douglas shook his head.

'Ach away, it's my last night. I'll away and get them in.'

Richard returned cradling two double whiskies, nodding in the direction of the bar. 'Did ye see that man that just came in, the one wi' the blue vest and the wee shorts? His belly's hanging doon tae his knees. It's like a sack ae tatties, so it is. I think he'd have right trouble finding his willie in the morn, eh, Douglas.'

Douglas laughed and raised his glass. 'It's the beer, Richie. These Australians drink a lot of beer. The Scots are amateurs by comparison. We're no in the game.'

Douglas sipped his drink. 'Do you think she'll come back?'

Richard swirled his whisky about, watched it lap up against the sides of the glass. 'No, I cannae see it myself. I had my chance, but I wisnae paying enough attention tae take it. I got distracted by other things, other less important things. But if Annie did decide to come back tae me, I'd be a different man, I tell ye. But it's too late now, I know that in my heart. I'm away back tae an empty house.'

He reached across the table and clasped Douglas's arm, pierced the man's eyes with his own. 'I can see myself in you, son. Don't get distracted like me. I know you've got your demons to wrestle wi'. But so has everybody else. Don't let time slip away from ye.'

Suddenly the front bar jumped with the sound of excited male voices as Vince, Archie, Angus, the Walker brothers, Perry McIntosh, Lively Ernie and Andrew burst into the bar like a steam train into a station, full of bravado, bluster and minor explosions of hot air.

'Jesus, Mary and Joseph, what in God's name has Andrew got on there?' Richard said. 'He looks like he's away tae the jungle for a bit ae big game hunting.'

'It looks like he's collected his safari suit from the lay-by,' Douglas replied, thinking to himself that it was quite an attractive shade of purple.

'Is that right? If it had any more pockets it would be a pool table.' Richard raised his glass and winked. 'Cheers son. Here's tae Andrew's new suit. And tae you. And mind what I said to ye. Mind now.'

'I don't remember exactly how old I wis, maybe seven or eight,' Wullie recalled, kicking distractedly at the bag full of school books that lay at his feet on the tiled floor outside Douglas's classroom.

'I wis comin' hame fae school, up Shettleston Road, ye know. Mind how busy it used to be then, Mr Fairbanks, wi' the buses and trams and a' those shops? There were so many shops ye could get anythin' ye wanted. There were ay people everywhere, women oot wi' their weans daein the messages and crowds ae people on the pavement. Well, our hoose was just aff the main road there. Anyhow, I wis walkin' hame and I stopped at that wee fruit shop near the corner. I'd usually buy an apple or an orange or somethin' wi' the money I wis supposed tae use for my bus fare, but if I walked hame I could buy fruit or sweeties wi' it, ye know. Sometimes I just used tae thieve somethin' fur the hell of it and keep the money as well.

'Mind that shop that sold a' the clothes? Well I was walkin' past that and I heard this scream. Eileen! All panicky an' that. Eileen!

And here, this wee lassie comes runnin' right oot ae the shop and right oan tae the road. It wis so quick, so it wis. She must've been four or five. She had a blue anorak oan and a wee tartan skirt, ye know the wans that hive the wee buckle oan the side.

'So she runs right oot in front of this big Corporation bus. A double decker. The driver saw her but he couldnae stop the bus, there just wisnae time. The next minute there's this thud, like somebody's dropped a sack ae tatties, and she's lyin' there on the road in front ae the bus. And she's aw twisted up. She's just lyin' there no movin' and there's blood coming oot her heid. It was right in front ae the clothes shop. Mind whit it wis called?' Wullie asked.

'McCall's,' Douglas replied.

'Aye, that was it. McCall's. Anyhow, the shop wis really busy and there wis people all o'er the place and this man comes flying oot the shop and he's screamin' Eileen! Eileen! And then he saw his wean there on the road and he ran tae her but he didnae know whit tae dae, ye know. It wis like he couldnae believe it. He just kept sayin' aw naw! Aw naw!

'Then the wean's mammy comes runnin' oot the shop and she just fainted oan the pavement. Just like that. Wan look and she fainted. Meantime the conductress came oot fae the bus and she was greetin' and greetin' and she's goat her hands tae her face and her face is a' red and streamin'. Then there's aw these women greetin' as well and tellin' their ain weans no tae look and takin' them aff hame. And the faither's tryin' tae get at the bus driver and he's screamin', I'll fuckin' kill ye! I'll fuckin' kill ye! But the polis were haudin' him back, ye know, but he still tried tae get at the man. And he wis greetin' as well, the bus driver.

'Then the ambulance came and the ambulance men covered the wee lassie up with a blanket and put her in the back ae the van. And the faither and the mother goat in and it drove away tae the hospital. But she wis deid, ye know, so I don't know why they took her tae the hospital.

'Some ae the women stood around greetin' and bletherin' for while about the wean's name but naebody knew her. Somebody said they thought she might be fae up Barlanark way. Then McFadyen the butcher came oot wi' a shovel full ae sawdust and threw it o'er the blood on the street and covered it a' up. But ye could still see a wee bit ae it. And that wis that.'

'And what did you do then, Wullie?'

'Ach, I just went hame, but there wis naebody in.' Wullie shrugged. 'So do ye think that'll make a good essay aboot childhood an' that, sur?'

'Aye Wullie. I do, son. I do.' Douglas patted him on the shoulder. 'Make sure you get your story in by the end of term, now.'

He watched Wullie amble down the corridor to his locker, swinging his schoolbag as he went. Suddenly, Douglas felt beyond breath. The boy's simple story had knocked the stuffing out of him. He went to his desk and sat himself down on the chair beside it. Some folk get a good go at life, he thought, some folk don't.

Kirstin stretched to reach the suitcase on top of the wardrobe. She could touch it with her fingertips but it was too far back against the wall for her to get a decent grip on it. She fetched a chair from the kitchen and was reminded once again that bright green vinyl was not her first choice for interior dècor. She placed the heavy old brown leather case on the bed. It had been Douglas's father's. It had been left to him by his older brother when he was killed in the Great War. Rab had then passed it on to his son, a farewell gift on his departure to Australia.

'Take it,' he'd said, 'I'll no be gaun anywhere at my age, nowhere that needs a suitcase anyhow.'

Kirstin drew her palm across the surface. Much of it was still smooth to the touch even after so many years, but here and there were the scratches and scores and small accidents of life that couldn't be erased or repaired. She took a cloth and wiped away the dust that had gathered on the lid. She undid the two thick straps wrapped around it like a lover's arms. The locks were lightly flecked with rust but they snapped open with an easy squeeze of forefinger and thumb. Whatever lining had once been inside had long since disintegrated. She gave the inside a rub with her cloth. It wasn't that long ago that she had unpacked it. She placed her hands on the sides of the case and lowered her face into it. It smelled complex, like history, like other lives and memories of happy holidays by the sea or in the highlands. It smelled of moving to better places. It had, she knew, the musty smell of death, of those who were no longer here.

Kirstin went to the chest of drawers and began to remove items of clothing. It would be cold, so she took out thick vests and socks, two pullovers, a scarf and a pair of woollen gloves. She placed them in the case, gently, as if she was putting a baby in a cot. She opened the wardrobe and removed some shoes and what other clothes she thought might be necessary. When she had placed everything in the suitcase there was still plenty of room and she wondered whether she had forgotten something. After checking her list and ticking off the things she'd already packed, she decided that she hadn't, that everything was here. She went to the kitchen and made herself a cup of tea, which she took back to the room. She sat on the bed, resting her drink on her knees, and gazed through the venetian blinds, which she had drawn slightly to keep out the hot late afternoon sun.

After a little while, before the sun had began to fade into a tired glow, she watched Douglas get out of Andrew's car, push the door shut and watch his cousin disappear down the street. She had watched him do this before when she'd come home from work early, or had had a day off due to her. It was as if he had to collect himself before he entered the house, to rouse himself into a feeling of joy at being home, at the prospect of being with his wife. For some reason, she didn't know why, she knew it was there inside him, but he just couldn't seem to summon it. It was as if there were too many other things going on inside his head.

But today, watching through the half-drawn blinds, she could tell he was different. He was actually smiling. He grabbed his briefcase from where it rested on the grass and, although he didn't actually bound towards the front door, he was moving faster than usual. She heard the key turn in the lock and the creak of the flyscreen door. She could swear she heard him sing a few tuneless bars of some terrible song that was in the charts. She felt the thump as his briefcase, full of his students' exercise books, dropped to the floor. She heard the echo as his voice filled the house.

'Kirstin. Kirstin! Are you in? Where are you?'

Kirstin stroked the handle of the suitcase. The stitching had frayed and the leather was wearing thin. 'I'm in here, in the bedroom.' She'd pulled the blinds shut and sat still on the bed in the half-light.

'Kirstin, there you are,' Douglas said, standing in the doorway. 'What are you doing sitting in the dark?'

Kirstin was uncertain about what to say. She should have thought about it more, rather than packing a suitcase. She'd managed to keep her mind off the subject rather than confronting it.

'Come and sit next to me, Douglas,' she smiled. 'There's something I have to talk to you about.'

'No, there's something I have to tell you, love,' he said, taking her hand and bouncing onto the bed beside her.

'No, Douglas, just wait, it's important.'

'No, no, just wheesht a wee minute,' he said, running his finger down her cheek. 'Hear me out, if you can.' Douglas sighed deeply, emptying his lungs of his spent self. 'I don't know where to start, Kirstin.'

'Look Douglas—'

'No wait, wait,' he said, letting his elbows slump onto his knees and running his hands through his hair. 'Wullie Henderson told me a story this morning. It was about a wee girl—'

Kirstin squeezed his hand. 'Douglas, please there's something I have to tell you.'

'No, no, Kirstin, a minute, please,' he said firmly. 'It was about a wee girl. She was just a wean, a wean for Godssake, and through no fault of her own, she got killed. There were no heroes in the street and no God in the heavens to save her, and in just a few seconds she was gone. It was that quick. She had no chance to make a life for herself, Kirstin, no chance to go to school, or to go to the dancing wi' her pals, or hold hands at the pictures wi' her boyfriend or to fall in love and get married. She didn't get the chance to grow up. Can you imagine that?'

Douglas gripped Kirstin's thigh. 'But I have. I have the chance and the time and . . .'

'You're hurting me, Douglas,' Kirstin said, wincing.

'And you. I've got you, and I'm a lucky man. Did you hear me, Kirstin? I'm a lucky man,' he said, releasing her, but jumping up to pull her towards him. The brown leather suitcase standing upright by the window was at first an apparition, but a second look confirmed its presence. He walked towards it.

'What's this then? Are you going somewhere?'

Kirstin took the envelope that sat on the bedside table, clutched it momentarily and handed it to her husband.

'This came an hour ago, a telegram from your Auntie Mary in Glasgow.' She wrapped her arms around him. 'I'm so sorry, Douglas.'

'Come on in son. Here, give me yer coat. Ye must be tired, comin' all that way.'

'I'm fine, Auntie Mary. Where is he?'

'Ben the back room.'

Douglas placed his bag behind the settee and removed his coat. It was stiff with frost and slightly damp. It felt strange to be cold, even after a relatively short time away. Warmth and sunshine had infiltrated his being. They were what he was used to now, what he expected.

The room looked just the same. Nothing had changed. The furniture was in the same place, as if it had been fixed to the floor. His father's chair was still slightly closer to the hearth than the other chair, as it had always been. The coal was burning down, long past flames, and making occasional noises of satisfaction, like a child asleep in a cot by its mother's bed. Mary had lit some candles and placed them on the mantelpiece, and together with the crimson coals, they provided the only light in the room. They made the room feel warm, even if it wasn't. There was always a chill in the air in these old tenements.

'You'll be wanting to see your father now.'

'Aye.'

'I'll make you a wee cup of tea first, Douglas.'

'That would be grand, Auntie Mary.'

Douglas went to the window that looked out on to the back. It was still a wasteland of dirt and broken glass, washing lines and middens. He could just make out the gap in the buildings opposite that had been there since a bomb hit during the war. When the German planes came to bomb the dockyards on the Clyde, his mother would pull the weans out of their beds, wrap them in blankets and rush down the stairs and along to the shelter. Everybody would put on their gas masks and they would sit there silent and terrified as they listened to the wail of the sirens and the rumble of engines in the sky. One day he overheard one of the women saying that the tenement across the back had been hit by a bomb and everybody in it had been killed. She said they found a headless body in a close.

When Douglas was evacuated to a farm in Fife near the end of the war, his father would travel up to see him on a Sunday. He'd bring him money and food and sweeties and they'd go for a walk around the countryside. They'd marvel at the fields and the things growing in them. He'd have a cup of tea with the farmer and they'd go outside and smoke a cigarette, leaning against a fence and blethering away. Douglas never wanted his father to leave and he'd always be asking to be able to go back home to Glasgow with him. He wanted to be somewhere familiar, where he felt he belonged. His father usually said no, but once he said all right because Douglas went on at him that much.

They walked to the bus stop together, and Douglas skipped some of the way, he was that happy. When they got there, his father patted all his pockets as if he was searching for something. 'Ye know what, son? 'I've left my cigarettes on the kitchen table back at the farmer's hoose. Will ye no go and get them for me?'

'Aye, Papa, I'll get them for ye. I'll be back in a wee minute,' Douglas said, already scampering away up the hedge-lined road.

When he got back to the bus stop, all out of breath from running so hard, his father was gone away home without him.

Douglas felt like a cigarette himself now but it didn't seem right, not in the circumstances. Anyway, his father always went outside to have a puff. He'd stand at the front of the close and nod to passers-by or talk to people he knew.

Douglas finished his tea, surprised at how good it tasted, and walked to the door of the bedroom. He stood there, tentative, unable to turn the handle and gently push it open. He'd spent so much of his life in there, asleep on the fold-down bed, or when he was just born, in a drawer on the floor. It always made him laugh that, the thought of sleeping in a drawer.

He walked in, and although the room was silent, it echoed with the past. Sounds, smells, voices raised in the night. Fleeting and terrifying glimpses of Santa Claus on Christmas night. His cousin Jackie stuck under the bed and unable to get out with her hair all tangled in the springs. The neighbour's cat on top of the wardrobe with their canary in its mouth. His mother on the bed weeping into her pillow because her husband didn't buy her a Christmas present. The sound of the gasman's boots clicking on the pavement as he lit the lamps with his long pole. His father stumbling drunk and singing up the street on his way back from the pub.

'He wisnae a bad man, yer faither,' Mary said. 'He just lost his way.' She sat on a straight-backed wooden chair by the side of the open coffin.

Douglas's father's face glowed in the soft light from the candles Mary had placed on top of the chest of drawers. He was wearing his only suit. He'd had it made by a tailor in town for Mary's eldest boy's wedding many years before. He'd had one other suit which he wore to the dancing and when he was courting Douglas's mother, but he had grown out of it as he aged and spread out. He used to joke that his stomach had a mind of its own. Douglas noticed that his father's tie was done up tight around his neck. After a couple of drinks he always liked to loosen it and unbutton the collar of his shirt. He would probably prefer it that way now, if the truth be known.

'He was a lovely wee boy, ye know. Always laughing. Me being ten years older than him, I used to give him his tea when he came home fae the school because oor mammy, your granny, didnae get home fae her work until half past six and your grandda was ay on the nightshift. So he'd eat his tea and he'd be away doon the stairs tae play bools. He loved to play the bools. He'd ay be on the street playin' bools wi' his pals.' Mary tugged a hanky from her sleeve and dabbed at her eyes. 'It was me that brought him up, ye know. He was like my ain wee boy.' She chuckled to herself. 'Sometimes he'd forget and call me mammy. It was that funny, so it wis.'

In his previous life Douglas had had to visit the dead and the dying, to administer last rites, to console those who had lost their parents or children, sons or daughters. He would tell those in mourning that their loved one was at peace now. But towards the end, he began to doubt that this was truly the case. He said it because he was expected to, and he wanted to believe it.

He wanted to have faith. But so often, as they lay on their beds, or in their coffins, people just looked weary and afraid, their faces cold and grey and shrunken, their mouths slightly open, their teeth bared as if they had been visited by some strange terror, an unexpected and devastating revelation that there was nothing beyond death after all, that it was all just a myth, a wee fairy story to keep you going while you were alive. Perhaps they knew there was nothing ahead, and everything from that moment on was past, that the memories you left behind in the minds of other people, your little stamp on the world, was all there was. The things you said, the way you laughed, how you brushed your hair, your favourite dinner. Whether you were good at your work or not. Were you a good father or mother; did you smoke too much? Could you sing a song? Did you love with all your heart?

Douglas took a chair and sat and quietly watched his father. He seemed to look less like himself by the minute. Everything was in flight. And he did not look like he was asleep. He was just not there. There was nothing of what made him who he was. Whatever spark had animated him had been extinguished, and Douglas knew in his heart that it would never reignite. He'd had his time and that was that. He touched his father's face with the palm of his hand, caressed his cheek. It was rough, like a cat's tongue. When Douglas was a boy his father would come home from his work, dirty and unshaven, and he would grab Douglas and rub his scratchy stubble against his son's soft cheeks and Douglas would scream and wriggle and laugh with the pain and the sweetness of it. In the years to come, would he remember this? Or would he remember his father, Robert 'Rab' Fairbanks, his face gorged red with anger and frustration, his fist hanging in the air like lightning ready to strike? Would he remember his father as the man he was, or the man he became?

'Yer faither wisnae sick, ye know. But he became awfy quiet after you left. He wisnae his usual self at all. The doctor couldnae find anythin' wrong wi' him.' Mary rose from her chair and crossed herself. 'I'll just leave you a wee minute, then eh.'

Douglas, too, crossed himself, as his auntie would have expected him to. In the name of the Father, the Son and the Holy Ghost.

For a while, Douglas stood over the coffin, just watching. He brushed some fluff from the lapel of his father's jacket, undid the top button of his shirt and loosened his collar. From the inside pocket of his own jacket he took out a small white envelope and removed a worn black and white photograph, which he placed between his father's folded hands. 'I will remember you,' he whispered.

The young dark-haired man on a bicycle smiled back at him, his eyes bright with hope and anticipation.

'It sounds like it was very sad, Douglas.' Kirstin lay beside him on the bed, stroking the hair on his chest. Even though the blinds were closed, it was like an oven in their bedroom. It was thirty-six degrees outside and, fanned by a north wind, the heat blew through every crack in the wall, every gap in the floor, every loose tile on the roof. It invaded them. They had been making love for most of the afternoon and their bodies were slick with sweat and tears and relief.

'It was sad. There weren't many people there. My da hadn't kept up with his friends, not since he left the pit, anyhow. The ones that did turn up told me a lot of his former pals had died. I suppose that's what happens when you get auld. The world you knew just expires around you. My sisters were there, except for Carol. She hadn't spoken to my da for years. She would never take her kids to see him. It's funny, I remember when she was a wee girl, she wouldn't leave him alone for a minute. She was always climbing all over him, following him around the house. My big papa, she called him. My big papa.'

Douglas kissed his wife's forehead. It was hot, moist. He pushed her hair back to let some air at it. 'But you know, in a funny way it was liberating. When the coffin was lowered into the grave—don't get me wrong, there were tears in my eyes—I felt as though I could get on with my life. That we could get on with our lives. It was if I was shaking him off, shaking his life with my mother off, letting go of all the stuff in my childhood that made me what I used to be.'

'Used to be?'

'Aye, used to be.'

'Will you miss him, Douglas?'

He sighed and stared at the ceiling. 'I don't know. I don't know if I'll miss him. I'll miss some things about him, maybe. But I'll remember him. I'll certainly remember him.'

Douglas reached for the glass of water on the bedside table. He noticed that the table was new. He passed the glass to Kirstin who took it gratefully. She sat up against the bedhead and sipped at the water. He gazed at her breasts as if it were the first time he had seen them. He had always known that she was beautiful— that was one of the things which attracted him to her in the first place—but it was as if he were rediscovering her, and he marvelled at the softness of her skin, the hardness of her nipples when he kissed them, the way he seemed to sink into her when they made love, the way he disappeared. Had it been like this before?

'Where did you bury him?' Kirstin asked.

'At the Royston cemetery.'

'I don't know it.'

'It's a depressing place. But I suppose they all are.'

'Where was the wake?'

'At my Auntie Mary's house. It was okay, quiet. Folk didn't have that much to say. Mary had made some sandwiches.' He turned to face her. 'After everybody had gone away home I caught the bus down to Shettleston Road. I wanted to have a walk up and down. I wanted to see if it had changed much.'

'And had it?'

'No, not really. It was still busy and most of the shops are the same. The Odeon's still there. And the State. Some of the tenements are away though. Demolished.' Douglas rubbed the sheet against this chest. It came away wet. 'McFadyen the butcher is still there. And so is McCall's.'

'You went to where the wee girl was killed? The one that Wullie told you about for his story?'

'Aye.'

Kirstin had never seen him cry before. She took his hand, and held it tight.

'I don't know why, but I expected something to be there, a reminder. I don't know, maybe a plaque or something. But there was nothing. It was as if it never happened.'

'But it did, Douglas, you know that. And that wee girl helped you. I understand that now. She made you realise that you have an opportunity she will never have. I hope you are going to make the most of it.'

'Aye. I'm—'

She quickly placed a finger against his lips. 'Don't say anything.'

Douglas kissed her neck. She tasted salty. 'I went to see your mother.'

Kirstin was surprised. 'That was nice of you, Douglas. A man who visits his mother-in-law of his own accord is rare indeed.'

'She told me I wasn't good enough for you, that you deserved better.'

'What? And you a former priest. That sounds like my mother,' Kirstin laughed. 'She never was one to mince words. And what did you say?'

'I told her she was right, and that I'd try to do better.'

'Well, I'm glad to hear that, Douglas. Do you have any idea what it's been like for me? I feel like I've been alone for all this time. I've been alone in a new marriage, in a new country, in a new job. I've had no family to help me, no real friends, no one to talk to. Do you know how that feels?'

'I . . .'

'I bet you do, Douglas. It feels just like you used to feel when you were alone in that chapel when you were a wee boy, alone in that seminary for all those years, alone in that big house with no one but drunk old Father Docherty to keep you company. It feels, Douglas, like you must have felt when your parishioners didn't want to have anything to do with you except for an hour or so on Sundays.' Kirstin stared at him and Douglas saw her eyes were thick with tears. 'If you ever do this to me again, if I ever have go through what I've been through in the last twelve months, then I will leave you and I won't look back. You either love me with all your heart, or you don't love me at all. Do you hear me, Douglas?'

Kirstin got up from the bed, moved to wrap a sheet around her but decided against it. It felt good being hot and naked. 'I'm away to make some tea. Oh, and by the way, you'll have to support me for a while, Douglas.'

'What do you mean?' he said, surprised.

'While you were away I quit my job. I'm unemployed.'

'Of course I'll support you. I'll always support you. But I thought you liked your job?'

'Clive was in on that whole land scam thing with Brian Myers, the bugger. So I had no choice. I couldn't work with him any more.'

'My God. Brian and Clive? I don't believe it. And I thought Clive was a good man.'

'So did I, Douglas. But as my mother always says, a good man is hard to find.'

'Come to think of it, she said that to me too. Quite a few times, actually.'

'You wanted to see me, sir?'

Douglas turned to see Jeremy Spencer standing quietly at the door to the classroom, his blond fringe draped over his right eye. His schoolbag hung off his shoulder, making him seem lopsided. He looked young for his age, and with his fair skin and small frame, and a disinclination to speak unless encouraged to do so, he came across as shy and vulnerable. He reminded Douglas of himself when he was a boy.

'Come in, son. Take a seat.' Douglas pointed to the chair he'd placed next to his own desk at the front of the classroom. It was lunchtime and the school building was quiet. The boys would be in the playground or in the canteen stuffing themselves with pies and cream buns or having a game of kick-to-kick on the football oval.

'I won't keep you long. You'll be wanting to have something to eat.'

Jeremy pushed his hair away from his face and sat down on the chair.

'So,' Douglas said jovially, 'two more days of school and then it's the summer holidays, eh. Are you going away anywhere?'

Jeremy thought for a minute. 'We might be going to my auntie and uncle's house in Colac. They've got a swimming pool.'

Douglas pushed his books and papers into a neat pile on top of his desk. 'Listen, son, when I spoke to your mother and father at the parent-teacher night they mentioned that you are thinking of joining up with the brothers here, that you believe you have a vocation. Is that right?'

Jeremy raised his eyes from the floor. 'Yes, Mr Fairbanks.'

'It's a big thing to be thinking about.'

'Yes, sir.' Jeremy's gaze had returned to the floor.

'Why do you want to become a brother?'

Jeremy took a pen from the top pocket of his blazer and began flicking the nib in and out. 'I don't know, sir. It just feels like the right thing to do. I like going to the chapel. It's nice and quiet in there. You can get away from things, you know. And I like to pray.'

'Aye, it is lovely and quiet in the chapel, especially of a morning. What do you pray for?'

'Aw, you know, things.'

'What sort of things?'

The boy, laughed, his eyes suddenly bright. 'Aw, that I might grow taller.'

Douglas laughed with him. 'Anything else?'

Jeremy pulled his socks up from around his ankles and turned the tops down so that they sat neatly below his knees.

Douglas drew his chair closer. 'Is there anything else you pray for, son?'

Jeremy shifted on his chair. 'I pray that my mum and dad might be happy.'

'Aren't they happy?'

'Sometimes, but not much. They fight a lot. It makes my sister Angela cry.'

'Does it makes you cry, son?'

'No, I just go to my room and do my homework. Sometimes I walk up to the chapel and see if Father Walsh is in, or I just sit there by myself.'

'It's comforting, isn't it?'

'Yes.'

'You know I used to be a priest?'

Jeremy nodded.

'It's a very difficult life, Jeremy. Some people can cope with it just fine, but I found it hard. It was good at first; it was a refuge for me. When I was young the chapel kept me company. It made me feel like I belonged to something. It was good like that. But as time went on, and I got older, I felt like I was missing out on things, that the life was passing me by and there was stuff going on out there that I didn't understand. And, you know, when I was ordained as a priest, it wasn't what I expected at all. There are a lot of rules, things you can and can't do. The Church is against a lot more things than I had imagined.'

Douglas took a long breath as if it would organise his thoughts. 'You know, sometimes I'd go out to visit people. And I'd walk into the close and up the stairs and I'd knock on the door. But, you know what? No one would answer. I knew the people were in because I'd seen their light on from the street. I'd seen shadows moving about behind the curtains. So I'd push open the letterbox and look in, and sometimes I could hear the telly on. I could smell what they'd had for their dinner. But you know what it was, Jeremy? They just didn't want to see me. They didn't want to see the priest.'

'My mum and dad try and do that, sir, when Father Walsh comes round to our house. They make us kids stay quiet and hide. But Angela always starts giggling, so we have to let him in. I don't know why they don't let him in straightaway. I think he's a very nice man.'

'I'm sure he is, son. A lot of priests are very nice men, but a lot have problems too. All I'm saying, Jeremy, is that this is not something to rush into. Why don't you finish school and go on to university before you make a decision? Get a job, even. Wait till you grow up and have lived a bit. Till you've met some nice girls. Do you understand what I'm saying?'

Jeremy hinted at a smile. 'Yes, Mr Fairbanks. You mean sex.'

'That's right. All that stuff we talked about in class.

'Chapter 11.'

'Aye.'

'It sounds awfully messy, sir.'

'Well, it's not that bad when you get used to it.'

Jeremy looked unconvinced. 'But I'd like to be a missionary. I'd like to help people. The poor people in New Guinea or the Aborigines.'

'They're fine things to want to do. But you don't need to be in a religious order to do them. You can just be a good human being.'

Douglas rested his hand on Jeremy's shoulder. It felt slight, like it still had a lot of growing to do. 'Look, son, will you promise that you'll come and see me before you make any decision? Will you do that?'

'Okay, sir,' the boy said, shrugging his shoulders. 'I promise.'

'All right, good man.' Douglas ruffled the boy's hair. 'You'd better go get your lunch.'

Douglas watched the boy trudge out the door, his schoolbag, and the weight of the world, on his shoulders.

'Oh, and Jeremy,' he called out.

'Yes, sir?'

'Are you interested in soccer at all?'

'Don't talk tae me aboot broccoli, Ma. I hate fuckin' broccoli. How many times have I telt ye? An' ye can stick that caulifloor up yer erse as well,' Wullie said, staring at the plate in front of him with no small amount of disgust.

'Listen, you, I told ye aboot the fuckin' bad language, did I no,' Agnes scolded, swiping her vegetable-wary son across the side of the head with her open hand. 'I telt ye whit Mr Fairbanks said aboot it. He said it'll stifle yer progress. Stifle it, dae ye hear me? He's yer teacher so he fuckin' well knows whit he's talkin' aboot. And I'll tell ye somethin' else an' a', if ye don't eat yer vegetables, ye wullnae grow, ye wullnae get intae the fitba team and ye'll get the cancer as well.'

Wullie sighed. Here we go again. 'Ach away an' bile yer heid. Ye don't know whit the fuck yer talkin' aboot. Vegetables don't make ye grow, they just make ye shite. And while we're at it, I've had enough of a' this cancer keech, so I huv. That's a' it is wi' you these days. Cancer this, fuckin' cancer that. Ye'll gie me the cancer the way yer gaun oan.'

Wullie took a bite of his sausage and, assessing its flavour and texture like a French chef with a rare truffle, decided it needed more tomato sauce. He bit into it again and was satisfied. 'Look, whit is it wi' you an' these vegetables, eh? Ye didnae make us eat fuckin' broccoli back hame.'

'But this is no Glesga, Wullie, this is Australia and ye know whit they say, when in Rome dae whit yer Romans dae.'

'Whit dae yer Italians know?' he protested. 'I'll tell ye whit they know. Shite. European Cup Final 1967, Glasgow Celtic 2, Inter-Milan 1. Nuff said.'

'Ye've got tae adapt tae yer new surroundings, son, if ye want tae get on.'

Wullie sighed, glared at his mother. Christ, she could go on. 'Ach, fucksake, gies a fuckin' carrot then,' he said, resigned to his fate and presenting his plate like a soldier offering a gun to his enemy and saying 'shoot me'.

Agnes smiled, the proud mother, her dentures bright as a moonbeam on a winter's night. 'That's my boy,' she said, squeezing her son's downy cheek between her forefinger and thumb. 'That's ma boy. It'll dae ye the world ae good for the game the day, eh.'

'I'm only the orange boy, ma. Fucksake.'

Agnes ruffled his hair, which she'd noticed had crept an inch and a half below his collar. She'd just give it a wee trim when he was asleep the night. 'Aye, I know son. But you're ma wee orange boy, eh.'

She placed another carrot and a clinically depressed piece of broccoli on his plate. 'Moan, get that doon ye and get a move on or ye'll miss the kick-aff. And mind ye polish yer boots and wash yer face and fucksake wid ye look at the back of yer neck, ye'd better gie that a wash as well while yer at it. And Wullie.'

'Aye, ma?'

'Will ye no gies a wee kiss?'

'Fucksake Ma,' Wullie moaned, fleeing to the safety of the bathroom, his sausage safely tucked away in the right-hand pocket of his tracksuit trousers.

Ayrshire Archie tipped his hat back until it revealed an inch of hairline, placed his large guitar-pickin' hands on the silver rodeo buckle on his jeans and nodded. He appraised Andrew from head to foot and nodded again. He said nothing and turned away.

'What's up wi' him?' Andrew asked.

'What's that you're wearing?' Joyce inquired.

'It's a kaftan.'

'Folk can see your nipples through it.'

Andrew shrugged. 'Well, it's no as if I'm a woman.'

Archie raise his eyebrows, said nothing.

'What's it made of, your—what was it again?' Joyce asked, rubbing the flimsy material between her fingers.

'Kaftan.'

'Aye, kaftan.'

'It's made of cheesecloth.'

'Did ye hear that, Archie? Cheesecloth. It's made of cheese-cloth.'

Archie, who was in the process of pulling on a pair of snakeskin boots, looked up, his face flushed with the effort. 'Fine bit ae embroidery around the neckline there, son. Aye, very fine indeed. What kind of cheese is it made out of then?'

Andrew sighed in exasperation. 'We'd better be getting on. That's all the gear in the van, is it Archie?'

Archie was tying a yellow kerchief around his neck. 'Aye, just this one guitar and that will be it and we'll be ready for the concert after the game.'

Andrew looked at his watch. 'Right we'd better be away then. Douglas will be expecting us. Are you ready now, Joyce?'

'Ready to rock and roll, big boy?' she laughed, patting him on his maroon-velvet-wrapped arse.

As they drove past the council offices and down Myers Parade towards the Baytown Soccer And Sheep Trial Club, Archie, Joyce and Andrew smiled at each other and began to sing.

'Oh Rooh– ooh be-ee,
Don't take your love to town'

Abigger car, that's what he needed, Vince Vella thought to himself as he continued to try and squeeze Teresa, the nine kids and Alfredo the goat into the Chevy. Alfredo was not a kid himself any more. He had been growing fast, especially since he managed to get into the neighbour's veggie garden at least once a week, twice if the kids chucked him over the fence. But how much bigger can you get than a 1958 Chevrolet Bel Air? Shit, that's it! Two 1958 Chevrolet Bel Airs! You bloody beauty! He could drive one and Teresa the other. And if they had more kids there'd be no worries. They would be able to fit in another four at least.

'All right everybody, we bloody have to go now, no bullshit,' Vince yelled, counting heads as he turned over the engine. 'One, two, three, four, five, six, seven, eight . . . There's one missing. Charlie, where's Charlie?'

'He's just gone to get a carrot for Alfredo,' Teresa explained, shouting at her son to get a move on because Kirstin would be waiting for her so they could open the hamburger, snags and pastizzi stall.

Vince chuckled to himself. Ever since that animal had been made the club mascot in a close contest with Archie's greyhound Hank, Charlie had been treating him like royalty. There had been mutterings about discrimination against the disabled but Douglas had rightly pointed out that Hank, being blind in one eye and with only half a tail, not only raised questions about the dog's long-term fitness but also its ability to parade around the pitch in something resembling a straight line. Vince felt that Alfredo ate better than he did. But nothing was too good for the King of the Goats, as far as Charlie was concerned.

'Bloody Jesus, Teresa, that boy love that goat more than he love me.'

'That's all right, lover man,' she said grabbing a handful of what she called her Little Man's Big Maltese Falcon. 'I still love you. Many, many times.'

Frank O'Connell sat back in his chair, comfortable as a cat on a cushion, his feet up on the desk, a glass of the good stuff in hand, his new shoes glistening in the soft light from the old desk lamp he'd brought with him from the *Argus*. Well not exactly brought, stolen might be a more accurate description if you wanted to get all subeditorish about it. He polished his already gleaming brogues on the back on his trouser leg. He'd gone out and bought a new pair to match his new suit. It had been pointed out to him by Bettina, Baytown's own Queen of Beauty, that a man occupying a position such as his should strive to look his best at all times. Indeed, she had invited him down to the salon for a shampoo, cut and blow job with an introductory ten per cent discount, an offer which he had found too good to refuse. After all, who was he to ignore the advice of someone who had dedicated her life to helping others blossom and bloom and dye their roots once a month? While a good perm did not necessarily maketh the woman, nor a well-tailored suit maketh the man, they didn't appear do any harm either. For the first time in a long while he was feeling good about himself and, to be truthful, Bettina the widowed Princess of the Perm felt pretty good too.

Frank cast an appreciative eye over the proof for next week's front page: BULLDOG BUILDING SCALES BACK NEW ESTATE PLANS. Not bad, not bad at all. And there would be plenty more exclusives where that came from. Funny, that—the more you had folk by the balls, the more they agreed with your view of the world. For a right bastard, Brian Myers wasn't a bad bloke when you got to know him. Well, maybe not. When it came down to it, Brian was an arsehole and would always be an arsehole. Some blokes were just like that.

Frank looked at his watch, brand new from Dunklings the Jewellers. Bettina had helped him pick it out, even strapping it around his wrist for him. 'Quel elegant,' she had whispered in his ear, allowing the tip of her tongue to slip in for good measure.

Jesus, where did the time go? He'd better get on up to the soccer club quick smart. He was supposed to be doing the match report. Now, what exactly was offside again?

Kirstin stood dumbfounded and floundering in the broad and highly polished aisles of the new supermarket in Bay Street. My God, there were some roads she knew back home that were smaller than these corridors. Everything gleamed, all so perfect in its newness. Endless aisles, straight as a parson's walk, burst proudly with packets and boxes and bundles and bottles of everything that was available for consumption across the six continents. Rainbows of fruit tumbled out of sparkling perspex bins. Cheeses, a hundred shades of yellow, fought for attention in refrigerated shelves. Row upon row of biscuits, enough to satisfy a century's worth of tea-swilling grannies, beckoned to be nibbled, dunked and munched. Women with freshly starched, snow-white hats baked bread in a corner. Crimson displays of cooked meats and sausage looked mouth-watering and attractive. What was cabana exactly? What did it taste like? Bright-faced girls smiled at the checkout counters. Smiled! So this was the way of the future. You could do all your shopping in the one spot, instead of traipsing up and down the road like you did back home, with your trolley or your basket, from one wee shop to the other.

Summer was best back then, when you'd be holding your mother's hand and she'd be talking to her pals outside the shops, gossiping away like sweetie wives. You'd have a nice summer dress on and you could feel the hot sun on the back of your legs, and you could squish your toes around your plastic sandals because they made your feet sweat. Ally Morrison the grocer always gave you a chocolate wafer biscuit or a sweetie for being a 'wee cracker'. And Mrs Gourlay, she had that funny, dark wee shop that had pens and pencils and jotters and needles and thimbles for the sewing classes at school. Whenever you ventured in, it was as if the undertaker was about to arrive any minute and take away the coffin in the corner. Her mother liked the McVeigh brothers the best. They had the butcher shop their father had started after the war. They were right handsome the two of them, like dark polished stones, and they'd tease the women and make them laugh and blush. 'Just get yer hons aroon that sausage, hen. That'll put a bit ae colour in yer cheeks' one of them would laugh. They sold a few fish as well and had an ashet of salmon paste in the window. The street was always that busy. The women did their shopping every day. It got them out the house and out of the close. But it'd all be away soon, Kirstin thought to herself. Just like here. All the wee shopkeepers, all the funny stories, all the laughs.

Milk, where was the milk? That's all she'd popped in for, a pint of milk for the tea after the match. Well, maybe that and bit of a gander. She'd seen that huge advertisement for the opening in the *Baytown Star*, a whole page it was. Frank O'Connell would have been happy. She could picture him now, lighting up another cigarette, head back, feet on his desk, ash on his tie, thinking about having another go at Brian Myers and maybe bumping the paper up to twenty pages.

'S'cuse me,' Kirstin said to the young woman distractedly pushing an empty trolley past her. 'Can you tell me where the milk is?'

The girl shook her head, her long brown hair flirting with her bare shoulders like loose skirts rippling in a sea breeze. 'It could be anywhere. I've been lookin' for it meself.'

Kirstin realised she knew the girl, had admired her fine features before. Karen Myers. Douglas had pointed her out one day at the beach. She had been massaging suntan oil into her legs, legs that were milky coffee brown and slight at the ankles. They sprung from strong hips that proclaimed her womanhood. Kirstin remembered that she looked wonderful in a bikini, although now she saw that it would be difficult for her to squeeze into those small scraps of teasing yellow cloth.

'It's Karen, isn't it? Karen Myers.'

'Yeah, Karen,' she said, pleased. 'You're Kirstin, aren't you? You're married to Malcolm's teacher, the soccer choc bloke. I saw you at the council offices that night. I was there. Sometimes I do a bit of cleanin' there, you know, just to earn a bit of pocket money for clothes an' that.'

'You'd know Agnes, then.'

Karen smiled, tossed her hair back with her hand. 'Agnes Henderson? Yeah I know Agnes. Can't understand anything she says though. I thought people spoke English in Scotland.'

'After a fashion,' Kirstin laughed. She glanced at the girl's swollen stomach and offered up an uncertain smile.

'Six month's gone,' Karen sighed. 'You?'

Kirstin was surprised. Perhaps that's why she blushed. 'I didn't think you could tell yet.'

'You've got the look. The look of ripe fruit. That's what me mum calls it.'

Kirstin laughed, placing the palm of her hand on her stomach. 'I'm still ripening then. I'm just nine weeks, so there's a wee while to go yet.'

'Well, it doesn't go quickly, in case you want to know. I'm sick of it. It buggers you up being pregnant, deadset. I've got piles. No bullshit. They don't tell you that in school, do they?'

Kirstin made a mental note to tell Douglas to discuss the physical side effects of pregnancy on girls in his Health Education class. Those horny wee boys should be made aware of what women have to go through after they've had their way and gone off to boast about it to their mates down at the pool hall.

'What are your plans, if you don't mind me asking?'

'Nah, no worries. At least you've got the guts to talk to me. A lot of the women around here, they just stare at me and talk behind me back. Bitches. I thought women were supposed to stick together at times like these?'

'Only when it suits them, dear. Are you going to stay here for the birth?'

Karen laughed again. 'Nah, I'm bein' packed off to me auntie's in Benalla. Then I don't know what's gonna happen. Me mum says she'll look after the baby so I can go back to school and do matric, but me old man can't handle the idea. But Mum thinks once he's seen the baby he'll come around. But I dunno, I'm not his little princess any more.'

'Och, you never can tell. People can surprise you, they can be better than you think.'

'Or worse than you think in my old man's case.' Karen fixed her gaze on the floor for a moment. 'Listen, I'm sorry about what me dad did to your soccer club. It was a real rat's act.'

'Well, he's making up for it now, isn't he? The new clubroom he built is magic, so much bigger than what the boys had originally intended. And a grandstand and everything! So you see, a leopard can change its spots.'

Karen sniggered. 'Yeah, especially when you've got it by the short and curlies, eh.'

'I suppose that's one way of putting it,' Kirstin laughed.

'Dad says there won't be anythin' in the paper about all the goings-on with the land an' that. He said Frank O'Connell promised 'im.'

'I think Douglas had a wee word with Mr O'Connell. He thought that you and Malcolm had enough to deal with already. But I'm sure there will be a fair few council scoops coming the *Star*'s way in the future.'

Karen examined the brightly polished floor tiles, saying nothing, her hair falling in front of her face.

'So,' Kirstin said, quickly changing the subject. 'How is Shane then? Are you going to get married?'

Karen scoffed loudly. 'Shit no. Fair dinkum, I don't know what I was thinkin', goin' out with him. He had that van, I suppose, and deadset when he's in the water, on his board an' that, he looks just beautiful. He's like a god, no bullshit.' She giggled. 'He's got a grouse body, you should see it. But, you know, he's a bit of dropkick. He makes Malcolm look like Albert bloody Einstein.' Karen shrugged. 'Me teachers at school reckon I can still go on to uni if I repeat the year. That's what I wanna do, not be stuck at home washin' Shaz's dirty jocks.'

'Good for you, pet,' Kirstin said, squeezing her hand. She looked searchingly across the aisles. 'I'd better go and find that milk. I have to be at the ground in five minutes. Come and see me when you get back from Benalla. I mean it. Bring the baby so I can see what I'm in for. Take care of yourself, Karen.'

'Call me Kaz,' she said, smiling, all bright eyes and skin like velvet, and looking every inch the seventeen-year-old girl she was.

Malcolm Myers smiled to himself as he pushed the marking machine across the grass and watched the lime drop through the hole to make a reasonably straight white line. He wiped his face with the back of his hand and peered ahead. Since he'd done such a good job cutting the turf, Angus had left him to do the final twenty-five yards of marking out the pitch. What an honour. They'd mowed the grass that morning and Angus said it looked just like Celtic Park on a bright summer's day. The old bloke had had some interesting things to say, too, about how to get a border collie to coax a sheep through a gate in a wooden pen. He said it wasn't as easy as it looked. 'Takes a lot of skill, aye a lot of skill,' Angus said. Malcolm could believe it. He'd tried to get his own little beast into Christine Morrison's front gate when her olds were at the pictures, but had given up in despair. He didn't get it. If she had the potential to push a nine-pound baby out of there, why couldn't he manage to get an eight ounce willie in? The mysteries of the human body, eh?

Maybe he hadn't paid enough attention in Health and Education. You thought you knew it all but when it came to the crunch you didn't know shit. Perhaps he should ask Mr Fairbanks to revise The Rooting Chapter. Wullie could do with a few extra pointers as well. He still thought babies came out of women's ears or just appeared one morning from the coal bunker. That older brother of his had a lot to answer for.

'That's it, boy, you're doing a grand job there, a grand job,' Angus said, taking a nip from a half-bottle of the Famous Grouse. 'Just concentrate a wee bit more, eh, you're mind seems tae have wandered.'

Angus turned and waved to the Walker brothers who were at the other end of the pitch putting a final coat of paint on the new goalposts. There was only an hour till kick-off, but on a glorious day like this they would be dry in no time. And that would be that, he thought, as he did a gratifying sweep of the ground. The pitch was in tip-top condition, lush and green as a Scottish meadow, the flags on the corner posts fluttering in the breeze that waltzed in from the sea. There was hardly a cloud in the sky. The smell of the sausages and the hamburgers and the onions sizzling on the barbecue made his mouth water. And he had a right thirst on him as well. He and Lively Ernie had packed the beer into the fridge before sun-up so that it would be nicely chilled for the beginning of the game. Ernie had supplied the drink and insisted they unload it under the cover of darkness but was reluctant to explain why. Some folk had already found themselves a shady position in the grandstand, including the mayor who would officially open the new facilities in about half an hour, ably assisted by the club's new benefactor, Councillor Brian Herbert Myers JP.

Angus felt his heart waver with regret. If only Richie were here. That would be the icing on the cake, the vinegar on the chips. But he had things to sort out in his own life now. Richie had sent a postcard saying Annie had moved in with her sister in Canada, and that she wouldn't be returning to Pittenweem. And some Australian pop group called The Easybeats was about to play a concert in the village so he'd have to get in reinforcements from Anstruther and Kircaldy. Pittenweem was also being overrun by American tourists with a spendthrift appetite for tartan hats, malt whisky and haggis. Poor Hughie Cameron was being run off his feet in the butcher shop and he'd had to take on an apprentice to help prepare all those haggises.

'Are you all right, Angus?' Malcolm said, biting into a meat pie with sauce.

'Aye son, aye,' he replied, rousing himself from his thoughts. 'Just you keep going there, time waits for no man. Dree oot the inch as ye hae done the span. Remember that now.'

Malcolm spat out a piece of gristle from his pie. 'No worries, Angus mate, I will.'

'That's a good laddie. Right then, I'm away tae see tae my sheep.'

Shane McGowan sat slumped over on the side of the bed and scratched his arse. His eyes felt like they had been glued together. When he finally managed to force them open with a supreme act of will power and two unsteady forefingers, he got such a shock that he immediately shut them again. He took deep, slow, lung-cleansing breaths, in and out, in and out, but the world refused to keep still, insisting rather on spinning like a top with a malicious streak. Jesus, what a night! Just like the old days. Him and Chook and Wozza, down the Pines, getting shit-faced. It was great to see the boys after so long. He'd been distracted by a sheila for a while there but he wouldn't let that happen again. He knew now who his true mates were.

Shane stuck his fingers in his mouth. Thank God for that. His tongue was still there. He'd had this nightmare that he was pashing Kaz down by the beach and she'd sucked his tongue right out of his throat and swallowed it. He'd tried to scream at her to give it back but because he didn't have a tongue any more she couldn't make out what he was trying to say so she'd gone ahead and swallowed the bloody thing. 'Needs salt,' she'd giggled, and run away down the beach doing cartwheels on the sand.

What a night, fair dinkum. They must have had two dozen bottles between them. Chook chucked at least eight times. No bullshit, eight times at least. The poor bastard still hadn't got over his girlfriend Corinna dropping him for the little prick Frankie Disabato.

They'd all fallen asleep in the van and had been woken by the sun blazing through the windscreen. He had no idea how he got home. He remembered he'd had to stop on the road a couple of times and have a bit of a heave himself. Great to see the boys though, eh? Grouse.

Shane weaved, wandered, bumped and stumbled his way into the kitchen. He felt quite pleased with himself when he finally made it to the bench. He took a breather and then managed to get the kettle filled and hissing away nicely on the stove. He peered into the cupboard. 'Fuck, no fuckin' bread,' he cursed. No bread meant no toast, no toast meant no Vegemite. Bugger it, he'd just dip his finger in the jar for a scoop anyhow. Beautiful! A nice hot cup of tea would see him right, no worries. He yanked open the fridge door, noticed that the little light wasn't working, made a mental note to fix it one day. He scanned the shelves as though he was checking out the waves at Barwon Heads. Things were moving inside the fridge, undulating and shimmering like the summer sun on a bitumen road. There were strange chirps and squeals. His head fell to his chest. 'Fuck, no fuckin' milk,' he mumbled to himself. Wearily he searched for the sugar in the cupboard above the sink, the cupboard below the sink, on the benchtop, under the couch, in the toilet and behind the television. 'Fuck, no fuckin' sugar!' he screamed at no one in particular.

Shane sat by the kitchen table, confused and uncertain what his next move should be. Go to the shop for some supplies? Ring Chook? Ring Wozza? Ring Kaz maybe? He slurped his black tea and picked up the *Baytown Star*. When he got to the back page he felt his stomach leap into his mouth, as though he'd just fallen from the scaffolding at work. He couldn't believe his eyes. What was that prick O'Connell playing at? A soccer preview as the main story on the back page, the fuckin' sports page for Christ's sake. BIG DAY FOR BAYTOWN blazed across the full width of the paper in type as thick as his wrist. And there in a little box in the bottom right-hand corner, 'See Inside For Football Reports'.

He couldn't believe it. No, he bloody well could not. Shane McGowan yanked up the kitchen window, thrust his head out and screamed at the bright blue sky. 'What's goin' on, eh? Just what the fuck is goin' on?'

Douglas watched Kirstin turn another sausage on the barbecue with the special tongs Teresa had given her. He couldn't recall ever seeing her cook outside before. In Scotland, the open air tended to be afflicted with sleet, snow, fog or coal dust and was certainly not blessed with a period of sufficient sunshine to allow the cooking of a sausage or a hamburger, never mind a thick slice of rump steak. But here she could stay outdoors and flip and toss and turn lumps of flesh for weeks on end. They were certainly getting through the food today and there was still another hour to go before the game started. The pastizzi were going down a treat too and Minh Thanh's spring rolls were winning a few converts. A sense of belonging certainly seemed to give people a ferocious appetite. Look at them, you could feel their excitement in the air, settling like confetti on their shoulders.

He had been up half the night working on his team selection and tactics for the match and was still fiddling as he sat on the bench outside the home team changing room, lost in his calculations and strategies. He frowned and licked his pencil. He was still drawing arrows and little circles all over his piece of paper. He was keen to try and give all the lads a run on the first day of the season, an appreciative baptism for everyone who had worked so hard to get the club up and running.

Any moment now and he'd have to go inside and get changed into his boots and strip. Then he'd give the boys their pep talk. All those sermons he had given on Sundays, had finally come in handy. From a Glasgow pulpit to a sweaty-arsed wooden bench on the outskirts of Melbourne. Life's journey took some strange detours, did it not?

Douglas sensed Kirstin's eyes upon him, could feel them warming his body. During his previous life there was rarely a day when he had not talked about blessings, but it was only recently that he had learned how to count his own. He looked up at his wife and he smiled and winked at her. She flipped a hamburger, laughed and winked back.

ACKNOWLEDGEMENTS

Many thanks to Amanda Paxton, Grace Reilly, Caitlin Reilly, Rista Fuller, Randall Fuller, Caroline Lurie and Fran Moore.

The following books were particularly helpful in researching Glasgow tenement life:

Haud Yer Wheesht, Alan Morrison, Neil Wilson Publishing, Glasgow, 1997.
Shattered Vows, David Rice, Triumph Books, Chicago, 1992.
Up Oor Close, Jean Faley, White Cockade Publishing, Oxford, 1990.

Graham Reilly was born in Glasgow, Scotland and emigrated to Australia with his family in 1969. He currently lives in Melbourne and has also lived for extensive periods in England and Vietnam. He has worked as a cook, a truck washer, a maintenance man in an abattoir, but mainly as a journalist and mostly at *The Age*. His first novel, *Saigon Tea*, was published by Hodder Headline in 2002.